Catherine Cooper is a journalist specialising in travel, hotels and skiing who writes regularly for the *Telegraph* and the *Guardian* among others. She lives near the Pyrenees in the South of France with her husband and two teenage children, and is a keen skier. Her debut, *The Chalet*, was a top 5 *Sunday Times* bestseller. *The Chateau* is her second novel.

www.catherinecooper.net

🐦 @catherinecooper
📷 @catherinecooperjournalist
f @CatherineCooperAuthor

Also by Catherine Cooper

*The Chalet*

# The Chateau

## CATHERINE COOPER

HarperCollins*Publishers*

HarperCollins*Publishers*
1 London Bridge Street
London, SE1 9GF

www.harpercollins.co.uk

HarperCollins*Publishers*
1st Floor, Watermarque Building, Ringsend Road
Dublin 4, Ireland

Published by HarperCollins*Publishers* 2021
1

A catalogue record for this book
is available from the British Library

ISBN: 978-0-00-840025-5

This novel is entirely a work of fiction.
The names, characters and incidents portrayed in it are
the work of the author's imagination. Any resemblance to
actual persons, living or dead, events or localities is
entirely coincidental.

Set in Sabon LT Std by Palimpsest Book Production Limited,
Falkirk, Stirlingshire

Printed and Bound in the UK using 100% Renewable Electricity
at CPI Group (UK) Ltd

MIX
Paper from
responsible sources
FSC
www.fsc.org    FSC™ C007454

This book is produced from independently certified FSC™ paper
to ensure responsible forest management.

For more information visit: www.harpercollins.co.uk/green

With heartfelt thanks to the scientists, researchers, the medics, the health workers and the volunteers, you are all amazing.

*I hold your hand as you take your last breaths, hooked up to countless machines in the hospital. Your eyes are closed and you look at peace. I stroke your cheek, which feels clammy and cold, but you don't respond. I'm not sure if you even know I'm there. You are so young to have your life snatched away, so unfairly. None of this is your fault. Someone will have to pay.*

# Prologue

*October*

Chateau Amaryllis is a fairy-tale French chateau – the kind you might expect a princess or Sleeping Beauty to live in. It's so picture-perfect it almost looks fictional. Like a castle in a theme park or a film.

Many of the chateaux in the area look stunning at first glance, Aura and Nick have learned since they arrived in the Mozène region in the South of France a few months ago. But once you look closer, things might appear a little different. In some of the wine-producing chateaux, for example, the tasting rooms will be impressive but if you peek into some of the non-public rooms on your way to the loo, like Aura always tries to if she gets the chance, the surroundings are often much shabbier. Things are often not as they seem.

But at Chateau Amaryllis, things are just as they appear from the façade throughout – at least when it comes to physical appearance. It's not open to the public – its owner Thea would consider that crass – but if you are lucky enough to be invited in, you'll find that wherever you go, everything is pristine. The four turrets are each topped by immaculate slate without a tile out of place – there's no running around with buckets in the attic every time it rains in Chateau Amaryllis. The leaded picture windows don't have cracks – and this evening every single one is lit up with bright lights so it looks even more impressive than usual as you come down the drive, which is lit with real flambeaux. In daylight you would see that the enormous, freshly-painted shutters are a gentle pale blue colour, not quite typical of the region, but created especially by an artisan paint colourist in Morocco. Now that it is almost dark, the shutters give the place a somewhat menacing look, but even so, no one can deny the beauty of the chateau.

Inside, the huge atrium and its several floors of balconies with intricate metalwork are lit with what looks (and smells) like hundreds of Diptyque candles, the light from their flames making the enormous crystal chandelier at its centre twinkle. Young waiters and waitresses wearing old-fashioned black and white, with the addition of zombie make-up and dripping fake blood for tonight, circulate with silver trays of champagne flutes.

It's Hallowe'en, and the usually spotless chateau is draped with fake cobwebs. A couple of aerial performers dressed as demons perform twists and turns in two large hoops suspended above the polished flagstones without any obvious safety ropes, drawing gasps from the costumed guests below.

Passing through the atrium into the garden, more flambeaux

light the way. Aura, Nick and the rest of their little group walk across the lawn to reach the marquee – almost as black as the night and also covered in fake cobwebs. Zombies and ghosts jump out to give the guests a minor fright as they arrive, prompting squeals of both delight and terror. Later, these ghouls will be part of a show, created especially for this party. Thea doesn't want her guests presented with something they may have seen before, certainly not.

Seb and Chloe, dressed as a devil and a cat respectively and carrying a camera and sound boom, follow Aura and Nick. Helen trails afterwards, feeling somewhat exposed in a sexy nurse's uniform which has been customized for the occasion with fake blood and ripped fishnet tights. She is carrying Bay, who is dressed as an adorable pumpkin. Little Sorrel, in his favourite Spiderman costume which he is rarely allowed to wear, trots alongside, holding her hand tightly. The children are wide-eyed and breathless – they've never seen such drama and spectacle before. Aura is secretly pleased with her witch costume and Nick feels a little awkward, dressed in a black robe with a giant hood and carrying a huge scythe – Death itself.

A young woman dressed as Mary Poppins but with the addition of zombie make-up (not too much though, so as not to scare the little ones) spots the children and accosts Helen, showing her where to take them. One corner of the garden has been set up as the children's area with a haunted house bouncy castle and a small marquee kitted out as a playroom for the evening. Inside there are several similarly dressed nannies, a low table shaped like a coffin with silver-coloured plastic crockery already laid out, and a darkened area with cots for sleeping. Inside the cots, the fleecy blankets are pumpkin-orange with printed black spiderwebs, and the tiny pillows are small, padded ghostly figures. Everything has been thought of.

It wouldn't be quite true to say that all of the voices are British – there are American accents, some Dutch and a smattering of German and Italian. And while no one is speaking French, you can catch the odd hint of a French accent here and there. Thea doesn't speak French, so to be admitted into her circle, you have to speak English. She hasn't got round to learning the language; she hasn't felt she's needed to as yet.

There are around two hundred guests. Many of them, like Aura and Nick, have been invited because they live in other chateaux in the area. Thea assumes that if someone lives in a chateau like she does, they'll probably be her type of person. So far, she hasn't been too far wrong. But obviously, that can change.

The rest of the people here are the best of the other expats that Thea's found so far. Some retired bankers, a few creative types such as wedding photographers and musicians, some families with high-flying husbands commuting back and forth and usually unambitious wives staying put in the countryside with the kids. A disproportionate number of retired policemen. It's not quite the crowd she would have chosen for herself, but most of them are OK in their way, or at least useful to her in some way or another.

Dinner is a huge success. A hog roast is always a crowd-pleaser, even if a little redneck for Thea's tastes. She's endowed it with more class by having it served by waiters at the long table set out on the lawn (buffets are so declassé, Thea thinks) to follow the massive seafood platters created from the raw ingredients brought in from Brittany this morning. It's so important that seafood is absolutely fresh – she wouldn't want to take any risks.

To accompany the roast, there are exquisite salad creations placed in the middle of each table, designed by a food artist she had a brief affair with in London and recreated by a small catering company from the local town. They're not quite as good as the real thing would have been, but impressive enough, Thea thinks.

She is particularly pleased with the dessert, which is a huge contrast to the rest of the meal – one corner of the garden has been set up to look like a fairground where guests can order ice cream made in nitrogen, artisanal candy floss in several all-natural flavours, or dip home-made marshmallows into a six-foot-tall chocolate fountain.

Everything is simply perfect. It's a party that none of the guests will ever forget, Thea is sure. Extravagant parties aren't really a thing in the Mozène – even among the few people like Thea who can afford to throw them. But Thea has money and she enjoys extravagance, so she doesn't see why she should hold back. She watches with a satisfied smile as Seb zooms in on the blue ice cream as it emerges from the white vapour. She's delighted her chateau is going to be on TV now, too.

Suddenly, there is a scream. And then another. Someone Thea doesn't know, one of the waitresses, is crying and yelling hysterically.

'Call an ambulance!' she is shouting, in between sobs. 'There's a body. Someone's been killed.'

5

# PART ONE

# 1

**Aura**

'I can't believe we're actually living here!' I say. 'Look at this view! I'm never going to get used to it.' In front of me fields roll almost as far as the eye can see, until you get to the snow-topped mountains. It is amazing.

Nick looks up from the table where he is browsing through a catalogue of what looks like about a thousand different types of drill and sighs. 'Yeah. It is amazing. Or it will be once we've renovated.'

He stands up and turns to face the chateau. It's a typical French chateau, like the ones you see on all the property programmes, only all the shutters are half-rotten and many are hanging off the walls, plus there's a huge crack running from the top to the bottom of one of the turrets. 'I mean, look at this place!' he says, waving his arm. 'Why is it so bloody big? And falling to pieces? What on earth were we thinking?'

'Nick! Don't be so silly! It's going to be incredible. When it's all finished there'll be a part for us and the boys to live in, another part for the paying guests, like we said. Maybe a multipurpose studio for yoga and painting and the like, so we can run themed weeks. Who *wouldn't* want to come and stay somewhere like this?'

He smiles. 'Yeah. I guess. It will be pretty special once it's all done.' He puffs out his cheeks. 'A lot to do though . . .'

We both look at the crumbling render, the ancient wood-work with paint so badly peeled you can't even tell what colour it once was, and the muddy field where you can still see occasional hedges and perennial flowers popping up from when it used to be a formal garden.

I shift Bay over to my other hip and he nuzzles into my neck, drooling. 'I know,' I reply. 'But what an amazing place for the boys to grow up, isn't it? And anyway,' I continue, 'I had an idea. I've found someone to help us out. And it won't cost us a thing.'

Just then Sorrel starts wailing from deep inside the house. Nick rolls his eyes. 'Nap time over, then. I'll go.'

I put Bay down on a blanket with some wooden building blocks and sit carefully on a rickety old chair which was left behind by the previous owners – along with pretty much all the furniture that's ever been here for the last century or so, or so it seems – and open Facebook on the iPad. I log on to Expats in the Mozène, which has been my go-to Facebook page since all that stuff happened back home and we decided that a fresh start in France was the best thing for us all. I don't think I could have made the move without it.

I take a picture of the view and post it with a caption: *Finally made it to France! So excited.* ☺ There is a flurry of congratulations messages from loads of people, sending animated balloons flying all over the screen. I smile to myself – I feel like I know some of them as well as I know my friends from home, we've been speaking so much over the last few months.

Almost instantly a private message balloon pops up in the corner of my phone. It's difficult to see properly as it's so small, but I know from having seen the profile picture before it's an image of a middle-aged man in a high-end sports car.

*Welcome to France! Can't wait to come and see your new place xxxx*

I smile. Frank has been so helpful since I've joined this Facebook site, advising me on everything from how to find someone to help with the garden and install a pool to the rules around home-schooling in France. Frank lives nearby too, so I'm hoping we can become friends and maybe he can introduce me to some of the other locals. Obviously we don't *only* want to mix with the expats, but my French isn't that good so I figure the expat community will be a good place to start.

*Thank you! I'll give you a shout in a week or two when we're a bit more set up x*

Nick reappears with Sorrel, who is grumpily rubbing his eyes.

11

'Hey, baby! Did you have a good sleep?' I say.

He shakes his head and shoves his finger in his mouth. 'Noises in room.'

I pull him onto my lap and kiss the top of his head. 'Old houses like this creak and groan, sweetie, it's nothing to worry about.'

He puts his head on my chest and carries on sucking his finger.

'OK, darlings,' I say, passing Sorrel back to Nick, 'I'm going to leave you both to play with Daddy now while I go and do some work inside.'

The interior of the chateau is cold compared to the surprising heat of September outside. I still can't believe we were able to sell our tiny house in London and buy something like this. The uneven terracotta tiles are beautiful but cold on my bare feet and also a little gritty. It's dark down here in the hallway, but as I go up the spiral stone staircase housed in one of the turrets, light spills in from the huge upper-floor windows. At the very top is a round room which I've earmarked for my study and counselling room. At the moment some of the windows are cracked and the wooden floor is so rotten that it's probably dangerous – I wouldn't want the children to come up here – but once it is all renovated, it will be fabulous.

I sit down at my laptop – thankfully, Frank sorted out the internet installation for us before we even arrived. I'm sure I couldn't have done it with my limited French.

To: Seb@frenchfancy.co.uk; Chloe@frenchfancy.co.uk
From: Sorrelsmummy@gmail.com

Hi Seb and Chloe, hope you're both well.

We're really looking forward to you arriving tomorrow. Is there anything we need to prepare for you? We are also expecting workmen first thing to start digging the pool and as far as I understand that will be going on for several weeks.

Let me know what time we should expect you? I've made up a room for each of you – they're a bit rough and ready, but I'm afraid you'll have to take us as you find us!

Best wishes,

Aura

Nick wasn't keen on me inviting the camera crew into our new home, especially after everything that went on back in London – he thought it might bring us more unwanted attention. But I pointed out that it would be amazing publicity for the chambres d'hôtes – after all, there are so many people doing this sort of thing now that it's important to do what you can to stand out. The programme is following people who are moving to France and setting up a new life there – I've been watching it for years, dreaming of doing the same, and I still can't quite believe I'm going to be featured myself. I've promised Nick that he can stay in the background; I will deal with the camera crew and make sure they don't bother him more than is absolutely necessary. I also think it will be fun for the kids to learn how making

13

a TV show works, plus, if I am entirely honest, I quite fancy seeing myself on TV and making my old friends envious about our amazing new place. All the stuff that happened before is in the past now. Yesterday's news. We are only looking forward.

# 2

*September, Mozène*

**Aura**

The film crew and the pool diggers arrive at almost exactly the same time. I leave Nick to sort out the workmen as his French is a bit better than mine and I show the TV people to their rooms. They're going to be with us for about two months (to start with – then they'll come back now and again after that to see how we're getting on). They will be with us round the clock, apparently, so they can be fully immersed in our lives. I don't mind at all, it gives me an excuse to try out the hospitality skills I'll need once the chambres d'hôtes is up and running.

The 'crew' consists of just two people who are much younger than I was expecting – in their very early twenties. Seb is the producer/director and Chloe is the researcher/

runner. I don't *think* they're a couple and it seemed impolite to ask, so I've made them each up a room on the top floor of the chateau – if I've misunderstood and they want to corridor-creep, that's their own business.

Chateau Ricane came with a lot of furniture – most of it isn't anything special, as far as I can see, and I doubt there is anything of real value. I am slowly sorting through it to see what can be kept and what can be upcycled – I think it will be nice to keep as much of the original stuff as possible. There are some half-decent armoires and the furniture being here at least meant that there was already a bed in most of the rooms when we arrived, even if the mattresses are a bit saggy. Obviously I will buy new ones before any paying guests check in, but I haven't had the time yet. The TV crew will just have to make do.

Once Seb and Chloe have dumped their bags they appear back downstairs in the kitchen. The kitchen is my favourite room of the house, or at least I think it will be once it's been tidied up properly. There is a huge Aga which is about the only thing in the house which looks vaguely new and will make it nice and cosy in winter (though admittedly, it's making it a little too hot at the moment), lovely flagstones, a window which overlooks the grounds, and hideous cupboards which will need to be pulled out ASAP. It's the boys' lunchtime and they are at the table eating pasta and pesto (from a jar but organic) – one day I will grow basil in the garden and make my own. I've also made a pot of tea for Seb and Chloe.

'What would you like to do first?' I ask them. 'Are you going to get started with the filming today or do you want to have a look around first, settle in and the like? Do a recce, isn't that what they say in films?'

Seb takes a large gulp of tea. 'We'll start shooting this afternoon, if that's OK with you. But we really want you to get on with what you'd normally be doing day to day and we'll just take the bits we need. That's why we're having this extended stay with you – the idea is to make the finished product seem more natural than some of the other programmes in this vein.'

I nod. 'OK. Well, as you know, outside the men are starting to dig the pool, so that's maybe something you might like to have a look at. Nick's supervising them. As for me, I'm mainly keeping an eye on the boys. Then mid-afternoon I'm off into town to collect our HappyHelp person from the station.'

'HappyHelp?' Chloe asks.

'Yes! It's brilliant. It's for young people who are travelling – you put them up and feed them and they do a few hours' work for you each day – well, five days a week – they get time off, obviously! The girl who's arriving today is mainly going to help look after the boys while I get on with other stuff, though we'll probably have her doing a bit of cleaning and the like too.'

'So like an au-pair, only unpaid?' Chloe asks.

I frown. I know they've only just arrived, but of the two of them I definitely prefer Seb so far.

'No, not really,' I say. 'I see it more as a labour exchange. We offer her something – bed, board and experience of French life, and she offers us something – help with the children. No one is making her do it – she wants to come here.'

17

Chloe nods, but I see her try to hide a smirk. 'Great. Ideal, I'm sure,' she says.

'I think so. If it works out well, we might even see about getting some others in – we have so much space here. There are people in my Facebook group who have whole teams of them helping with their renovations and stuff. But it's easier to get people in July and August when all the students are travelling, apparently. At this time of year, you have to take who you can get to a degree. Especially when you live as rurally as we do – we're not much of a draw for young people. No nightlife here!' I laugh, but it sounds false even to my own ears.

'OK,' Seb says. 'In that case, I think we'll leave you to get the boys sorted out and go and have a look at what's happening out by the pool. And then obviously we'll want to meet your new arrival later. What's her name?'

'It's Helen. She's already in the area, which is why she's able to start at short notice. I'm delighted.'

# 3

*September, Mozène*

**Aura**

I drive really slowly to the station to collect Helen – I'm still not used to being on the wrong side of the road. I've seen a photo of Helen on her HappyHelp profile and have told her what kind of car I'm driving, so hopefully we will be able to recognize each other.

As it is, only two people get off the train at our sleepy little station and one is a man, so it's pretty clear which one is her.

'Helen?' I say, approaching her with my hand outstretched. 'I'm Aura. So lovely to meet you. How was your journey?'

She is not quite what I was expecting – the picture on her profile must be an old one. She's got a good few years on me, and is definitely older than the average backpacker.

It's difficult to place her age. Late thirties maybe? Perhaps even early forties – she's rather mumsy-looking with her shoulder-length, nondescript hair and somewhat dowdy jeans and T-shirt.

'It was fine, thank you,' she says. 'I haven't come that far – only a couple of trains.'

'Ah yes. Where was it you were before?'

'Near Montauban,' she replies. 'Been there about a month, helping out on a farm.'

She's not exactly forthcoming, but maybe she's tired. Or shy. 'Sounds lovely!' I trill. 'And the family there seemed very impressed with your help.'

I blush. I've never had any 'staff' before – not even a cleaner – and I don't know how our interactions should be. Not that Helen is staff, exactly, this is a labour exchange, a cultural experience, like I told Miss Judgy Pants Chloe. I contacted the family she was with before for a reference and they couldn't have been more complimentary. And I don't feel ashamed to let Helen know that I checked her reference; I'm not going to have just anyone in my house, after all, am I?

'Yes, it was a great place to be and they made me very welcome,' Helen says. Maybe she is making her own point there, that she doesn't expect to be treated like a servant. 'But it was time to move on – the whole idea of taking a year off was to travel, not spend all my time in one place.'

'Well, I hope you'll enjoy staying with us just as much,' I say. 'It's all a bit rough and ready at home at the moment as we've not long arrived, but I think you'll agree that the setting is beautiful, especially if you're a nature-lover.'

20

She nods. 'I'm looking forward to it. I'm excited at the prospect of staying in a chateau.'

My heart swells with pride. I still can't quite believe that we live in a chateau now, even if it is falling down around our ears.

I show Helen her room, which is nicer than the ones I've given to Seb and Chloe as I'm keen for her to stay as long as possible. She is one floor down from them and one up from us and the boys. And that still leaves several rooms spare – I can't get over the novelty of having so much space.

'Thank you, it's lovely,' she says, although she seems somewhat underwhelmed. Perhaps she was expecting something a little less shabby round the edges.

'Why don't I leave you to get organized, and then I can make everyone some tea and introduce you to Nick and the boys?' I say.

She nods. 'Great – thank you.'

My phone pings. It's a message from Frank:

*Hey. How's it going there?*

I smile. He's so sweet and thoughtful.

*OK. Busy. My HappyHelp's just arrived – not entirely sure what I think of her yet – and we've got the film crew here too. Lots going on!*

*Sounds like you need a break! How about I come over and make you a cup of tea? If you're lucky I might even bring cake . . .*

I smile. Frank's been so helpful since I joined English Speakers in the Mozène, and it would be nice to meet someone local. It strikes me with a pang of loneliness that we know absolutely no one here.

*Why not? Why don't you come tomorrow? Would be lovely to meet you.*

*Looking forward to it xxxx*

At dinner Helen seems more relaxed and starts to grow on me a little.

'So, Helen, what made you come to France?' Nick asks.

'I'm taking a year or so off from normal life. I was offered voluntary redundancy from my IT job with the council, and for various personal reasons I needed a change of scene, so it seemed a case of now or never.'

'Absolutely! Do it while you can, while you've got no ties, yes?' Nick says.

She nods. 'Yep.'

I assume by 'personal reasons' she means she's been through a relationship break-up, but obviously I'm not going to pry.

'Wish I'd done that too when I had the chance,' Nick says. 'Too late now!' I slap him gently on the arm as if I'm being playful but, actually, his words cut deeply. Given our time again, I think we'd probably both do things differently.

'Not that I'm not delighted to be here with my lovely family,' he adds hastily, seeing the expression on my face.

We were only a couple of years out of university when I got pregnant with Sorrel. I'd been doing a lot of reading about hormones, chemicals and Big Pharma at the time and had stopped taking the pill. We thought we were being careful, but obviously not careful enough.

Initially, I panicked. We were too young to have a baby, surely? But then I thought about it more and it became apparent to me that this was what Mother Nature had intended – who was I to go against that? Nick wasn't keen at first, but we talked and talked and I went for an angel reading which made it very clear I should keep the baby. Eventually I brought Nick round to my way of thinking – this baby was meant to be and I was going to have it, with or without him.

We'd been together almost four years by then and one night Nick took me out to our favourite restaurant and proposed. He is from a very traditional family and I've always wondered if his parents told him he should 'do the right thing', even though he denies it. We got married shortly after Sorrel was born; I didn't want to be a comically pregnant bride. His parents are still annoyed about their first grandchild being born before Nick and I were married.

'You're very lucky to live here,' Helen adds. 'It's a beautiful place you have and I'm so looking forward to getting to know you all. What would you like me to start with tomorrow?'

# 4

*September, Mozène*

**Aura**

The main reason for having Helen here is to help with the children, so in the morning I start by introducing her to the boys. She described herself in her biog on the HappyHelp site as a 'very hands-on auntie'. Her sister apparently lives just down the road from her and has four children, so she has lots of experience with babies and toddlers. She also helped with the children at her previous HappyHelp posting.

Until Sorrel and Bay went to nursery, I was always very reluctant and nervous about leaving them with anyone. In fact, Nick and I had only one night out together in between Sorrel's birth and setting off for France, when he pretty much forced me to let his mother babysit, and even then we ended up coming home before dessert because I felt too anxious.

But since they started nursery and I've grown more accustomed to them being away from me, I feel much calmer about leaving them with other people. Now that Helen's here to help look after them, I will be able to get on with setting up the chambres d'hôtes and my counselling business. And it's not like I'll ever be very far away from them anyway, is it? It really couldn't be more convenient.

Helen seems like a natural with them over breakfast, making Bay giggle by playing peekaboo and helping Sorrel mash his bananas into his porridge the way he likes to.

'Is everything OK in your room, Helen?' I ask. Even though she seems reserved almost to the point of frostiness, I can already see she'll be such a help with the boys. I want her to feel comfortable here so that she'll stay as long as possible. 'Did you sleep OK?'

'Yes, it was all great, thank you,' she replies. 'It's so lovely and quiet here!'

'Noises in room,' Sorrel says sombrely, his mouth full of porridge. Sadly, this has become a bit of a theme since our arrival. I'm trying to be patient as I'm sure the move has been unsettling for the boys, but his constant night-waking is leaving me exhausted.

'Yes, Sorrel, I know, you woke us up several times last night, didn't you? But as we talked about, at great length, old houses like this make noises. It's not something to be scared of.'

After everything that went on back in London, Nick and I attended couple's counselling where we both set out what we felt we needed to make our relationship work. I said we needed an entirely fresh start – hence the move to France.

25

Nick's number one wish was that the boys needed to stop sleeping in our bed so that we could feel more connected as a couple. That was how he put it, at least, but what he actually meant was so we might have more sex. Even though my wish seems like the bigger life change, I still worry about how not having the boys close to me at night will affect them. I don't know why I let Nick persuade me.

And yet, I could sort of see Nick's point. *If* we had been more connected as a couple (and having more sex), paying more attention to each other, the whole thing in London probably wouldn't have happened. And I *do* want us to stay together – for the sake of the boys, if nothing else. So in the end I agreed to the new sleeping arrangements, just as Nick agreed to the move to France. And while Bay has taken to sleeping apart from me fairly well (after a few nights of screaming, though less than I'd expected), Sorrel is clearly not enjoying it at all and tries to come back into our bed every single night. Even though we have so much space here, I have put the boys in the one room together for company. In retrospect, this may have been a bad idea. Sorrel is still unsettled and he ends up waking Bay most nights.

Nick is standing firm and taking Sorrel back to his own bed every time he comes into our room, but every single time it breaks my heart. Last night, once I could tell that Nick was properly asleep, I crept across the landing and cuddled up with Sorrel in his tiny bed. I miss the feel of his warm little body and the organic baby shampoo smell of his hair. They're small for such a short amount of time. I want to make the most of it.

'I've got an idea, Sorrel,' Helen says, winking at me. 'How

about after breakfast we give your room a really good tidy so we can check there's nothing in there that shouldn't be? Then, once we're sure, if Mummy can find me a couple of old wire coat hangers, we can collect some bits and pieces from the garden and make a dreamcatcher – how does that sound? I've heard they're pretty good at keeping strange noises away from little boys as well as bad dreams.'

I smile at her and mouth 'thank you'.

'Make 'catcher,' Sorrel agrees solemnly, nodding.

'That sounds exciting, doesn't it, Sorrel?' I say. 'I'll find you some hangers right after breakfast, Helen. I think there are some ancient pillows in the loft – maybe you'd like the feathers from them? Or you might be able to find some in the garden?'

Helen gets up, clears away the breakfast things and puts them in the dishwasher. 'Don't worry – I think we'll find everything we need in the garden. I'm sure you've got things to get on with. Would you like me to make lunch too?'

'Well, if you're sure you don't mind, that would be lovely, thank you.'

She nods. 'No problem. Kids always like to get involved in cooking, I find. I'll have a hunt around in the fridge and see what there is, if that's OK with you. It'll be fun for all of us.'

Frank arrives on the dot of 11 a.m. with a bunch of wild-flowers and a pot of home-made jam. 'I'm afraid I didn't have time to make cake, so I hope these will do instead,' he says. Once he has handed them over to me, he kisses me on both cheeks, as everyone of all ages and both sexes seems to do here. I'm not sure if I love it or hate it; either way, I certainly haven't got used to it yet.

'Aura!' He steps back a little but hasn't yet let go of my shoulders. His proximity is making me uncomfortable – even though we've spoken a lot online, this is the first time we've met – so I turn away to fill the kettle. 'How are you settling in?'

'Fine, I think,' I say. 'It's a bit daunting – there seems to be so much to do. I really appreciate you helping out with everything before we got here – it would have been a nightmare to arrive with no electricity or internet.'

He waves his hand dismissively. 'Honestly, don't mention it. Keeps me out of trouble. People were kind to me and helped me out when I arrived – I like to pay it forward where I can. Everything working OK? Lights on? Internet?'

'Yes – the internet is a little slow but, given where we are, I think that's to be expected, isn't it. Tea?'

Frank isn't at all what I'd imagined. He's probably in his late fifties and his profile picture must have been taken at a very flattering angle and with some kind of filter. He's overweight, a little sweaty, and wheezes when he moves. His belt holding up his unfashionable jeans is straining and his thin T-shirt has ridden up, exposing his flabby white tummy.

This man has been very kind and helpful to you, I tell myself. Be nice. He doesn't talk about himself a lot online, but from memory, I think he's divorced, with grown-up children back in the UK, and owns a couple of small properties in France which he rents out.

'I see they've started work on the pool already?' he says.

28

'Yes, very exciting. Nick's out there keeping an eye on what they're doing.'

'Your husband? And how is he finding it here so far?'

'I think he's slightly overwhelmed by it all. Like me!' I laugh, trying to make light of it, but suddenly I do feel overwhelmed. There's so much to take on board.

Frank nods. 'I'm sure you'll both settle in quickly. There's a lot to get used to at the beginning and it can feel like a lot to get your head round. Plus, I think with most couples, there's usually one who has led the move and one who follows, so it's often harder for one than the other.'

'I'm sure you're right. In this case, it was me who led. I manifested it.'

Frank looks confused. 'Manifested?'

'Yes,' I say, struggling to keep the sigh out of my voice. I get so bored of trying to explain manifestation to sceptics. 'It's basically when you bring something into your life through belief. Though obviously it's not quite as simple as that.'

He nods. 'I see. So in other words, you wanted to move to France more than your husband did?'

'Yep,' I agree, for simplicity's sake.

To be honest, even 'led' is understating it. Though I wanted us to stay together, I pretty much gave Nick an ultimatum – it was my way or no way. We would move out of London as a family, or I would take the boys and leave him. After everything that had happened, we needed to start again somewhere totally new and different. Where no one knew who we were. Where I didn't feel like people were pointing and whispering every time we went out. It didn't have to be France, but in many ways, it made the most sense.

29

I bring the tea over to the table and sit down. Frank sits in the chair next to me instead of opposite me, which feels weird. I shift away a little.

'So, remind me of your plans?' he says, helping himself to a biscuit from the plate I've put out. I wish there was cake. I had visions of myself as some kind of domestic goddess in our new life in France, but so far I haven't done any baking at all. It's been impossible to find the time and, apart from the Aga, the kitchen isn't particularly inviting in its current state. However much I wipe and mop, it never really feels clean.

I pour myself some tea from the blue-and-white-striped pot. At least I've made a pot rather than simply putting teabags in the mugs. And it's only thanks to Frank that, before we left London, I loaded up the removals van with so many teabags; it isn't something that would have occurred to me to do.

'We're hoping to run a chambres d'hôtes,' I say, though we've talked about this already at length online, 'but obviously we need to renovate first. In the meantime I'm hoping to find some counselling clients among the expats, and we thought maybe Nick could do a bit of English teaching – he was a teacher back in the UK. But to start with, I think we'll mainly be busy with the renovating.'

He nods and takes a noisy gulp of his tea. 'And you're going on that TV programme, aren't you?'

'*French Fancy*. Yep. The crew arrived yesterday – I'm not sure where they are at the moment. Maybe seeing what's happening at the pool, or following the kids around with Helen. The deal is they're here 24/7 and they can film what they like. Nick isn't keen, but it'll be amazing publicity for the chambres d'hôtes once we open, don't you think?'

I take another sip of the tea. Even though the teabags are from home, the drink tastes weird because of the UHT milk and different water, and I feel a pang of loss for what we have left behind.

'Yes, all publicity is good publicity, don't they say?' he agrees.

At that moment the back door bursts open and Sorrel barrels in, sobbing. He launches himself at me and buries his face in my lap.

'Sol?' I ask with a stab of alarm, stroking his hair. 'What is it?'

He lifts his head and wails 'Bunny!!!!!!!' before burying his head back in my lap. He is sobbing so hard I can feel his little body shaking.

'Shhh, Sol,' I soothe. 'What bunny?'

Helen rushes in carrying Bay, who is also screaming his head off, followed by Seb and Chloe, filming. Bay reaches his arms out towards me and I take him from Helen, edging Sorrel over a little so as to accommodate the two boys. 'What happened?' I ask. Even Helen looks pale and shocked, though maybe it's just because of all the screaming.

Helen sits down at the table and I pour her a mug of tea. Her hands shake slightly as she lifts it to her lips.

'Thank you,' she says, as she sets the mug back down. The boys' cries have subsided now into gentle sobs and Sorrel's tears, snot and dribble have soaked my jeans. 'We were looking for twigs and feathers for the dreamcatcher and I'm afraid we came across a dead rabbit under a bush.

It was bloody and crawling with maggots and . . .' She shudders.

'I'm so sorry,' she continues. 'I feel terrible that the boys saw it, but they ran into the bushes ahead of me and . . . obviously I had no idea it was there. But I can't apologize enough.'

I pat her arm. 'Don't be silly – it wasn't your fault. These things happen. They'll get over it.'

'And they'll have to get used to seeing that sort of thing now they're living in the countryside,' Frank chips in, somewhat unhelpfully. I flash him a look.

'Tell you what,' he adds, getting up, 'if Helen can point me in the right direction, why don't I go and dispose of the bunny before it can upset the boys again? Where can I find a dustpan and a bin bag?'

I feel a whoosh of relief – as a semi-vegetarian I don't think I could cope with getting rid of a dead rabbit. 'Would you, Frank? That would be such a help, thank you. You'll find everything you need under the sink there.'

Sorrel sits up and wipes his eyes. 'Poor bunny,' he says, wistfully.

I kiss the top of his head. 'I know, Sol. Poor bunny. You need to remember that he probably had a very nice life though, hopping around in the fields eating lovely green grass. Try to think of him like that.'

He gives out a little sob, sticks his finger in his mouth and leans his head against my chest. Seb moves in closer with the camera and I feel a flash of irritation.

'Who was that guy who came round earlier?' Nick asks over dinner. It's about 9 p.m., the boys are finally asleep (for now

32

at least) and Helen has made a tartiflette which she's served with green salad. It's very good.

For once Seb and Chloe aren't filming – I guess even TV crews have working time directives and while they insist on access 24/7, they can't actually film all of the time. Tonight they are having dinner with us, and clearly can't eat and film simultaneously. They have their own little kitchen upstairs where they can make their own food if they want, but I make a mental note to invite them to dinner often. Probably worth trying to keep on the right side of them, after all.

'Frank?' I reply. 'I met him on that expat Facebook site. He's been great about helping me sort out loads of boring admin things. Without him, we probably wouldn't have had electricity or internet when we arrived, and possibly not even water.'

'Hmm. Don't you think it's a bit weird though?'

'No. Weird how?'

I notice Seb and Chloe glance at each other and then carry on eating. I don't want to start a row even though they're not filming because I don't want them deciding that this little discussion might make a 'storyline' for them.

'Well, we don't know him at all and yet he's piling over almost the same second we arrive. What does he want?'

'Want? I don't think he *wants* anything. He said that people helped him when he got here and he wants to pay it forward. Nothing wrong with that, is there? In fact, he's coming over again tomorrow to help me with my website.'

Nick takes a forkful of salad, saying nothing. I think he's being ridiculous – he can hardly be jealous of someone like Frank.

'I think he's probably lonely, to be honest,' I add, which is true. 'But he's been a massive help and the Facebook page is great – the expats really help each other out. There's the odd row, certainly, but even those are rather entertaining.'

He shrugs and goes back to eating. 'Rather you than me,' he says. 'Those Facebook groups seem to be full of egotistic losers, from what I can see. It's beyond me why you spend so much time on them.'

# 5

*September, Mozène*

**Aura**

Frank turns up as promised on the dot of 11 a.m. again, this time with a USB stick and a very glamorous woman. 'I bumped into my good friend Thea at the boulangerie this morning and brought her along to say hello,' he explains. Thea smiles blandly at me and then casts her eye around the kitchen with an obvious look of disdain.

'I thought it might be nice for you to meet,' Frank continues. 'Thea lives in a chateau too. It could be useful for you to have a chat about artisans for the renovation and the like.'

'Lovely to meet you,' I say, extending my hand, though I can already tell we are not going to be friends. Thea takes my hand gingerly as if it's a smelly fish, and shakes it at arm's length. 'You too, I'm sure,' she says. She'd struggle to sound less sincere if she tried.

'How are you settling in?' she asks.

'Oh, you know, it's exciting to be here but there's an awful lot to do!' I reply. 'It's so daunting. What's your place like? I'm sure there's always something that needs fixing, don't they say? That owning a chateau is like painting the Golden Gate Bridge? As soon as it's finished, you have to start all over again?'

She sniffs. 'Not really. I had Amaryllis renovated before I moved in – I can't bear dust – and now I have Graham, who lives in the cottage and does jobs around the place as and when they need doing in lieu of rent. Easier all round that way.'

'Gosh! Well, we have Helen here helping us out with the boys with a similar arrangement, but I'm not sure she'll want to stay long term. And we don't have a cottage, or at least not one that's remotely habitable so . . .' I realize I'm babbling but there's something about Thea that makes me nervous. 'We're planning a chambres d'hôtes once we're up and running. Do you rent your place out at all?'

'No. Well, very occasionally as a location for photographic or film shoots, but that's it. I'm not interested in being a *landlady*.'

She says landlady as disdainfully and incredulously as if she might have said streetwalker and I feel my dislike for the woman growing. I'm looking forward to welcoming guests and I don't care what she thinks.

The door opens and Nick comes in from the garden, treading mud all over the floor I've just mopped. I bite my tongue; I'm not going to tell him off in front of Thea or the film crew.

'Thea, Frank, this is Nick, my husband,' I say, emphasizing *husband* in light of the way Thea's demeanour totally changes the moment Nick enters the room. She visibly preens, and then leans in to kiss him on both cheeks while holding his shoulders. 'Nick!' she cries. 'So lovely to meet you. And what a delightful place you have here – so much character!'

Character. So patronizing. I mentally compare Thea to myself. She has immaculate auburn hair topped with designer sunglasses and is dressed in what look like Louboutins, skinny jeans and a crisp Ralph Lauren shirt. I haven't ironed a single thing since we got here. I am wearing ancient cut-off jeans, a manky old T-shirt with a baby food logo on, which I was given as a freebie, and Birkenstocks. I haven't washed my hair this morning and I'm still wearing my gym headband which I put on to keep my hair off my face when I was mopping. I hastily pull it off and wrap it around my wrist.

'Anyway,' Thea continues, 'I should get on and leave you and Frank to sort out your little website. But I wonder if you'd like to come to dinner this Saturday? I'm having a few friends over and it would be lovely for you to meet some of the other people in the area?' she asks, looking directly at Nick.

'Oh, that's very kind, Thea, but I don't think we can. We don't have anyone to look after the boys,' I say quickly, before Nick can respond. It's a reflex reaction – the truth is I don't want to go. There's totally negative energy coming from Thea and I don't like it. That, or the way she's looking at Nick.

'What about the woman you have helping you – Helen, I think you said? Can't she do it?' Thea asks, not bothering to hide her somewhat exasperated tone.

'Helen?' I bluster. 'Oh. Yes, maybe. I'll ask her. I don't want to take liberties, especially as she's not long arrived and she's not expected to work weekends, but . . . can I check with her and get back to you?'

She nods. 'Of course. But it would mean a lot to me if you both came. And I think you'd enjoy it. Frank can give you my number – if you could let me know by Thursday at the latest? I'll need to let the caterers know how many we'll be.'

Caterers! I was imagining she was suggesting having a few friends round for a kitchen supper. Clearly not.

'We'd love to come,' Nick says, 'I'm sure Helen will be fine about it. We can always pay her like a babysitter if need be.'

'But we'll call to confirm once we've spoken to her,' I add, furious with Nick for speaking for me. How dare he? 'But many thanks for the invitation; we'll look forward to it. If it turns out we can make it, that is.'

Frank had pretty much set up my website for me even before he arrived. I sent him the wording I wanted a while back and a few ideas about the kinds of things I was after design-wise, and I have to say, he's got it spot-on. He's even done a French version. I can't speak French, so there's no way I can take on French clients, but he thinks it makes the whole thing look more professional.

'Wow, Frank, it's amazing!' I say. 'How did you learn to do all this stuff?' He's a far cry from the 25-year-old bearded hipster I imagine a typical web designer to be, but obviously I don't say this.

He shrugs. 'It's pretty easy – they make all the website builder sites so user-friendly these days. You don't need HTML or anything like you did in the old days. You could do it easily yourself if you put your mind to it, I'm sure. It's not difficult.'

'I'm sure I couldn't. I only use tech at all because I have to – I barely even know how to use my phone properly! You must let me pay you for your time, Frank. How much do I owe you?'

He shakes his head and holds up his hand, still looking at the screen. 'Nothing. Honestly, if it weren't for doing these little jobs for people, I'd be a bored old bloke sitting on my own with next to nothing to occupy me. I'm happy to help. It hasn't cost me anything other than my time and I have more than enough of that, so please don't worry.'

'Well, that's very kind, Frank. I owe you one,' I say.

'And how are you finding the Astrid I set up for you?' he asks. 'Are you using it much?'

'Astrid?'

'The virtual assistant,' he says, pointing at a black object close to the kettle which I had totally forgotten about.

'Oh! Astrid. Um, no, I'm not using it much,' I say. By not much, I actually mean not at all. 'I'm not all that sure what to do with it,' I add.

'Aura! I'm shocked. You must give it a go,' he says. 'It's great once you get used to it. Astrid does loads of things. Changed my life at home. Let me show you . . . I know, what do you need shopping-wise at the moment?'

'It does the shopping?' I ask, incredulous.

He laughs. 'No! Sadly not. But look: "Astrid, add potatoes to the shopping list."'

A blue ring lights up on the top of the device and a disembodied voice I've never heard before says: 'I added potatoes to your shopping list.'

'What list?' I ask. I still don't see the point.

'Every time you realize you've run out of something, you tell Astrid and she makes a list. Then when you go shopping, there's a list in your app.'

'What app? It all sounds very complicated.'

'It's not complicated at all – it's very simple. But you need to download the app – do you want me to do it for you?'

I hand over my phone. 'Great, thank you.'

'You can ask it to play music,' he adds, as he swipes and jabs at the screen, 'the kids can make it tell jokes – there's all sorts of things it can do. The internet company was offering it as a freebie when I got you set up, so I thought I might as well sort this out for you too – I did mention it at the time, but perhaps you don't remember?'

I shake my head. I don't, but there was always so much to think about during the move that I'm not surprised I've forgotten.

'If you don't like it, you can ignore it or get rid of it, obviously,' he adds. 'I think they take a little getting used to, but I find mine invaluable. There' – he hands back my phone – 'all set up. So when you want to go shopping, you go into lists here' – he scrolls and jabs – 'and the list will be there ready for you.'

I look at the screen where it does indeed say 'potatoes'.

But honestly, what a faff! Wouldn't it be easier to jot things down in a notebook like I normally do? In any case, once we get the kitchen sorted, I'm hoping to have one of those blackboard walls I've seen in interiors magazines, so the boys can draw pictures with chalk and I can write my shopping list – which will include things like terrine and macarons now that we live in France and will be buying things like that.

But Frank seems so excited about the device and so eager to help that I say: 'Brilliant, I'm sure it will be super useful,' though I can't actually see myself using it at all. What would be the point?

# 6

*September, Mozène*

**Aura**

Once my site is up and running, Frank also helps me navigate another website which is all in French and which will set me up as a business in just a few clicks, apparently. 'Don't worry – you don't have to pay anything unless you earn, and it will help you get into the health system more easily,' he adds. Then we look at various Facebook pages and other sites where he thinks I could advertise my fledgling counselling business.

By the time we've done all that it is lunchtime, so it seems rude not to ask him to stay and eat with us. Helen and the boys arrive back in the kitchen just as I'm putting bread, cheese, ham, tomatoes and anything else I can find in the fridge on the table. It's a far cry from the nourishing home-made soup I envisaged myself making for lunch, perhaps with some sourdough bread (also home-made, naturally) – but there never seems to be any time. And I really do need to go shopping.

Helen is carrying a bunch of wildflowers she has picked. She takes an old carafe down from the dresser, fills it with water, arranges the flowers prettily and puts them on the table. Sorrel is carrying a fistful of dandelions and weeds and thrusts them at me. 'Fowers, Mummy,' he says.

'Sorrel! They're lovely, thank you!' I say, pretending to smell them. I put them in a glass of water next to Helen's rustic-chic arrangement where they look even more bedraggled, but Sorrel seems pleased with them.

'Pretty,' he says.

'Thank you so much for keeping the boys occupied, Helen. We've got so much done! Did you have a good morning?'

She unclips Bay from his buggy and lifts him into his highchair before taking the large supermarket bag which is hanging off the back of the buggy and showing it to me. It's full of twigs, leaves, tiny stones, feathers and some more flowers.

'It was great! We collected these. I'm not entirely sure what we'll do with them, but the boys had fun picking up anything that caught their eye. They're mainly too big and heavy for a traditional collage, but I thought maybe we could create something with them out in the garden this afternoon? Unless you had any other plans for the boys, Aura?'

'Oh gosh, no, that sounds an ideal activity for them, as long as you're happy to do that? I know you're only officially supposed to work five hours a day and I don't want to feel

43

like a complete slave driver!' I laugh, but even to me it sounds forced. I'm mindful of what Chloe said about our 'unpaid au pair' arrangement with Helen, and don't want her to feel exploited.

'It will be a pleasure,' Helen says. 'Anyway, it's not as if I'm doing anything else this afternoon, is it? I'll get them back to you in time for their tea, perhaps you could take over then?'

Nick comes in, treading mud as usual, and sits down at the table. 'Speaking of childcare duties, Helen, we wondered if you'd be happy to babysit this Saturday?' he says. 'We can either pay you the going rate, or you can take some extra time off during the week – whatever works best for you.'

I bite down on my anger – we haven't discussed this yet. I don't want to go to Thea's party and I don't know if I'm ready to leave the boys all evening with someone who, although she seems brilliant with them, I don't know all that well. It's different during the day when I'm always around. And it's quite obvious why Nick's so desperate to go, having seen what Thea looks like.

Helen's face falls. 'Oh, I'm sorry. Normally I would, but I'm going to see a friend in Toulouse this weekend. I would have checked with you, but I assumed the weekend would be my two days off? We've got a cheap hotel room booked and are planning to see the sights while the weather's still good – I was going to ask if you could drop me at the station but it's no problem if it's inconvenient – I'll just get a taxi.'

'Of course the weekends are your own, Helen,' I interject before Nick can say anything, 'and it's absolutely no problem

44

to give you a lift to the station.' She's so amazing with the boys and it makes my life so much easier to have someone around to help. The last thing I want is for her to think we're unreasonable or inflexible. 'It's no big deal – there will be other parties, I'm sure.'

'I can babysit, if you like?' Frank interjects. My feeling of relief immediately turns to panic – I don't want to go to this party and neither do I want to leave my precious boys with a man who I've only just met, however helpful he might seem.

'Frank, that's very kind but won't you be going to the party too?' I ask desperately.

'No. Thea's dinner parties aren't exactly my scene,' he says. 'I won't be invited to this one. I'm not the right sort of person. Chateaux-dwellers only, I think you'll find!' He laughs, but it sounds hollow. It seems like he's making a joke, but I don't entirely understand it.

'That's very decent of you, Frank, if you're sure,' Nick says, making me boil with rage. Only yesterday he was saying he thought Frank was weird and tragic, wasn't he? And yet suddenly he's good enough to look after my darling children.

'I don't know,' I bluster, 'the boys aren't used to being left in the evening and        '

Frank takes both my hands across the table. His palms are clammy and I want to pull mine away but that would be rude. 'Aura. Look at me.' He looks directly into my eyes and it feels too intimate. 'I have three children of my own and I did a lot of the day-to-day care when they were small. I now have two grandchildren. You'll only be down the road at Thea's place. I'll be at the end of the phone and you can

45

call me whenever you like, if it makes you feel better. It'll be good for you to meet some new people. Go on – get out there and enjoy yourself.'

I still don't want to, but I can't think of a way to say no that wouldn't seem insulting after everything he's done for me.

'OK, thank you, Frank. If you're sure.'

'Thanks, mate,' Nick adds. 'Appreciate it.'

# 7

*September, Mozène*

**Aura**

That night I'm dreaming I am in a cinema watching a film I don't understand when Nick shakes me awake. 'Where the fuck is that music coming from?' he shouts.

It's so loud I can barely hear what Nick is saying, though I can hear the boys screaming from their room next door even over the din. The music is creepy and dramatic with massive choral cadences and loud bangs – it sounds familiar but not in a good way – it makes me think of horror films. What the hell is going on?

I scramble out of bed to go to the boys, shouting at Nick, 'I think it's coming from downstairs – can you go and see?' and bump into Seb on the landing, who is bare-chested, wearing only pyjama bottoms and – for fuck's sake! – filming.

'What's happening?' he shouts.

'I don't know,' I snap. 'Get out of my way. And stay out of the boys' bedroom – you know the agreement.' The bathrooms and bedrooms are out of bounds to the crew.

Nick rushes down the stairs and suddenly the music cuts out, giving way to the boys' screams.

I lift Bay out of his cot and hold both of my sons in my arms in Sorrel's bed. 'Sssshh, ssshhh, it's OK now,' I soothe. Their sobs are already subsiding.

Seb has obeyed my instruction to stay out of the boys' room, but I see with a flash of annoyance he's filming Nick coming up the stairs.

'What was with the Verdi?' Seb says.

'Verdi?' Nick asks as he arrives on the landing.

'The music,' Seb persists. '*Dies Irae*. I was in the orchestra at uni and we did it for an end-of-term concert. I played percussion – brilliant fun, especially for that piece of music. Massive drum.' He mimes hitting something with a drumstick as he says 'Ba DUM Ba DUM Ba DUM Ba DUM. Fantastic.'

Nick puts his hand to his forehead. 'Right,' he says. 'I don't know what happened. It was the Astrid thing playing it. I unplugged it. Some kind of malfunction, I imagine.'

They continue to talk in low voices so I struggle to hear what they are saying and soon the boys are asleep again. I tuck the boys back into bed and join Nick and Seb on the landing. 'A malfunction?' I hiss. 'Why would that thing suddenly start playing demonic music in the middle of the night?'

Nick shrugs. 'I dunno. These things happen, don't they? Like when you go to a hotel and you get an alarm call at

3 a.m. because someone's given them the wrong room number. It feels weirder than it really is.'

That did happen to us once, what now seems like a lifetime ago. And I don't want to discuss this in front of Seb, who I'm not entirely sure didn't somehow set this up to give himself something more interesting to film for his programme. We've been pretty boring so far, after all.

'I guess. Anyway, I'm going back to bed. Night, Seb,' I say pointedly. 'See you in the morning.'

'Sorry about the music last night, Helen,' I say at breakfast as she helps the boys eat their porridge, 'I'm not sure what happened there.'

'Yes, it woke me up,' she said. 'But it went off again so quickly I figured you'd got it sorted and so I stayed put. Very odd,' she says.

'Music!' Sorrel cries, waving his spoon around. 'Very loud.'

'That's right, Sorrel,' Helen agrees. 'Very loud music.' She looks out the window. 'On another note, though, I was thinking about what to do with the boys today and wondered if you'd be happy for me to borrow the car this morning, if you don't need it? The weather looks awful, so I thought it might be nice to take the boys to soft play in town – let them burn off some energy. Assuming it's OK with you, of course. I had a look at the website and it's only a few euros – no charge at all for Bay.'

I feel a lurch of panic – do I want someone I don't know all that well driving my beloved children around?

'Oh, um, I'm not sure, I thought maybe I'd . . .' I bluster, but I don't know what to say. I would love to get on with disposing of some of the junk from various rooms – the skip arrived yesterday – and it'll be much harder to do it with the boys around.

'It's all right, if you feel weird about me driving the boys, I understand. I'm sure we can find something to do here,' Helen says.

'No, it's OK,' I say. I need to get over this. I trust Helen. They'll be fine with her. 'Soft play sounds a wonderful idea – thank you.'

Soft play is a resounding success – the boys always loved it when Nick took them back in London too. Later I drop Helen at the station as promised. As soon as I get back to the house, I miss her. Nick is simultaneously trying to strip ancient wallpaper while keeping an eye on the boys, so everyone is absolutely covered in dust, scraps of paper and God knows what else.

I wish he wouldn't try to get on with other jobs while he's meant to be looking after the children, but I can't be bothered to get into a row about it now.

I usher the boys into the kitchen and put them in front of the iPad (I promised myself I wouldn't do that anymore once we were in France, but needs must) and achieve my first cooked-from-scratch meal since I've arrived – a lasagne. I figure the boys can have it for their tea and I can leave some for Frank for his dinner when he's babysitting tomorrow. I know he won't accept any payment, so the least I can do is provide him with something to eat.

I remember what he said about Thea's parties 'not being his thing' and wonder again what he meant. What is it going to be like? I'm not going to know anyone and Thea wasn't exactly warm and welcoming when she came round. She made it very clear it's Nick she's interested in, not me. Going to this party feels like a terrible idea in so many ways. I should have stood my ground and said no.

# 8

*September, Mozène*

**Aura**

I'm feeding the boys earlier than usual as I want them to be asleep by the time Frank arrives. It's highly unlikely they'll stay asleep the whole evening, but at least that way he might be able to enjoy a quiet dinner, hopefully. Also, I'm not sure how the boys are going to react to us going out; if they start screaming and crying and begging us not to go, I don't think I'll be able to bear it. Nick would probably insist we go anyway, and the whole evening would get off to a horrible start. Again I find myself wishing we didn't have to go at all.

I manage to get the boys to eat their tea (incredibly slowly, but we get there eventually), and we skip bath time, going straight to the three of us lying down on our bed, reading stories and cuddling until they are both asleep.

Nick refuses to stop stripping wallpaper until about fifteen minutes before we are due to leave, at which point he jumps in the shower and gets dressed. His shirt isn't ironed but I wasn't going to offer to do it for him (even if I had the time). It'll have to do.

Frank arrives and I give him a quick debrief (with Seb and Chloe filming; sometimes I really wish they'd just fuck off) and show him where the lasagne and salad are before diving in the shower.

I half-dry my hair and put on an old Hobbs dress – it hangs off me these days, as the stress of everything that happened in London and the move seems to have resulted in me losing some weight. I suppose that's something. There isn't enough time to do my make-up properly as I don't want to be late, so I'm feeling far from perfectly groomed by the time we are downstairs ready to go.

'It's likely the boys will wake up,' I remind Frank, 'they usually do. I've told them we're going out this evening and they seem fine with it, but they're so little it's difficult to know how much they take in.' I feel another pang of unease. Is it really OK to leave them with someone I barely know? I wish Nick and Frank hadn't railroaded me into this. Suddenly I wonder if Nick had approached Frank behind my back and talked him into offering to babysit. My anger flares again at the thought.

Anyway. Too late now. 'So what we usually do is sit with them until they go back to sleep,' I continue, even though, as far as Nick is concerned, this is not part of the new regime. 'They're not allowed to come downstairs, and they have water in their room in sippy cups, so you just need to sit there for a while, or maybe read a story with the light as dim as you can. Normally it's fine, but if they won't settle, I would a hundred times rather you called me than allowed them to get too distressed. For your sake as well as theirs!' I add, trying to sound light-hearted and jokey but failing.

Frank nods. 'Understood. I'm very happy to read stories until they drop off again. But if there are any major issues, I'll call, I promise. Now go! Have fun! Thea puts on quite a spread. I'm sure you'll enjoy yourselves. The boys will be fine – please don't worry. And I won't be offended if you want to call – as many times as you like.'

Thea was very clear that the film crew were not to come with us this evening. 'I'm holding my annual Hallowe'en party next month and they are very welcome at that,' she said. 'But this is an intimate dinner party with some of my closest friends, most of whom are very private people. They wouldn't want to be on TV. For some of them, it might even put their security at risk.'

I'm certain this isn't true; Thea is simply trying to make herself and her friends sound important. But I don't care because I'm delighted to have a night away from the film crew. I'm sick of having them hanging around all the time. Seb was annoyed when I told him they couldn't come and grumbled it 'wasn't in the spirit of the show', but fuck him. I told him there was nothing I could do about someone else barring them from their private property. Chloe didn't seem to care at all – I think she was only too pleased to have the night off.

# 9

*September, Mozène*

**Aura**

Chateau Amaryllis is a fifteen-minute drive away from our place and I'm totally unprepared for how stunning it is. Thea said it was finished but, wow, it's like something out of a film.

'Don't park right in front,' I tell Nick, embarrassed by our battered old Renault Scenic in such grand surroundings. 'Let's park round the side.'

I take Nick's arm – partly because I'm unsteady on my now-unfamiliar heels and partly because I'm feeling possessive after the way Thea flirted with him when she came round before. We walk up the stone steps and Nick pulls a brass lever like you'd expect to see on the front of Downton Abbey. Deep inside the chateau, a bell chimes.

When the door opens, it isn't Thea who greets us but a beautiful young woman wearing a full-length red sequinned evening dress. I feel underdressed in my at-least-five-years-old simple black dress, which might as well be a rag in comparison.

'Good evening. Monsieur et Madame Dorian, I think? I am Emilie, your hostess for the evening.' Her English is grammatically perfect but she speaks with a French accent. 'May I take your coats?'

I hand over my Zara wrap and grip my Accessorize clutch bag tightly. I checked several times before leaving the house that my phone was fully charged, the volume was turned up to high and vibrate was also switched on – I even got Frank to help me give him his own 'Flight of Valkyries' ring tone so that I'd know straight away it was him calling, in the event of a problem with the boys. Even so, I'm desperate to check I haven't somehow accidentally switched it off, but don't feel I can take my phone out now. I'll pop to the loo as soon as I can to check it's all set up OK.

Emilie leads us through an enormous atrium with a crystal chandelier into a small lounge with an oversized fireplace. Though the days are generally still warm, the fire is lit, no doubt because it makes the room look more impressive. There are two huge antique leather sofas on either side of it with a glass coffee table in between, on which rest two giant copper urns. There is a couple on each sofa, the women a little older than us – about the same age as Helen, but way more glamorous; the men a decade or more older than them. There's also a man in his mid-twenties sitting in an armchair at the end of the coffee table.

'Monsieur and Madame Dorian, may I present Monsieur and Madame Byng,' she indicates the couple to the left, 'and Monsieur and Madame Silverthorn. And also Monsieur Hervé who is joining us this evening. Would you both like a glass of champagne?'

'Yes, please,' Nick and I say at the same time. I am not planning to drink much this evening – I offered to drive, pretending that I was being generous so that Nick could relax, but really I want to be in charge of when we leave in case the boys need me. But having seen the other guests and the surroundings, I'm even more nervous than I was before. I tell myself it will be OK to have a glass or two to help me ease into the evening.

They all get to their feet and come over to welcome us, and everyone does the *bise* – one kiss each side. Both women are wearing floor-length dresses – one I recognize from a magazine as a Temperley – and again I feel underdressed and awkward. One of the women has clearly fake boobs and the other looks like she's recently had lip fillers which haven't settled down yet. Thea had said the dress code would be 'smart casual', which the men seem to have taken on board – they are all dressed similarly to Nick, except for Hervé (is that his first or second name? It wasn't clear), who is wearing a traditional dinner jacket. The women are perfectly coiffed and dressed as if they are gracing the red carpet at a film premiere. I wonder if Thea deliberately downplayed the smartness of the occasion, wanting me to feel awkward and on the back foot. If that was her plan, she certainly succeeded.

Where is Thea anyway?

Nick and I sit opposite each other, one on each sofa, and Emilie returns with the champagne and a fresh plate of canapés.

'You're new to the area, I believe?' one of the men asks. He looks vaguely familiar, but I can't quite place him.

I nod, quickly chewing and swallowing the quail's egg dusted with paprika. 'Yes, we are. We arrived a few weeks ago; we've bought a chateau about fifteen minutes away to renovate and run as a B&B, eventually. And you? Have you been here long?'

He takes a large gulp of his champagne. 'We've had the house around ten years. Tiggy's been here most of the time for about the last five or so; I'm mainly in London and come for weekends and holidays and the like.'

'Sounds idyllic!' I say, wondering if I would love or hate being alone in our chateau, just me and the boys. 'And what do you do in London?'

'I'm an MP,' he says. Ah. That's why he looks familiar. And I guess Thea wasn't merely trying to impress by saying that her dinner guests needed privacy. 'So it's a little tricky to get out here too often as it's the done thing to be in the constituency at weekends, but I can usually fly over every other weekend or so. Plus during recesses obviously.'

'Gosh. Must be hard to spend so much time apart,' I say, though I've already decided I am a little envious. Especially the way things are between Nick and me at the moment.

'You get used to it,' Tiggy says. 'I have our two girls to keep me busy, during the school holidays at least, and a little landscape gardening business.'

'I see. And you, Mr . . .' I've totally forgotten all the names

Emilie gave us and it only now strikes me as weird that she introduced everyone by their surnames. Does anyone even do that anymore outside of school?

'Tristram,' he says. 'We live out here full-time, bar popping back now and again to sort out the various property investments we have in the UK. This is my wife, Celia.'

The one with the fake boobs. 'Lovely to meet you,' I say. She smiles in reply, but doesn't say anything.

'And you, Hervé?' I ask. 'Do you live locally?'

'No, I live in Toulouse,' he says, his voice more heavily accented than Emilie's. It's the first time I've looked at him properly and he really is extraordinarily good-looking. 'I am, 'ow you say, in the entertainment business.'

The champagne is slipping down nicely and I'm already starting to feel more relaxed and am about to ask Hervé something else when a gong sounds. It's so unexpected I can't help but laugh.

'What's that?' I squeak.

Emilie is standing at the door holding a small brass gong and a mallet.

'Mademoiselle Thea d'Arbanville,' she announces.

Everyone stands up and I suppress an urge to giggle. What the fuck? I glance at Nick, but he isn't looking at me. Thea is gliding across the room in a bodycon white gown (also floor-length, naturally) with a gossamer cape.

'Darlings! So pleased you could all make it this evening. Dinner is served – shall we go through?'

59

# 10

*September, Mozène*

**Aura**

We cross the atrium to the other side of the chateau and enter the dining room, which is smaller and cosier than I had imagined. A fire is blazing in another oversized fireplace and a table covered in white linen is set for eight. There are place cards with our names on in elaborate cursive script, but there is no need to read them as Emilie and two butlers in tailcoats show us to our places. I am in between Tristram and the other man, whose name I have forgotten. Thea is between Nick and Hervé. The room is lit entirely by candlelight from ornate holders placed around the room. Elaborate candelabras on the table narrow at the bottom so they don't obstruct the table or our view of each other and branch out higher up to light the table from there.

Looking around at the others I can see it's a very flattering, sensual light.

As I sit down, I remember that I wanted to check my phone or even call home before we sat down for dinner, but it feels too late to get up from the table now. I put my bag on my lap rather than on the floor to be sure that I will hear the phone if Frank rings.

The two butlers circle the table, offering more champagne.

'Only a half-glass for me,' I say, 'I'm driving.'

'I or my colleague will be happy to drive you home if you prefer,' he says, 'and arrange for your car to be delivered back to you. Mademoiselle d'Arbanville likes everyone to be able to fully relax into the evening. But that is up to you, of course. As you wish.'

'Oh. OK.' A large part of me wants to stay sober in case I need to go home before the end of the evening – I don't want to feel *trapped* – but I catch a glance of Nick and Thea, heads together at the end of the table and her touching him on the arm as she throws back her head and laughs uproariously at something he's said, and realize that a drink or two might help me get through the evening. 'If you insist, I'll have some more, thank you.'

'I don't insist – everything that happens this evening is your own decision,' he says, which seems a strange thing to say, but maybe it's because he is not speaking his first language.

'Sorry, it's just a turn of phrase. Yes, please, I would like some more champagne. Thank you.'

He nods and tops up my glass. Nick is now whispering something in Thea's ear. It is too intimate a position between

61

two people who barely know each other. The sexy lighting reminds me how good-looking Nick is and why I fancied him so much all those years ago when we first met. He and Thea look like something from a film or a photoshoot, leaning in together like that, lit only by candles. Hot fury courses through me. Has he forgotten I'm here?

I turn to the man on my left, who I've remembered is called Bertie.

'So tell me, Bertie, what brought you to the Mozène?'

Bertie launches into a long and boring story about how he was great friends with a previous prime minister who recommended the area so he came on holiday and fell in love with it and blah di blah di blah. I say 'mmm-hmm' and smile and nod in the right places, but all the while I'm keeping an eye on Nick and only half listening. I'm relieved to see Thea has now turned her attention to Hervé and is flicking her hair about like a show pony as he unashamedly casts approving glances at her ample cleavage. Nick is now talking to fake boobs woman, but I can tell by his face he doesn't find her attractive or even interesting. I allow myself to relax a little.

The butlers have distributed a cold *amuse-bouche* tomato soup and I eat it (all of two teaspoons) while Bertie drones on about the buying process for their chateau and how difficult it was to get planning permission for the home cinema extension. This time when the butler passes with the wine I ask for a glass of white without hesitation. It is cold, crisp and delicious.

The *amuse-bouches* are cleared away and two enormous platters of oysters on crushed ice are brought out, with little jugs of shallot vinegar and intricately cut lemon halves. By now Bertie has moved on to some of the various problems they encountered with their builders and the difficulties of French paperwork. Nick is glazing over as fake boobs lady (Celia?) tells him a story about her housekeeper being deported; from the snatches I can glean, it's a wonder he hasn't died of boredom.

'And you, Aura,' Bertie asks as the oyster shells are taken away and Chateaubriand steak is carved at the table and dished up onto piping hot plates with dauphinoise potatoes and asparagus spears, 'do you have children?'

It's the first time he's stopped droning on about himself all evening to ask me a question, so I'm a bit taken aback. I take a bite of the steak – it is incredibly tender – before answering. 'Yes, we have two boys, Sorrel and Bay,' I reply.

'Interesting names,' he says, somewhat patronizingly. 'And . . . how old are they? Are they out here with you?'

I know I don't look like much compared to the other women here tonight, but surely I don't look old enough to have grown-up children? I'm not even thirty years old! Lost for words, I reach for my glass. It's empty, but a butler appears and I accept a glass of red to go with the steak.

'Bay's fifteen months and Sorrel's nearly three,' I say.

He nods. 'Lovely ages. Ours are a bit older, but they're at boarding school most of the time now anyway.' Ah – that was what he was asking. He thought they were away at school. That I was someone who would have children only to send them away, like him. It's clear I have absolutely nothing in common with these people. 'So where are your children tonight?' he continues. 'Did you bring them with you?'

'No, I didn't realize that was an option.' Was it? I'd much rather have done that. Thea didn't offer – I'd have remembered if she had. Then again I can't see the boys fitting into this set-up. Even if I'd managed to get them to go to sleep upstairs somewhere, they'd probably have been awake and shouting for me by now. Or they'd be toddling around, covering some of Thea's no doubt priceless *objets* in sticky handprints. Or even worse, breaking things. I feel a pang of guilt that I haven't phoned to check on them yet or even looked at my phone. I touch my bag again. I'd have heard if it had rung, surely? After this course I will excuse myself and at the very least see if I have any messages – or call Frank, if I can.

'We've got a guy called Frank babysitting them, you might know him?' I say. 'Been out here for ages. He's a friend of Thea's; he introduced us to her, actually.'

'Ah! Frank. Yes. I know. Oh, they'll be fine with Frank – he'll do anything for anyone. Salt of the earth type – I know he helped Tiggy out a lot, especially when we first arrived. And he's always happy to pop over to fix a blocked sink or minor IT issue when I'm not here. Or even if I am – I'd be the first to admit I'm not very good at getting my hands dirty,' he guffaws.

My wine has been topped up yet again, and I'm feeling slightly drunk, which gives me the courage to ask what I was wondering about earlier. 'I was surprised when Frank offered to babysit – I thought he'd be invited this evening too, being that he said he and Thea are good friends?'

Bertie laughs. 'Frank can be something of a liability at parties, especially ones like these. Gets a tad . . . overexcited, shall we say.'

What does he mean by that? That he drinks too much? I left him a couple of beers to have with the lasagne but . . . oh God. Is he an alcoholic?

'But you've got nothing to worry about with your nippers – he used to babysit ours often. I'd trust him with my life – but probably not with my wife!' He laughs uproariously at his own joke and I titter along politely, even though it doesn't seem particularly funny.

The plates are cleared away and I seize the opportunity to go to the loo to check my phone. My head spins as I stand up and it is a struggle to walk straight.

Emilie is waiting outside the dining room – has she been there all this time? – and leads me to a door at the end of the corridor.

Inside there is an anteroom with a pink chaise longue and a vanity unit with perfume, hairspray, disposable hairbrushes in a pot, hand cream and even a discreet dish of tampons. It's so feminine I can only assume this is actually a bathroom especially for female visitors and there's a separate one for men. How weird. I go through the next door into the actual loo, put the lid down and sit on top of the seat.

I take my phone out and feel a whoosh of relief as I see that there are no messages. Even so, after Bertie's cryptic remarks about Frank, I can't help but call. Frank answers on the second ring.

'Hello?' he says. He doesn't sound drunk. At least, nowhere near as drunk as I am. 'Aura?'

'Yes, it's me,' I whisper, because I think Emilie is waiting for me outside the door and I don't want her to hear. 'I'm just ringing to check everything's OK.'

'Yes, all fine and dandy. I enjoyed your lovely lasagne, the boys woke up about an hour ago, I read them a couple of stories and they went back to sleep, good as gold. You've got nothing to worry about. You having fun there?'

'Um, yes,' I say, because it feels rude to say no when he was the one who introduced us to Thea. 'I decided to have a drink so one of the . . . I guess they're staff, said they'd drive us back, but we won't be too late.'

'No rush, you take your time. I'm a night owl anyway, and nothing particular to get back for.' I wonder if he's angling for an invitation to stay the night, but my head is too fuzzy to work it out, so I push the thought away.

'OK, thanks, Frank. And you'll call me if there are any problems?'

'In a heartbeat. Now go and have fun!'

I lift the seat, have a wee, flush and then wash my hands. I look at myself in the mirror. My face is blotchy from all the wine and my mascara is smudged, but in my rush to leave the house I forgot to bring any make-up with me. Ah well. I'll have to do.

Emilie is indeed waiting for me outside the door and leads me back to the dining room even though it's just up the corridor and I could have easily found my way. Bertie is now chatting to Nick and fake boobs lady, so I can't ask him what he meant about Frank. Though I'm not so worried now that I've spoken to him and it sounds like everything is fine at home, thankfully.

Dessert is crêpes Suzette – they are being flambéed on a trolley at the side of the table by one of the butlers. I glance at Nick, who is looking rather glassy-eyed – not sure if that's the drink or the conversation. A bit of both, I think. Thea is now practically in Hervé's lap, though he doesn't seem to mind. Perhaps they're a couple? There was nothing to indicate they were earlier, but who knows?

The man on the other side of me – Tristram – is now chatting with lip-filler woman and I can't be bothered to try to break in to either of the conversations. I take the opportunity to eat my crepe and appreciate the surroundings. I don't think I've ever eaten in such a beautiful room. There are French windows which open out on to a terrace lit with fairy lights. The walls are exposed stone and the two windows are framed with heavy curtains without a speck of dust. Over the table there's a smaller version of the crystal chandelier in the atrium, which is shimmering and glinting in the candlelight. Above the fireplace there's an enormous modern painting of colourful, geometric shapes which probably shouldn't work in a period room like this, but somehow does. And in each corner are huge, intricately sculpted flower arrangements, lit by strategically placed candles, the heady scent of both filling the room and making me a little dizzy.

The plates are cleared away and Emilie appears in the door with a gong again, which she taps seemingly without any sense of irony. Although, now that I've been here the entire evening, while the gong still seems incredibly pretentious, it no longer catches me by surprise as it did earlier.

'Coffee and digestifs will be served in the salon,' she says.

We all get up and follow her through to the room where we had champagne at the beginning of the evening, which now feels like a lifetime ago. The lights have been turned off and the room is lit purely by candles, like the dining room. They smell amazing. There's choral classical music playing – I'm not sure what it is, but it's somehow sexy.

The eight of us sit down on the two sofas – the armchair Hervé was sitting in earlier has vanished. Emilie manages to direct who sits where without actually saying so, and I find myself between Bertie and Hervé. The sofas suddenly don't feel so huge and I notice that both men's legs are pressed against mine. I try to shift away but there isn't enough room. In between the sofas, the glass table is topped with several bottles of Cristal champagne in an enormous ice bucket, a bottle of Remy Martin Louis XVI in a decanter that looks like an oversized perfume bottle, various appropriately sized glasses and a couple of plates of exquisite-looking petit-fours.

Celia takes a tiny pouch from her Chanel handbag, tips some white powder onto the table and starts expertly fashioning it into little lines with a platinum credit card. It takes me a couple of beats to realize exactly what she's doing. I've never seen it done in real life before – only in films or on TV.

She takes out a twenty-euro note and rolls it into a tube, before leaning down and snorting a line as casually as if she were checking her lipstick in the mirror. I try to arrange my face to not look as shocked as I feel right now. I sneak a glance at Nick, but he is leaning forward, helping himself to a canapé, and I can't see his face.

Is this OK? Most of these people are parents; at least one of them helps to run a country! No wonder Thea didn't want me to bring Seb and Chloe along tonight. And thank God I didn't try to bring the boys. I couldn't have had them innocently sleeping upstairs while people take Class A drugs downstairs or – oh my God – what if they'd come downstairs and seen what's happening?

Tristram pulls one of the bottles of champagne out of the silver bucket and says, 'Shall I be mother?' as he expertly rips off the foil and basket, pops the cork, fills the eight flutes and deposits the bottle upside down in the bucket. It looks like the butlers have been dismissed and I feel a tremor of alarm – they're still going to drive us home, aren't they? Nick and I have both drunk far too much to drive – so has everyone else, as far as I can tell.

Celia passes the twenty-euro note to Nick and I look on aghast as he takes a line. He doesn't look at me as he sits up, dusts off his nose and takes a swig of champagne. I'm not surprised he won't catch my eye – he knows I'll be horrified. We don't do drugs – never have done. Not even a bit of weed at university when we met. I thought we were still on the same page on this issue – clearly I was wrong.

I try to maintain a neutral expression as the note comes round the table towards me, and keep my voice light and steady as I say, 'No thanks, not for me tonight.' I look meaningfully at Nick, who is now talking to Celia and casting too many not-very-subtle glances at her fake cleavage for my liking. I pass the note on to Hervé, who takes a snort like all the others. To my relief, no one feels the need to comment on my refusal.

My face feels hot. I wonder what time it is but there are no clocks in here and I'm not wearing a watch. I want to go home. But I don't know how to extricate myself without looking rude or a prude. Does it matter? Should I just say I'd like to go now? Or pretend there's a problem with the

69

boys? I'm not sure, so I don't do anything, but I'm feeling more uncomfortable with every second that passes.

Tristram opens another bottle of champagne and tops everyone up. By the time he sits down again, Celia and Tiggy are openly kissing. What the fuck? Nick is staring at them and – oh my God – I can see a bulge in his trousers. Hervé puts his hand on the inside of my thigh and turns to look at me lasciviously.

I jump up in horror, spilling my champagne. Isn't he with Thea? Why is he touching me? 'I'm really sorry, we need to go, we have someone babysitting our sons,' I blurt.

I push past Bertie to extricate myself from the group; it's difficult as the table is too close to the sofa and I don't want to knock anything over. Thea catches my hand in hers as I pass.

'Aura,' she says, her voice low and gentle. I turn to look at her. 'I thought you might like to play with Hervé. I invited him with you in mind, I thought he might be your type, no?'

'I thought he was your boyfriend,' I say stupidly.

She waves her hand. 'Oh no. We all share here. You can go to one of the bedrooms if you like? Your husband is welcome to watch, or join in if he prefers. Hervé is very flexible.'

I glance back at the sofas where Tristram now has his hand up Celia's skirt and Bertie is watching the two women kissing, quite openly playing with himself. Nick is thankfully not touching anyone, but he's not exactly averting his eyes either.

'It's . . . not my thing. But thank you,' I say, even more stupidly, as if I'm refusing a cup of tea. Thea has now put

70

her hand on my leg and I back away, no longer caring if I knock things over. 'I really think we need to get back to the boys now. One of your . . . butlers said they could drive us so if . . .'

She shrugs. 'OK. Entirely up to you. I thought you'd enjoy Hervé, but I guess I got it wrong. I apologize.' She looks over to the other sofa. 'Nick? Are you leaving too?'

'Yes, he is!' I snap before he can say anything.

She sighs. 'Such a shame. I thought you'd enjoy tonight.'

'I did, I just . . .' I bluster.

She holds up a hand. 'No problem. Absolutely the last thing I want is for anyone to do anything they don't want to do. That's the only rule during these evenings. Emilie!' she calls.

Emilie appears in the doorway. Was she waiting out there all that time?

'Could you get one of the boys to drive Nick and Aura home? They'd like to leave now.'

# 11

*September, Mozène*

**Aura**

I don't utter a word in the near-silent Tesla we are driven home in as I'm aware the butler/driver might be listening. What the fuck was that? I stare out the window, silently fuming at Nick. Would he have stayed if I hadn't made him leave? Would he have let me 'play', as Thea put it, with Hervé, had I wanted to? Would he have wanted to watch? Join in even? I can't believe he took the cocaine. Do I even know him at all?

The butler pulls up outside our chateau and it's only then I realize we didn't need to tell him where to go – he already knew. 'Would you like me to pick you up tomorrow so you can retrieve your car?' he asks. 'Or you can leave me your key and I can have someone bring it back for you?'

'No, thank you,' I say. 'We wouldn't want to disturb you any further. I'm sure we'll be fine.' We only have one car so I'm not sure why I say that, but I can't bear the thought of being beholden to Thea and her minions in any way. Maybe Seb will give me a lift over. Whatever happens, I'm definitely not sending Nick there on his own.

We get out of the car and Nick walks away from me before the butler has driven off, probably to avoid me laying into him. I follow him inside to the living room, which looks like a hovel compared to the lavish surroundings we've just come from, even though I tidied up especially before Frank came over today. In spite of everything else which has happened this evening my heart sinks at the thought of the huge amount of work we have ahead of us – it's hard to imagine that this could ever become anything vaguely approximating Thea's place. And then there follows a wave of anger as I remember what she was suggesting. How dare she!

Frank switches off the TV and stands up. 'Ah! Back early, I see. How was your night? Thea's parties are quite something, aren't they?' he says.

Are all her parties like that? Does he know? He must do. Why didn't he warn me? Does he think that's the sort of people we are? 'Yes, quite something,' I say, frostily. 'Not my thing, to be honest. Anyway, was everything OK here?' I ask, wanting to avoid discussing what did or didn't go on this evening. 'Did the boys wake up again?'

'All fine,' he says, picking up his bag. 'I enjoyed our little story time – it's a long time since mine were that young. And they didn't wake up again, no. Your camera crew people popped out for a while and came back about ten thirty, I think. Guess they found the village bar wasn't very exciting.'

'Well, thanks again, Frank. Are you sure I can't offer you something for your time?'

He waves his hand. 'No, no, it was my pleasure. Any time. I don't get to see my grandchildren much so . . .' His eyes get a little misty. I know I should be polite and ask him to stay for a drink as he's put himself out for us like this but I simply can't face it. All I want is for this evening to be over.

I don't say anything and I guess he senses my mood. 'Anyway. I'll get out of your way now. Sleep well.'

'Thanks, Frank. Safe journey.'

After he's gone, I close the door behind me and turn to look at Nick, ready to give him two barrels. But the sight of him wide-eyed and buzzing makes me sick and I find I simply don't want to speak to him at all.

'You'd better find another room to sleep in tonight,' I tell him. 'There's no way you're sharing a bed with me.'

# 12

*September, Mozène*

**Aura**

In the morning the boys are up too early as usual – going to bed past midnight is a very late night for us these days. I didn't sleep well. Why did we come here, to France? Is everyone we meet here going to be like those people last night?

I make breakfast on autopilot, I am exhausted. Nick comes through, grabs some toast and mumbles something about getting on with pulling out an old bathroom. Fuck's sake. I need to speak to him about last night, but I don't want to do it in front of the film crew. I'll have to try to find a way to corner him alone later.

The prospect of having to entertain the boys all day alone

and with a crushing hangover looms ahead of me. I can't wait for Helen to come back this evening.

Shortly after lunch when, amazingly, both of the boys have decided to take a nap at the same time, there's a knock at the door.

It takes me a second to recognize her as she looks so different in jeans and a simple top with her hair in a pony-tail, but it's Tiggy from last night. She's not wearing any make-up and the freshness of her face makes her look younger and much friendlier. Even the lip filler is less obvious than it was yesterday.

'Hi, Aura? Sorry for calling in unannounced but I was passing and I thought I'd come in and say hello. I brought you a cake?' She holds out an old Quality Street tin. 'If I'm calling at a bad time, please say so, but I remember how lonely I felt when I first arrived here so . . . well, anyway.'

'Not a bad time at all, please, come in.' I'm grateful for the company. Nick is upstairs and the camera crew are currently with him, so we can chat in peace. 'Thank you for the cake. Shall I make some tea for us to have with it?'

I flick the kettle on and Tiggy settles herself at the table. 'How did you find the party last night?' she asks.

I feel myself go crimson as I remember that, the last time I saw her, she was snorting coke and snogging another woman. I laugh. 'Well, Thea has a beautiful place and dinner was amazing but the other stuff . . . a bit racy for my tastes, I'm afraid.' I realize with annoyance that I didn't say 'our'. 'We moved here for a quiet life,' I add.

She pulls a face. 'Yeah, I hear you. Thea's parties are . . . quite something.'

'Are all her parties like that?'

'No, not all. She loves a party and likes to show off. She holds a couple a year which are much more inclusive and family-friendly but the dinner parties . . . yes they do tend to be like last night.'

She blushes. 'I bet I know what you're thinking. Me kissing Celia like that . . . must seem weird to you. But we don't just do it for the men, if you know what I mean.'

I nod. 'None of my business, I'm sure,' I say, but actually, I haven't a clue what she means.

She sighs. 'You might as well know, it's no secret among our friends here that Celia and I . . . spend time together when we can. We can't be a proper couple because Bertie won't get divorced – he thinks it would be bad for his career. Neither of us want to do that right now anyway because we still get on OK and because of our kids, but . . . well. That's a big part of why I go to Thea's parties, I find them . . . liberating. It's about the only place I can be who I want to be in public, although I admit it is rather . . . voyeuristic. Or whatever the opposite of that is. Exhibitionistic? Is that a word?'

'Gosh,' I say, not knowing how to react.

'Anyway, enough about me!' She waves her hand dismissively as if she's just told me she prefers apples to oranges rather than that she's a closet lesbian who doesn't mind a bit of light exhibitionism. 'How about you? Did it all go OK with Frank babysitting? Your husband said you were worried about leaving the boys here.'

'Oh yes it was fine! It's kind of you to ask. It was only me being silly – we're not used to leaving them with babysitters. And they're not very good at staying asleep, sadly. But Frank seemed to have it all under control. Do you know him? He seems like a nice guy.'

'Yes, I do. Everyone knows Frank. And he *is* a nice guy. But, strictly *entre nous*, I'd be careful if I were you. He helped me out a lot over the years, especially when we first arrived – Bertie is away most of the time, obviously.'

I pour the boiling water into a teapot and bring it over to the table with mugs, plates, forks, milk and sugar on a tray. I cut a couple of slices of Tiggy's cake and put them on plates, hand one to her and sit down.

'Really? How do you mean?' I ask with a stab of panic. I should have followed my instincts and refused to go to the party. I knew it. I shouldn't have left the boys with him.

Tiggy takes a forkful of cake and chews thoughtfully. She swallows. 'Hmm. It's difficult to describe. There's nothing I can put my finger on exactly, but over time I started feeling slightly uneasy about Frank. He got a bit . . . clingy almost. He was always coming round, whether I wanted him to or not, day or night. He then did the same to Thea when she arrived, but she put a stop to it more quickly than me. She's more forthright, for one thing, and also she can easily afford to pay if she ever needs help with anything. Frank was livid when she stopped inviting him to her parties because he used to get a little . . . over-enthusiastic, shall we say. Thea likes people to enjoy themselves and feel free at her parties, but she's also very hot on consent. It appears the two of them have made up again now, but she still keeps him at arm's length. As do I.'

She pauses.

'I feel bad saying bad stuff about him though,' she continues. 'Ungrateful. I'd have struggled without his help in the beginning. But I was glad when Thea arrived and he latched on to her instead.'

But by now I am barely listening. 'Should I not have trusted him with the children?' I blurt.

'Oh gosh, I didn't mean that! He's great with kids.' I feel a whoosh of relief. 'He babysat ours loads of times over the years,' Tiggy continues, 'and I was never worried about it. They'd have told me if there was anything they were . . . uncomfortable with. No, he's not dodgy in that way, more . . . needy, I suppose. I dare say it's because he's lonely. But I'm sure he's completely harmless. And now I feel like a complete bitch.'

I laugh. It feels like about the first time I've laughed genuinely since we arrived in France. 'You're not being a bitch. It's helpful for me to hear about what other people are like here. We don't know anyone.'

Tiggy rummages in her bag and hands me a card. 'We're not far away. Come and see me any time – you're welcome to bring the boys too, if that's easier – I miss having kids around. With Bertie and the girls away most of the time, I'm usually on my own. To be honest, I'd welcome the company.'

'Thank you, I will.' I'd never have thought so last night, but Tiggy is the first person I've met since we arrived who I feel I could actually become friends with.

Seb and Chloe come in with the camera, so Tiggy and I continue our chat on much safer ground. She asks why Nick

79

and I decided to come out to France and our plans for the chateau. Obviously I don't tell her the real reason behind coming here, not with the camera running, but I think in time, and in private, I probably will. Our conversation isn't very exciting – I can almost feel Seb willing something interesting to happen. And then the boys wake up and the house descends into chaos again. I take Tiggy up on her offer to drop me back at the chateau to collect the car. I don't want to see Thea and will send a text later to say sorry that I didn't say hello when I was passing but I had to rush to pick up Helen from the station, which is sort of true. I very much doubt Thea would be bothered about seeing me anyway.

# 13

*September, Mozène*

**Aura**

By the time I get to talk to Nick alone, we are in bed. My fury has waned a little over the day, and I'm determined to be calm and reasonable and give him the benefit of the doubt. We came here, after all, to get over what happened, to give our marriage the best chance it could have. So that the boys could have the childhood they deserve.

I try to keep my voice light as he comes out of the bathroom. 'What did you think of last night then?' I ask.

He gets into bed next to me. 'It was a bit full-on, wasn't it? Although,' he runs his hand lightly along my leg, 'also just a little bit sexy, don't you think?'

I try to shift away but he carries on stroking my leg. 'A little,' I say, not that I mean it at all. It was hideous and seedy. 'I was surprised to see you taking the cocaine,' I add, trying to make it sound like I haven't been thinking about how to bring it up all day.

He stops stroking my leg, sighs and leans back so he is sitting up against the headboard. 'Right. We're going to do this, are we?'

'Do what?'

'You're going to have a go at me for having some fun, for once. It was only a bit of chang among friends; it's hardly the end of the world.'

*Chang?* Has he done this before?

Stay calm. Be nice. We need to make this marriage work. 'Of course I don't object to you having fun – I just thought we were both on the same page when it comes to drugs. I thought we agreed that nothing good ever comes from them.'

He takes my hand and sighs again. 'I'm sorry. I know. We are. It's all been so stressful lately what with everything back in London and with working these long days trying to get the house sorted – when it was there I kind of thought, "why not?" And it seemed easier than saying no, especially with everything else that was going on.'

'OK. I understand. So long as you don't make a habit of it.' I pause. 'And what about the rest of it? The sex stuff?'

He laughs. 'I certainly wasn't expecting that! I thought we'd come here for a simple life. I thought dinner parties around here would mean a beef stew and maybe a game of cards if everyone could stay awake long enough.'

I laugh. It's nice. It feels like the first time we've been together without bickering over who did what or whose turn it is to sort the boys out for months. Years, even.

I snuggle in closer to him. 'Me too.' I look up at him. 'And that thing with Hervé? Did she seriously expect me to have sex with him?'

He looks back at me. 'I'm not sure. Maybe she was trying to shock you. Though she was certainly all over him all night, wasn't she?'

I trail my hand lightly across his stomach. 'What if I'd said yes? What would you have done?'

He suddenly flips me over onto my back, lifting himself up so that he can look down at me. I can feel he is already hard. 'I'd have killed him,' he says in a low voice, as he thrusts into me for the first time in months.

# 14

*September, Mozène*

**Aura**

A few hours later I wake with a start. I look at the clock – it's gone 3 a.m. I assume one of the boys must have woken me but now I can't hear anything at all. I get out of bed and cross the landing to their room. The shutters on our bedroom window are too rotten to use and we don't have any proper curtains yet – only makeshift ones of blankets hung over old curtain rails where we need them. The moon must be almost full as it's quite light on the landing and the old mullioned windows cast a criss-cross pattern on the rickety floorboards. The floor is freezing cold and I wish I'd bothered to put my slippers on.

I creep into the boys' room and I'm surprised to find they're both still asleep. I feel a pang of regret; I miss them

84

being in our bed. But Nick insisted that if we were to make a go of things, that was what had to happen. In spite of what went on in London, I want us to stay together. It's best for the boys and, quite frankly, best for me too. I need to make Nick see it's best for him too. I'm sure it is.

I kiss Bay's forehead and smooth back his hair. He snuffles in his sleep and then settles again. Sorrel's squirrel has fallen out of his bed so I pick it up and put it back in his arms. He reflexively shifts it to his cheek and starts sucking his finger. I kiss his forehead too and move to the end of the bed to where I can see them both.

My heart swells. My boys. They are my world and I would do anything for them. Drinking them in once more, I turn away to go back to our room. But my foot hits something soft.

Thinking it must be a teddy bear or toy, I bend down to pick it up.

And then I scream.

*Your funeral is the worst day of my life. They say that funerals are for the living, don't they? To help us gain closure? Not for me. As I watch the pink balloons being released into the sky and floating away while your far-too-young body is lowered into the ground, my grief gives way to anger. There is no closure here. You should have lived. Grown up. Had a family if you'd wanted to. It isn't right that your life was ended so prematurely. I will never forget. I will never forgive. Never.*

# 15

*September, Mozène*

**Aura**

Both boys instantly wake up and start screaming too.

Nick appears at the door in his boxer shorts, bleary-eyed and dishevelled-looking. 'Christ, Aura, what's all the noise?' he snaps, flicking the light on.

My hand flies to my mouth and I point at the mess on the floor. The boys' eyes follow my finger and their screams redouble when they see what's there.

'Bunny!' Sorrel shrieks. 'Dead bunny!'

I sit next to him on the bed and take him in my arms. 'Ssshhh, darling, it's OK,' I soothe, but really, it is far from OK. What the fuck is it doing here?

Nick scoops up Bay and strokes his head. 'It's OK, Bay.

A cat must have brought it in. You remember how we saw some cats in the garden? It must have been one of those.'

Poor Bay is so tired his head almost instantly starts drooping onto Nick's shoulder. Nick puts him back into bed, tucks his little duvet around him and turns the light off. Sorrel is still shrieking; God knows how Bay can sleep with that noise going on.

'A cat?' I say to Nick. 'What cat?'

He holds up his hand. 'I don't know!' he snaps. 'A cat. Does it matter? I'll get a binbag and get rid of the rabbit and then maybe we can all finally get some sleep.'

I sit rocking Sorrel and his shrieks gradually subside into sobs. He buries his head in my lap so that he can't see the half-eaten rabbit with its glassy eye seemingly staring at me, even in the semi-darkness.

I don't see how a cat could have brought the rabbit in. We close and lock all the doors at night. Frank was telling me how he doesn't normally bother to lock up as he feels so safe out here in the countryside and that nothing ever happens. But I'm used to living in town – it would take a long time for me to feel safe leaving my doors open. It's hard to imagine I ever would.

Maybe a window was left open. Some of the catches are very old. It would probably be easy for a cat to find their way in, if they wanted to.

Yes, that must be it, I tell myself. How else could it have happened?

I hear Nick climb the stairs and go back into our room without a glance towards us. Sorrel is still whimpering. 'Hey, Sol, tell you what,' I whisper. 'Why don't I stay here with you for the rest of tonight?' If Nick can't be bothered to come back and check on his sons, I don't see why I should share his bed. Such a shame after what happened earlier – I hadn't felt so close to Nick for ages.

Sorrel snuggles against me, his finger still in his mouth, and we curl up together under the duvet.

# 16

*September, Mozène*

**Aura**

I barely sleep a wink; partly because I want to stay awake to enjoy the now-novel feeling of Sorrel's hot little body cuddled up to mine, the gentle *thock-thock* noise as he sucks his finger in his sleep and the little-boy smell of his hair. But I can't stop thinking about the rabbit and am almost grateful when Sol wakes at six (as usual) and we can get up and go down for breakfast.

He and Bay seem full of the joys of spring and not remotely upset by what happened last night. Obviously I don't mention it to them and I'm grateful that they seem to have forgotten about it already.

But I have not forgotten about it. The more I think about it, the less likely it seems that a cat brought the rabbit in. I haven't seen a cat come into the house once, and even if it did, why would it drag a half-eaten creature up a flight of stairs?

Maybe Nick is right – maybe there is a simple explanation. But the fact that it was left in the boys' room makes it seem all the more sinister to me.

I shake myself. I'm being ridiculous. It had to have been a cat, or a fox, or something like that. These things happen. Like Frank said when the boys saw that dead rabbit in the garden, we'll have to get used to this sort of thing now we're living in the country, won't we? Can't go around being all squeamish about things.

Nick seems to have treated himself to a lie-in as there's no sign of him yet. Helen coming down for breakfast is a welcome distraction. She sits at the table and helps Bay feed himself his porridge without me needing to ask her, and pulls faces at Sorrel to make him laugh.

'Did you sleep well, Helen?' I ask, putting down the pot of tea and a mug in front of her. I've even put the milk in a little jug as part of my quest to become the perfect French hostess.

'Like a log,' she says. 'It's so peaceful here, I love it. Did you?'

Seb and Chloe enter, fully dressed and already filming. Shit – I'm still in my dressing gown. Why have they started so early today? Are they trying to catch me out?

They've told us many times that when they're filming we should try to entirely ignore them and not acknowledge their presence if possible, so I do so, though planning to get out of the kitchen and get dressed ASAP. I don't want to be appearing on camera looking like this.

I sigh. 'Not really. I'm surprised you didn't hear us – there was a bit of a commotion.' I mouth: 'A cat brought a dead rabbit in.'

I see Chloe smirk. I ignore her. 'Oh dear,' Helen says. 'That must have been upsetting.'

'Yeah,' I agree. 'Not the best. But never mind – onwards and upwards! Is it OK if I leave you in charge of the boys again this morning? Do you have any ideas for activities?'

'It looks like it'll be a lovely day – I thought maybe we could go for a walk? I might take them down to the river. Is it OK if I get some bits and pieces together for sandwiches – I thought maybe we could have a picnic?'

'Yes, that sound perfect, thank you!' I struck gold with Helen. I can't believe we don't even have to pay her. 'If you'll excuse me, I think I'll get dressed and then get on with some clearing out.'

With the boys out of the way, I change into some old clothes and start ferrying junk out of the downstairs room which I hope will eventually become the breakfast room for the chambres d'hôtes. It's a beautiful, light room (or at least it will be once it's all been cleaned up) with three French windows leading out on to an old patio with cracked paving stones. It's calming, soothing work, and some of the stuff I find in there is amazing. Much is simply rubbish – there are endless broken toys, a scary Chucky-style doll, old shoes and countless rancid supermarket shopping bags, but I also uncover a mirror with a gilt frame which could almost certainly be cleaned up and hung somewhere, and a pretty armoire with a broken door which I'm sure can be fixed.

Frank arrives mid-morning. I wasn't expecting him and, bearing in mind what Tiggy said, I wonder if I should ask him to call ahead next time. But I can't think of a way of saying that to him without being rude and I don't want to do that when he has been so kind to me. Plus it is good to have him around when there is so much to do – he always seems happy to help with anything.

'How was your little coffee morning with Tiggy?' he asks as we carry on sorting through the debris in the room together.

'It was good, thank you,' I say. 'She seems like a nice woman. Not at all like I thought she was when I . . . first met her. I hope we can be friends.' I pause. 'But how do you know about that?' I ask.

He waves his hand. 'Dunno. Can't remember. I guess she mentioned it when I bumped into her sometime – I often see her at the boulangerie. And Tiggy *is* a nice woman, but . . .' He tails off, pretending to be fascinated by an old car door he's just unearthed under some manky old cushions.

'But what?' I ask.

He lifts the car door – why on earth is it in here? – carries it across the room, through the doors and deposits it in the skip outside.

'Oh, nothing, shouldn't gossip,' he says, picking up a box of old bottles. 'Skip or recycling?' he asks.

'Recycling,' I say. 'Could you put the box to one side of the skip for now and I'll get Nick to move it later. But what were you going to say about Tiggy?'

He sighs. 'Well, if you insist, I was only going to say don't be surprised if she's your best mate for a while and then suddenly drops you. She's got form for that.' His tone is bitter and biting. It's not a way I've heard him speak before. 'She doesn't have a nice word to say about anyone – you shouldn't believe everything she says about other people. And don't be surprised if she's saying stuff about you behind your back.'

His cheeks colour and he turns away, pretending to be looking through a box of ancient VHS tapes.

'Um, OK, thanks, I'll bear that in mind,' I say, wondering what Tiggy's done to him to spark such vitriol.

We continue sorting the room in silence.

# 17

*September, Mozène*

**Aura**

As usual, our night is not unbroken. Nick remains blissfully asleep as I go in to tend to Sorrel, as usual, when I hear him crying out.

'Sol? What is it?' I say, sitting on his bed and stroking his hair.

'Voices talk me,' he says.

Oh God. I thought this had gone away since Helen and he made the 'dreamcatcher'. The dreamcatcher is a hideous concoction of bent coat hangers and old feathers which hangs from the ceiling and quite frankly terrifies me when I catch sight of it at night. But for Sorrel it seemed to have stopped the complaints of 'noises in his room' in their tracks. Until tonight.

'What voices, Sol? I'm sure it was only a bad dream.'

'Nasty voices.'

'What did they say?'

Sorrel shakes his head. 'Can't tell.'

I feel a lurch of alarm. I turn his face gently to look at mine. 'Sorrel, did someone ask you to keep a secret? Because we've talked about this before. If a grown-up tells you to keep a secret, it's always wrong, and you must always let Mummy or Daddy know straight away. Especially Mummy. Always. You won't be in trouble.'

He turns away and I feel his head move against my chest in a shaking motion.

'No secret,' he says.

I squeeze him tighter. 'OK. That's good. We don't like secrets. Then why can't you tell me?'

'Scared.'

'Don't be scared, Sol. Things are always less scary when you tell someone.'

He shakes his head again and buries his face further into my chest.

'Come on, Sol. If you tell me what the voices said, I'll let you have ice cream after dinner tomorrow.' I know bribery isn't the best form of parenting, but I figure that if he tells me about his nightmare, it'll be the first step in being able to let it go. I learnt about it on my counselling course.

He sticks his finger in his mouth. 'Be scared,' he says again, taking his finger out of his mouth just long enough to say the words.

'You'll be scared?'

He takes his finger out of his mouth again briefly and says, 'No. Mummy be scared.'

I squeeze him tight. 'Aw, Sol. I'm a grown-up! I won't be scared, I promise. Mummies are *never* scared. It's our super-power.' That's exactly the kind of thing we were taught not to say on my course but whatever, Sorrel is a child, not a client.

'No, Mummy!' he says, louder and exasperated. 'Voice say it. Be scared. Your mummy be scared.'

He puts his finger back in his mouth and rests his head against my chest.

I stroke his hair again and make sshhing noises. It must have been a nightmare.

I am finally drifting back to sleep when the lights suddenly come on in our bedroom. I sit up and shake Nick awake.

'Nick! The lights are on. What's happening?'

He eyes me grumpily, still half-asleep. 'What do you mean? Turn them off then.'

'No, Nick! I mean they came on by themselves.'

He gets out of bed, squinting in the brightness, and flicks the switch. The lights go off and he throws himself into bed. 'There. Problem solved. Now can I please get some sleep?'

He has his back to me, but I flick my bedside lamp on and shake his shoulder. He turns onto his back and puts his hands over his eyes. 'Aura, please, I'm knackered. Can't this wait till the morning?'

'No, it can't. I'm scared. Something's going on.'

He sighs, turns towards me and props himself up on one elbow.

'What do you mean? What's going on?'

'Come on. The dead rabbit. The music. The lights. And then Sorrel woke up earlier and told me that a voice in his

97

room said I should be scared. It's not the first time he's said he's heard voices either. Or at least noises.'

He throws himself back on his pillows. 'You're a bit old to believe in ghosts, aren't you?'

I pause. 'Spirits. It could be spirits. Maybe someone who lived in the house in the past and doesn't want us here.'

He pulls a face. 'Seriously? Really, Aura . . . you can't possibly believe that.'

'You must see that something like this happening nearly every night isn't normal!' Tears spring to my eyes and my voice wobbles. 'I think someone is trying to scare us. If not spirits, then . . . someone else.'

He touches my arm. 'Who?'

'I don't know.'

'And why would they want to?'

I shake my head. 'I don't know that either.'

He pulls me over to him so that I can put my head down on his chest. Apart from the other night, it's been a long time since we've lain like this. Maybe coming to France was a good idea for our marriage after all.

'The rabbit was brought in by a cat,' Nick says patiently. 'The music was most likely someone accidentally setting an alarm, or a power surge making that device misfire. Same for the lights – the electrics in the house are ancient and dodgy – you know we're going to have to replace the entire system before we can open our doors to paying guests? It's going to cost a fortune. And Sorrel's always been prone to nightmares, hasn't he? That's all the "voices" are. None of this is a big deal.'

I move away so I can look at him. 'Don't you think it's

all rather a coincidence, though? All this weird stuff going on since . . . since the film crew arrived. I'm wondering if they're doing this to try to make out the place is haunted. Make their programme more interesting.'

He frowns. 'I can't see they'd do that. They seem like nice kids, and surely there are rules around that kind of thing? They were very clear that they were only filming what we're doing and not intervening in any way.'

'Yes, but maybe we're not interesting enough and they've decided they want to shake things up a bit.'

'I don't think so. But if you're worried, we could talk to them about it?'

I look at him in horror. 'No! We can't go accusing them! Imagine if we're wrong. No, I'm just going to keep an eye and see if . . .'

'See if what?'

'I don't know!' I say, exasperated. 'I don't understand why any of this is happening or if it's them, how they'd do it. I'm just going to . . . watch them more closely, I guess.'

Nick reaches over me and turns out the light. I turn my back on him so that we can spoon. It's nice – I feel cosy and protected. 'We can always ask them to leave,' he suggests softly. 'I know we've signed a contract, but I'm sure there must be some way of getting out of it.'

Nick's never wanted them here. But he's not going to get his way that easily.

'No,' I counter. 'The programme will be amazing publicity for the chambres d'hôtes. I want the crew here for now at least, but if things carry on this way, we might have to reconsider.'

# 18

**Aura**

The next day while we are having lunch the Astrid makes a strange 'bong' sound. I brace myself for a burst of loud music, but nothing happens.

'Why does it make that noise?' I ask the table in general. I'm still on edge and jittery from all the stuff that happened last night. I barely got any sleep at all. I couldn't get Sorrel's words out of my head: 'Mummy be scared'. Because the problem is, I *am* scared. Rationally, what Nick says must be right – it's hardly the first time Sol's had a nightmare and he's a very imaginative little boy – but it's been going round and round in my head. Why would anyone want me to be scared? They wouldn't. Sorrel had a nightmare. But then so much has happened lately that it can't all simply be coincidence, can it?

'That noise means someone's dropped in,' Helen says.

'Dropped in? You mean it's the doorbell?' I look at the device where there's a green light zipping around the top. 'That thing's linked to the doorbell now?' I ask.

'No, it means that someone's dropped into the system so they can talk or listen.'

'What? Who? Why?'

'Don't know. Nick maybe? He could do it from the garden on his phone. Nick, is that you?' Helen says towards the device.

Silence. The light on its top goes out.

'Do you want me to have a look at your app for you?' she offers. 'I might be able to tell from that. I have an Astrid at home and love it. In fact, I have them in several rooms, I find them so useful. Did you know you could use it as a baby monitor if you got an Elsie too – it's like a smaller version of the Astrid? You could listen out for the boys when they're asleep and, when they're bigger, tell them when it's time to come down for meals or whatever.'

'Really?' I say, but I'm not remotely interested. 'I hate that thing. It's been nothing but trouble. I'm tempted to unplug it and have done with it,' I say, tears springing to my eyes again. I desperately need to get some proper sleep, maybe then I wouldn't feel so on edge. 'I certainly don't think I'd want another one any time soon.'

'Hmm – only seems to be your account attached to the device from what I can see,' Helen says as she moves her finger up and down the screen on my phone. 'Maybe you dropped in accidentally yourself – it can happen. Or it could be a glitch. Like the one with the music the other night.' She hands the phone back. 'Thinking about it, if the internet trips out for a second, which I imagine is hardly unheard of somewhere like here, these devices have a tendency to go haywire when they first come back to life. I wouldn't worry about it.'

I look at the device again, which is still black with no lights on. But I decide to unplug it anyway to be on the safe side.

# 19

*October, Mozène*

**Aura**

Over the next few weeks, we settle into a routine – Helen looks after the boys in the morning while I work on the house with Nick. Nick and I are getting on better than ever and we've even had sex a couple more times, so he's in a better mood. Mid-afternoon I take charge of the boys again and we bake, go for walks, pick flowers and the like. Sometimes I take them over to Tiggy's and we sit on her terrace by the pool or let the boys splash about on the steps on warmer days. When it's cooler we chat in the kitchen while the boys play with her children's old toys in a massive playroom just off it. Our chateau is slowly coming together too. Though it's a very long way off being ready, I am starting to be able to imagine how it will look, and we're hoping to be able to open at least one or two guest rooms for next summer.

It's finally starting to feel like the life I came here in search of. The days are gradually getting colder, but it's still warm enough that the boys can spend most of their time outside. Thanks to Helen, I have the time to myself I always dreamed of, even if it is mainly spent clearing junk out of rooms, scrubbing old tiles and walls, endless trips to brocantes and Mr Bricolage, supervising the workmen who come and go to do the various tasks we can't do ourselves, paying bills and generally organizing things.

I've also had time to get used to the film crew hanging around all the time. They have become so much a part of the furniture that I self-edit a lot less than I used to when they were first here; if I want to have a go at Nick about something, then I will, whether or not they are listening. Not that it happens as much nowadays; we're getting on brilliantly most of the time.

Frank is still helping me out with my website and also with general grunt work around the house, but mindful of what Tiggy said, I am careful not to be too reliant on him. I've also asked him to call me before he comes round, giving the excuse that at the moment I am so often out buying things we need for the house. He said: 'Of course, of course!' and tried to pretend he wasn't offended, but I could see he was, so I immediately felt sorry for him and invited him for lunch the next day.

The only ongoing problem is Sorrel, who is waking up almost every night screaming and saying there are voices in his room, telling him that I should be scared. I've begged

Nick to let him sleep with us again, even temporarily, but he won't have it. He says that once Sorrel's back in our bed he won't want to get out again. Though it breaks my heart, I know he's right. Sorrel already has Helen's horrible dream-catcher and we've tried everything else we can think of – night lights, homeopathic sleep remedies, whale music, white noise, different teddy bears to 'guard' him – but nothing works. I've spent ages on the various Facebook parenting groups I'm a member of, looking for a solution but so far, no joy. Nick insists Sorrel will grow out of it and I guess he probably will. I only hope it's soon – we're both exhausted. At least, Sorrel and I are – Nick always sleeps through all the crying and shouting.

We haven't seen Thea again; I guess she decided that we (or rather, I) weren't her sort of people. Tiggy has been to a couple more dinner parties at Amaryllis, she tells me about what went on when I see her. She gets a bit wistful when she talks about Celia. She also tells me about her marriage; Bertie is apparently sleeping with his parliamentary researcher. Tiggy shows me a picture of her; whore-face, as Tiggy calls her, is very young and pretty. God knows what the researcher sees in Bertie. I guess she thinks he might be good for her career.

'But don't you mind?' I ask. My relationship with Nick may be far from perfect, but theirs makes us look like Romeo and Juliet.

She shrugs. 'Not really. Bertie provides for me and the girls well and he's a good dad. He puts up with me and Celia, as long as he gets to join in sometimes, and in turn I tolerate him being with whore-face in London. Somehow it works.'

105

In spite of what she says, it sounds to me like she does mind. I wonder whether it's time to open up to her about all the stuff that went on before we came here, but decide I'm not ready yet. We came here to get away from all that and it's nice being a totally different person and having a clean slate. I'm no longer 'the woman who' blah di blah.

'It suits us both,' she continues. 'I guess when the children are older we'll discreetly split and go our separate ways. But Bertie says it would kill his career to do it now – it's always better for MPs in his party to be married. The only issue would be if it came out in the press. But, given where we live, and as long as he and whore-face are as discreet as he claims they are, I think that's fairly unlikely, especially post-Leveson.' She waves her hand dismissively. 'Anyway, enough about me and my dysfunctional marriage. Much more importantly, have you got your costume sorted for tonight?'

Tonight is Thea's Hallowe'en party and I have to admit I'm excited about it. We haven't been out at all since the dinner party – there's pretty much nowhere to go here, we have the boys and we don't know anyone anyway. I wasn't sure I wanted to go, but Tiggy assures me that the Hallowe'en extravaganza will be nothing like the dinner party.

'This is a totally different thing,' she says. 'You'll love it – everyone brings their kids and Thea gets people in to entertain them. Her Hallowe'en parties are her way of showing off her wealth to as many people as possible. Champagne flows but there's a strict no-drugs policy – she likes to look squeaky-clean outside of her inner circle. She puts on a great bash – you'll adore it. So will your kids.

Mine are coming too – they're home from school for the holidays. Me and the girls are going as the three blind mice.'

I laugh. 'That sounds fun! I haven't given any thought to costumes, to be honest – I'll have to see what we can cobble together at home.' This isn't true – I got straight on to Amazon and ordered for all of us as soon as the creamy card invitation covered in classy silver cobwebs arrived through the post. I wasn't going to be shown up again by wearing the wrong thing like the last time.

# 20

*October, Mozène*

**Aura**

I am very pleased with how I look in my witch's outfit. I have lost weight since we arrived in France; probably from dragging large pieces of ancient stuff out of the house and being forever on the go. The dress is an old black one which now clings in all the right places and shows just enough cleavage. I've also got a hat from eBay, an old-fashioned witch's broom which I found here during one of my clear-outs, and a plush toy cat someone gave the boys at some point which I've tethered to the end of the broom. I think I look sexy without being slutty, as well as fun and inventive. Exactly the kind of image I want to portray in my new life out here. This party will be the first time we meet a lot of people who could potentially become our friends (assuming they're not all like the awful Thea), so it's important we give the right impression.

Bay is simply adorable dressed as a pumpkin – I try not to think about the poor kid who must have slaved over his costume in some godforsaken sweatshop, but sometimes needs must. Sorrel is in a Spiderman outfit he was given by a friend of Nick's who I don't like very much. I never buy the boys gendered toys or outfits of any sort, but Sorrel would wear his Spiderman costume every day, given the chance (which he isn't – special occasions only. Or when Nick lets him and I don't notice till too late).

I knew Nick wouldn't bother to find a costume himself and wouldn't want to make himself look too stupid or like he'd gone to too much effort either, so I bought him a huge black cloak and a plastic scythe – he can go as Death but wear his own clothes underneath.

Thea has also invited the film crew and Helen this time, which is a relief as, if she's happy to have them filming, it backs up Tiggy's assurance that this evening's party will be distinctly PG-rated. The only condition is that they'd have to dress up like everyone else, so I put in an order for costumes for them along with my own. Helen is a zombie nurse, Chloe a cat (in a skin-tight PVC suit which I wouldn't want any daughter of mine to wear, but whatever, she chose it) and Seb is a devil. Even if I say so myself, we make a good-looking group.

Seb says he has to stay sober during filming for insurance purposes and so he may as well be the designated driver and take us all to the party in the van. I wonder about taking our car too in case the boys find it overwhelming and one of us (i.e. me) needs to come back early with them, but Nick tells me to stop being so fretful. I don't want to spoil the evening before it's begun so I try to push the thought out of my mind and leave the car at home.

The chateau is looking even more spectacular than last time we were here, all candlelit and decked out in Hallowe'en decorations. With Helen, I take the boys to the designated children's area to check that it looks safe; their eyes light up at the sight of the huge piles of sweets, the bouncy castle and other toys. A zombie Mary Poppins shows me the darkened area for sleeping and assures me that no child will be left unattended at any point. There are five nannies to look after twenty children, most of whom are older than ours. She also tells me that I'm welcome to come and check on the boys at any time and promises that someone will come and find me if there is a problem. Sorrel is already flinging himself around the haunted house bouncy castle and I put Bay down in the ball pit, which is full of large plastic eyeballs and mini pumpkins, kissing his head as I leave.

Back in the main marquee I take a glass of champagne from one of the zombie waiters. I find Tiggy, who introduces me to her two tween girls. They are beautiful, like miniature versions of her, and are decked out in little ears, short black tulle skirts with dark glasses and canes exactly like Tiggy. They have that polite self-confidence which only seems to come from being public-school educated and I feel a sudden pang of doubt about our move to France – did we do the right thing? Would the boys have been better off being educated in the UK?

110

No, I tell myself. No sterile, loveless boarding school for them – not that we could ever have afforded it anyway. They will grow up bilingual, with two parents and with nature all around them. I'm actually keen to home school them – I just need to persuade Nick.

Frank comes over and does the *bise* with us all – he is also dressed as Death, like several of the men here, including Bertie. Celia and Tristram arrive – Celia looks stunning as Elsa from *Frozen* and Tristram is dressed as a skeleton, his paunch excruciatingly pronounced in the skin-tight suit.

Thea sweeps up to us and kisses everyone exuberantly. She is dressed as evil fairy godmother Maleficent and she looks amazing. Like last time, despite having been delighted with my costume when I left the house, the sight of her immediately makes me feel dowdy.

'Wow, Thea, you look incredible,' Frank says, his eyes unashamedly flicking up and down her body. 'What a great costume!'

She smiles smugly. 'Isn't it beautiful? It's one of the originals worn by Angelina Jolie in the film. I sent someone out to LA to bid for it especially – since I saw the film I simply had to have one. After tonight I'm going to re-auction it for charity though – it's not as if I can wear it more than once, is it?'

Tiggy rolls her eyes at me. 'Anyway, I hope you all have a wonderful evening,' Thea continues. 'I do appreciate you all coming along. Hallowe'en is my favourite night of the year. So pagan and wildly erotic, don't you think?'

She sashays off, all the men looking at her pert little arse, for fuck's sake. I rein in my thoughts and remind myself that

I am now tolerant and reasonable Aura, not fly-off-the-handle-and-harass-Nick-for-his-many-shortcomings Aura.

Given that last time I saw many of these people they were kissing or groping each other and Bertie had his penis in his hand, I'm struggling to get the various images out of my head and am a little stuck for conversation. I opt instead to talk to the tweens about their boarding school while Nick and the two men talk renovation and workmen nightmares. Celia and Tiggy chat quietly to each other, standing close. I wonder what they are saying. I reach out and stroke Nick's arm. Our relationship is far from perfect, but it could be a lot worse.

After an hour or so of champagne and watching the aerialists and roaming demonic fire-eaters, dinner is served. In many ways, though it's way less formal, this evening's event is more lavish than the dinner party – all gargantuan roasts, elaborate vegetable food sculptures and classy yet over-the-top decoration and entertainment wherever you look. By the end of dinner, thanks to the circulating zombie waiters who seem to constantly top up drinks, along with everyone else I am more than a little drunk. I've checked on Sorrel and Bay a couple of times during the evening – they were having such a great time in the playroom with the nannies that although they spotted me coming in, they barely gave me a second glance. I feel a pang; they are growing up so quickly. How long will it be before I am no longer the centre of their world?

After dinner the nannies bring the kids out to the garden and the performers put on an impressive show on a stage which has been erected for the evening – it's a medley of songs from musicals such as *Little Shop of Horrors* and the *Rocky Horror Show* (with any unsuitable lyrics suitably sanitized, thankfully) alongside more fire-eating and acrobatics. Afterwards the kids are taken back to their playroom and one of the nannies tells me the children are going to watch a film while they relax on colourful FatBoy cushions with babyccinos and popcorn. There will be plenty of blankets on hand to keep them cosy as they drop off to sleep, which they surely will. We can pick them up whenever we are ready to go home, but there is no rush – the nannies are here for the whole evening.

Before dinner I was keeping an eye on Nick, generally staying close to him or at the very least watching out for who he was flirting with, but he seemed to be behaving himself. Thea appears to have lost interest in him, and there's no Hervé character for her to flirt with; instead she's playing the bountiful hostess to perfection, circulating, talking to everyone, making sure we're all happy.

After dinner and all the wine and champagne I feel emboldened and decide I'm going to meet some more people – I don't need to watch Nick all the time. I latch on to various groups via Tiggy and Celia, occasionally even introducing myself to strangers all by myself, telling them I'm new to the area. No one minds. Some of the people I meet are dull and pompous, but others are interesting – everyone seems to have a very different story around how they arrived in the area. I find it fascinating. Who would have thought there would be such a variety of people in a place as rural as this?

I spot Nick mingling with others from time to time, both men and women, but it's fine. We're going to be fine. There must be around two hundred people at the party, spread out around the garden on this surprisingly warm night, others under the marquee and some in the chateau reception rooms, so I lose sight of Nick for an hour or more at a time. Seb and Chloe are flitting around filming – Seb seems to have stuck to his word of not drinking, but I see Chloe sneak the odd glass or two. Even Helen seems to be enjoying herself in her own quiet way.

At midnight there are fireworks. Not just a few – a full-on, twenty-minute display not that different to the ones we used to watch at the local park on Bonfire Night when we were still in London – when one of us (me) always had to come home early because the bangs and crashes would upset Sorrel and Bay. By now the children are all asleep, or at least I assume they are – the nannies don't bring them out to see the display. The final fireworks have been arranged to make the shape of a big red heart, shot through with an arrow and a flurry of smaller, red starbursts, as if it is dripping with blood. And it's in that quiet lull after the fireworks have stopped that there is a scream.

# 21

*October, Mozène*

**Aura**

Everyone rushes out to the front of the chateau where one of the waitresses is crying hysterically. The fact that she is dressed as a zombie somehow makes the scene almost ludicrous rather than frightening at first glance. I realize with a stab of panic I haven't seen Nick for a while – where is he?

Never mind. He's a grown man and first I need to check that my boys are safe. I rush back through the throng to the children's tent, where I'm relieved to see all the children are fast asleep, the nannies quietly fiddling with their phones as they watch over them. I guess they wouldn't have heard the commotion all the way back here. Bay and Sorrel are on a big red cushion, cuddled up together and covered with an orange-and-black blanket. I feel a rush of love for them.

If anything happened to my boys, I would die, I'm sure of it.

Confident that they are safely asleep, I run back out to the front of the building where the entire party is now gathered in a chaotic, frantic melee.

'Call an ambulance!' someone is shouting.

'Is anyone a doctor?' yells someone else.

'Is he breathing?'

'Don't move him!'

Some of the women are crying as another shoves through shouting, 'Let me see – I'm a surgeon.'

I follow in her wake. My hand flies to my mouth as I see that, on the ground, illuminated by the burning flambeaux, blood spills from the face-down prone figure who is wearing a big black cape. His scythe lies on the ground beside him.

I scream.

*The hurt doesn't diminish, and neither does the anger. Her short life taken away so cruelly and so young. She is never coming back. Grief is a long process, but the anger I feel is somehow harder to deal with. I know what I need to do. I know what will make me feel better. Taking revenge. It's the only way.*

# PART TWO

PART TWO

# 22

*TEN MONTHS EARLIER*

*December, London*

## Nick

I take a deep breath as I put my key in the lock, steeling myself. Inside someone is crying, loudly. I turn the key and push the door open, arranging my face into an expression of empathy in advance, as I know is required of me in this situation. The one I come home to almost every day.

Once the door is open I can hear that it's Bay screaming, and that he's upstairs. To my left I can hear the tune from some irritating kids' programme booming out from the TV in the living room – it's on far too loud. I put my head round the door where Sorrel is staring wide-eyed at the screen, sitting in his favourite position in the corner of the sofa, sucking his finger and clutching his squirrel.

'Sol?' I say. He doesn't hear me over the blare of the TV. 'Sol!' I repeat louder. He looks round at me and grins, his finger falling from his mouth as he does so. He waves his squirrel at me. ''Beebies!' he cries in delight. 'Me watch 'Beebies!'

I smile, feeling a surge of love for him. He's so adorable. 'That's nice, Sol.' He loves TV. He turns his head back to face the screen, putting his finger back in his mouth and clutching his squirrel against his face. Bay's screams are getting louder and more urgent. 'Where's Mummy?' I ask.

'Mummy 'sleep,' Sorrel says, not looking away from the colourful creatures dancing and singing on the screen. 'Me watch 'Beebies.'

I turn away and dash up the stairs into what is notionally Bay's room, though he never actually sleeps in it. He's on his back in his cot, fists balled and face puce. His cries are more like hiccups; it's almost as if he's struggling to catch his breath. I lift him up and cradle him against my shoulder. 'It's OK, little guy,' I soothe. 'I've got you.' His nappy is soaked and so is his Babygro. I put him down on the changing table and get him sorted, which is tricky as he's kicking and wailing so much. 'Shhh, Bay, it's OK,' I say. 'Look, you're all clean and dry now. That will make you feel better,' I add, though he is still crying his heart out.

Once he's dressed, I pick him up to cuddle him against my shoulder but he won't be consoled. 'You hungry, little guy?' I ask, as he continues to scream. 'Let's get you some-thing to eat.' I take him downstairs and put him in his

122

bouncy chair while I prepare him a bottle. His wails are getting more and more urgent as he tries to stuff his little fists into his mouth and kicks his legs furiously. I put a bottle in the sterilizer and whizz it through the microwave, then clip the corner off one of the 'emergency' ready-made formula packs and pour it in.

'Come on, come on,' I mutter to myself, in between saying to Bay, 'Sssh, sssh, little man, it's coming.' Why does all this have to take so long? You'd think someone would have come up with a better – quicker – way of doing this by now? Oh yes, they did – breastfeeding. I feel a stab of annoyance at how that didn't work out followed immediately by a rush of guilt. It wasn't Aura's fault.

I fill the bottle and put it in the microwave – Aura would be appalled if she saw me do this but the plug-in bottle warmer takes too long and I need to stop Bay crying. Thirty seconds later, the microwave pings. I squirt the milk onto my wrist to check its temperature and plug it into Bay's mouth without lifting him from the chair. He stops crying instantly, sucking greedily. My back quickly starts to hurt from the awkward position I'm crouching in but I don't want to take the bottle out of Bay's mouth and set him off again. I ease myself down to sit on the floor, still holding the bottle while Bay finishes, stroking his little foot through his stripy Babygro. Before the bottle is even empty, his eyes droop and he falls asleep. I gently ease the bottle from his lips, his rosebud mouth still making a gentle sucking motion before stilling. I carefully lift the chair, carry it through to the living room and put it on the floor, then take the remote control from the sofa next to Sol and turn down the volume.

Sorrel looks up at me, horrified, so I say: 'I'm turning this down so Bay can sleep, 'kay? You be a good big brother and come and get me if he wakes up.'

Sorrel nods and turns his attention back to the TV. 'Bay watch 'Beebies with me!' he says, smiling.

'Yes. I'm going to go upstairs and see Mummy, OK? You shout for me if Bay wakes up, OK? Don't forget.'

Sorrel nods, still staring at the TV. I run up the stairs to our bedroom. I'm expecting to find Aura asleep. She hasn't been sleeping well lately – none of us has – but even so, I'd be surprised if she could sleep through all the noise Bay was making.

But she's not asleep. She's lying flat on her back, eyes open, staring at the ceiling, a pillow pressed up around her ears.

'Aura? What's going on?' I say gently. Inside I am screaming, *Why the fuck did you leave our baby in a soaking wet nappy and bawling his head off because he was starving?* but I know I can't say that to her, not at the moment.

She continues staring at the ceiling. I'm not sure whether she's oblivious or if she's simply decided to ignore me.

I gently grasp her wrists and pull them away from her ears. She lets her hands fall on to the bed and finally turns her head to look at me. 'Aura. What's happening?' I ask, trying to keep my voice calm and neutral, the way we were taught to at teacher training college when the kids are playing up. 'Why did you ignore Bay? He was crying. Screaming, in fact.'

I hold myself back from demanding how long she's been here on the bed, how long Bay was crying for, how long Sol

124

has been watching TV, entirely unsupervised. She turns her head away from me and looks back towards the ceiling.

'I can't do this anymore, Nick,' she says. She is dry-eyed and her voice is flat.

'Can't do what?'

'All this. The full-time mum stuff.' She looks at me again. 'I really wanted to, but I hate it.'

A tear forms and runs down her cheek. I wipe it away. A surge of panic wells inside me. I kind of saw this coming, but I don't know how we can cope financially if she's not at home. Childcare is so expensive in London.

But I don't say that. 'Come on, Aura,' I say. 'You've had a bad day, that's all. You stay here, I'll get you a cup of tea – or a glass of wine, if you like – then I'll do the kids' tea and baths.' I lean forward to kiss her on the forehead. 'You'll feel better tomorrow. You'll see.' There goes the night out I'd planned this evening.

Aura sits up and rubs her eyes. 'No, Nick, I won't feel better. This has been going on too long. I can't take it anymore. I mean it. I need to think about me for a change. It can't all be about the children.'

I hold in a sigh. 'OK,' I say, trying to keep the irritation I am feeling out of my voice. 'How do you want things to change? I can't give up my job to be at home more – you know that, don't you? We have to pay the mortgage. Your inheritance was a good deposit but there's still a huge wedge to pay every month. It's already a stretch as it is.'

She bites her lip and nods determinedly. There's something child-like in the gesture. 'Of course.'

'And childcare is expensive so . . .'

She picks up the iPad which is lying on the other side of the bed and waves it at me. 'It doesn't have to cost as much as you might think. I've been looking into it. Sorrel will be eligible for free childcare in a few months.'

'You've been looking . . . since when?'

Aura gives me a look of exasperation. 'God, Nick, you don't know what it's like! You've got no idea! I put up with it when it was just Sorrel at home as I was pregnant again about five minutes later and feeling so sick I was in no fit state to even think straight let alone go to work but now! With two of them! It's too awful. I can't do it.'

I nod. It's not as if I didn't know she was finding it hard. Every day when I get back from work the house is in a mess, often no one is dressed and nine times out of ten Aura shoves a child at me and says, 'Take him – I've had him all day,' when I've barely had time to take my coat off.

And it's not as if we haven't talked about it. We have. But all those discussions degenerate into Aura wailing about how she's such a rubbish mother and how terrible she feels about never learning to breastfeed properly and if only, if only, if only . . . And I have to calm her down, tell her she's doing an amazing job. It's no wonder we haven't managed to come up with a solution.

I'm not some unfeeling and callous bastard. I get it. I know it's hard and I'm happy to do my share. I've said she should go out with the girls, let her hair down, maybe go to stay with an old friend for the weekend or something – have a proper break. But she won't do it. She's been out a couple of times locally, but each time she's come home early saying she missed the children. And she won't admit it, but

I don't think she trusts me to look after the children for more than a few hours. So I don't know what else I can do.

'I've been looking into it for a few weeks now, when I can get a moment to myself, which is almost never,' Aura says. 'I'm going to retrain.'

'Retrain? As what? Shouldn't we . . . discuss this?' I say, all the while thinking: how are we going to afford this? Aura hasn't worked since early in Sorrel's pregnancy and my teacher's salary barely covers the too-large mortgage Aura insisted on so that we could afford a house with a postage-stamp-sized garden in a nice area of South London close to a park and good schools so that our children could have the 'idyllic' childhood she pictured for them.

Aura sighs. 'I knew you'd react like this. I knew you'd only find reasons for me not to do it. So I decided I'd work it all out and present it as a *fait accompli*. I've signed up for a counselling course at the local college. It's something I've been thinking about for ages – I think I'd be a brilliant counsellor. I'm also going back to work part-time – which will pay for both the course and a nursery for the children. Since it won't affect our finances one way or the other, there's no reason I shouldn't go ahead and do it. And once Sorrel's free childcare kicks in, we'll actually be slightly better off than we are now.'

'What? What course? What job? And the one time I suggested scraping some money together to put the children in a nursery to give you a break, you said I was accusing you of being a bad mother and didn't speak to me for days.'

Aura gets up off the bed. 'Things change, OK? I've done the sums. I'm going back to my old job at Evergreen three days a week – well, not fundraising any more, it's more of an admin role as that's all they can offer me because I only want to work part-time, but that's OK. I'm doing the course in the evenings. The children will go to nursery three days a week. It's all arranged.'

I nod. 'Right. I thought we had the kind of relationship where we talked about fairly major decisions like this. Clearly I was wrong.' I am fuming. I knew she was finding things tricky, but I've always tried to help, and to talk to her about it. And this is the first I've heard of her wanting to be a counsellor. How dare she shut me out like this?

She wanders into our en suite bathroom and splashes her face with water. I follow her and stand at the door.

'Oh, don't be like this, Nick! I need something for me. I can't do this anymore, staying at home changing nappies and making food that almost invariably gets thrown on the floor. I've had enough.'

She turns round, walks over to me and takes my hand. 'You understand that, don't you?' she asks.

I pull my hand away. 'Yes. But I would have preferred that you'd discussed it with me first.'

'Is this the Fifties? Do I need your permission?' she says sarcastically.

I run my fingers through my hair. 'Of course not. But we are a couple, parents, with joint responsibilities. You could have at least told me what you were planning.'

'You've said several times I should get out of the house more. Find a hobby. Make new friends. Arrange my days so I'm not stuck at home with two small boys. This ticks all those boxes, except it's much better than going to baby yoga

128

or hanging about in Starbucks talking to dull women a decade older than me about mastitis and sleep routines. This course will get my brain working again and eventually be a new career for me.'

'You're serious about this?'

'Yep.'

'Starting when?'

'After Christmas.'

'What? In a couple of weeks?'

'Yes! Honestly, I don't understand why you're being so grumpy about it. I already feel lighter just thinking about it. You can see that, surely?'

'You didn't look very light when I came in,' I counter, remembering Bay's screams.

She smiles tightly. 'Yes, well, I haven't had a good day. Haven't had a good week or month, for that matter. But this will sort all that out – I'm sure of it.'

'Dada! Bay wake up!' Sorrel shouts from downstairs.

'I'll go,' Aura says. 'I'm feeling much better now I've got that off my chest. Positively buoyant, in fact. I'm really excited about starting my course. You still going out this evening?'

'Oh . . . I don't need to if . . .' Can I trust her to look after the kids right now? They didn't seem very looked after when I arrived home.

'You should go,' Aura interrupts. 'I'm totally fine now, honestly. Why don't you help me with teatime and baths, and then you can go off if you like?'

From her tone this doesn't *sound* like one of those loaded statements where I'm actually supposed to say no, no, no,

I'll stay here with you, but it's getting so difficult to tell with Aura these days. And either way, after her bombshell, I could do with being away from her right now.

'Well, only if you're sure. I'll keep my phone on and you can call me if there are any problems.'

# 23

*December, London*

Nick

I don't go out much these days, but tonight it's Dan's leaving drinks, and I'm glad to be here. We both started at St Benedict's High at the same time straight out of teacher training and we've been mates ever since. He's moving to Australia with his new (Australian) wife and I can't help but feel a pang of envy. I will still be here in rainy South London, same job, same old shit, dealing with an ever-increasingly-erratic Aura and a barely affordable mortgage. And apart from all that, I'll miss him. He's a good mate.

A couple of drinks turn into a few more and then suddenly it's closing time and someone is suggesting going to a club down the road. By now I am well on the way to being drunk and the thought of going home to three people in tears, as

131

has happened so often lately, seems too much to bear. So I check my phone – I'm delighted to see there are no messages or missed calls from Aura, so I send a text saying, *OK if I go on to a club with the boys? Don't wait up xxx*

Without waiting for an answer, I turn my phone off.

It's several years since I've been to a club and I'm surprised to find nothing seems to have changed, if this one is anything to go by. Almost as soon as I'm through the door I regret coming – it's too hot, too loud and too dark, but with too many lights at the same time. I'm about to tell Dan, sorry, I made a mistake and I need to go home, but then I remember I don't want to go home yet and that I'd really like another drink.

I get the first round in – that's the other thing about these places, fuck me, how can they justify these prices? I hand the bottled beers round and we lurk by the bar. I suddenly feel depressed – it's come to something when I'd rather be in a dive like this than at home with my wife and children.

A couple of the guys spot some people they know and drift off to join them. Another classic Eighties anthem comes on and Dan and the other two of us left go off to dance. I'd rather drink than dance, though. I finish my beer and order a double vodka. But this will be the last one, definitely.

I down it and weave over to the table where the rest of the group are now sitting with some women wearing lots of make-up and tiny tops. I am seriously drunk now.

I mean to tell them I'm going to leave but instead I take my phone out of my pocket and power it up. As soon as it comes to life I see there are five texts and two voicemails.

All from Aura. I scroll through the texts, the first sent at 11:30 p.m. and the last about twenty minutes ago – all variations on 'Where the hell are you, I can't get Bay to go back to sleep.' No doubt the voicemails are in the same vein – I delete them without listening and plonk myself down at the table. I just can't deal with this right now. I'm twenty-seven years old. I should be out having fun with my mates, not being summoned home by my wife because she can't get the baby to sleep.

There are several bottles of something fizzy and pink in the middle of the table. Someone pushes a glass my way and fills it up. 'Here,' she says. 'You look like you need a drink.'

Do I? I take a sip of the drink – it's too sweet but I can't be bothered to go back to the bar to get something else. 'Sorry,' I say. 'Bad day.'

She smiles at me. She is wearing deep red lipstick and her eyelashes are very long and dark. Her hair is blond and poker-straight and she is very pretty. I try not to look at her boobs, but I can't help noticing they are small and pert and she is definitely not wearing a bra. 'Want to talk about it?' she asks. She is slurring a little. I guess she's pretty drunk too. You have to be to want to be in a place like this, I suppose.

I shake my head. 'Not really. Don't want to bore you.' I take another sip of the vile drink and lean in closer to her. 'Tell me about you instead. How was your day?'

She continues looking me in the eye as I feel her hand on the inside of my thigh. 'It was OK,' she says.

'Yeah?' I ask. I feel myself getting hard and am not sure whether or not to be embarrassed. Aura has barely touched me since Bay was born, so it doesn't take much these days. She moves her hand up my thigh and I move a little to meet her hand.

She leans in closer to me so that I can feel her breath on my face. 'But it's getting better,' she whispers, and then we are kissing.

# 24

*January, London*

Nick

'Nick!' Aura is yelling. 'You need to come and help me get the boys ready!'

We have all been up since 5 a.m. Stupidly, when Sorrel was born I caved to Aura's demands that we all co-sleep, which means that I typically spend half the night being kicked in the head by Bay and the nuts by Sorrel. The idea was that Aura would be able to breastfeed the boys easily but as the breastfeeding didn't work out it usually means one or other of us getting up several times a night to sort out a bottle. I've taken to drinking more in the evening than I used to, partly because then Aura feels it's unsafe for me to be in bed with the boys and I get to sleep in the spare room, like I did last night. Those nights are the nearest thing I get to a proper night's rest, but Sol came in to see me at 5 a.m. this morning because he'd had a nightmare he wanted to tell me about, and that was that.

It's Aura's first day back at work today and, despite her saying that this was what she needed, that this would make her feel like herself again, that it would improve our relationship, the prospect seems to be totally stressing her out and she's been in a foul mood for days.

The fridge is packed with home-made organic hummus and carrots from the local farmers' market, while the cupboards are full of weird 'crisps' made of things like lentil and broccoli. Aura has been baking all week, making horrendous-sounding 'treats' like courgette muffins and sugar-free flapjacks. The nursery offers lunch, but Aura wants to keep control of what the children are eating and send them in with food and bottles of organic formula she's prepared herself. You don't need to be a psychologist to know that she's over-compensating for feeling guilty about sending them to nursery.

But obviously I don't say that. Taking the children to nursery is to be my job rather than Aura's, but that's OK as the nursery is next to my school.

I go down to the kitchen where Aura is cutting grapes into quarters and putting them in a little stainless steel can for Sorrel's lunch, with slices of banana in another can and some awful tofu wrap thing in a third. These are then deposited in one of the drawstring-muslin bags which Aura has made and embroidered with each of the boys' names. To be fair to her, even if her forthcoming course and putting the boys in nursery has put her on edge, it's also turned her into

136

some kind of story-book mum – at least from an outsider's perspective. But I've been at home for the last two weeks during the holidays, which obviously makes life easier for her. I may not embroider, but I'm pretty good at taking the boys to the park and soft play, reading stories, looking after bath time and things like that.

'There you are!' she cries. 'Can you get their shoes on? I don't want them to be late on their first day.'

I put my hands gently on her shoulders. 'Aura, calm down. It's nursery. It doesn't matter what time they arrive.'

She tuts and shrugs me off. 'Can you just get their shoes on, like I asked?' she repeats, not looking up from the chopping board.

The drop-off at nursery isn't easy. It's the first time the boys have been without either me or Aura, pretty much ever. Even when Bay was born, because he was born at home in a rented birthing pool, Sorrel was upstairs, thankfully asleep. Bay cries as I hand him over to a smiley girl who doesn't look old enough to be out of school – I can still hear him crying as she walks him round the corner out of sight.

Leaving Sorrel is even worse. He clings to my leg screaming: 'No, Dada, me stay with you!' over and over. The staff seem unconcerned and unsurprised – I guess they deal with this sort of thing all the time. No amount of head-patting or re-assurance from me seems to make any difference so eventually I simply prise Sol's tiny fingers from my legs as gently as I can and thrust him at a rotund, kind-looking lady, then bolt. Outside I pause to take a deep breath, surreptitiously swiping at the tears in my eyes. I can still hear poor Sorrel screaming.

I walk briskly down the path, open the gate and carefully slide the lock back in to place as I leave. They'll be fine, I tell myself. Perfectly safe. Thousands – millions? – of parents do this every single day. It'll be good for the boys. Make them more sociable little people. The people who work at the nursery are professionals. My sons are probably safer here than with Aura half-heartedly looking after them at home.

# 25

*January, London*

Nick

'OK, let's settle down, please,' I call as I walk into my Year 12 classroom. The shrieking and shouting stills to a gentle murmur overlaid by the scraping of desks and chairs as everyone settles down into their usual places.

I've no sooner begun taking the register than there is a knock at the door. I look up as the school secretary opens it – she's with a girl I don't recognise.

'Mr Dorian? This is Ella – she's just moved to the area and will be in your class.'

I smile at her – she looks terrified, poor thing. It's always difficult starting at a new school when everyone else already knows each other – especially part way through the year. And so late in her school career.

'Ella – lovely to meet you. Ah yes, I can see you've been added to the register now. Why don't you go and sit there by Molly?' I indicate an empty desk towards the back, next to Molly, who is at least reasonably kind and might make an effort with the new girl.

Ella nods, slouches over to the desk and sits down.

I thought the first day back at school would be distracting enough not to think about the boys and how they are managing at nursery, but I find that every time I am not actually speaking, every time I give a class a few minutes to get on with a specific task and stroll between the desks or sit at the front pretending to be consulting some notes, my mind drifts to Bay and Sorrel. How long will it have taken them to stop crying? They will have stopped crying by now, won't they? Will they have eaten their lunch? Did they like the food Aura packed for them? Should I have tried to talk her into letting them have the lunch the nursery provides – wouldn't it be better for them to have a hot meal at lunchtime, in the winter at least? It's freezing cold at the moment, even for January.

As soon as the final bell goes, I'm out of the door and straight over to the nursery. The boys are allowed to stay as late as six, which will no doubt prove to be necessary some days once after-school clubs, parents' evenings and the like kick in, but as today is their first day and I'm worried they're going to have found it hard, I want to pick them up as early as I can.

I'm expecting a wall of noise as I'm buzzed in, but actually it's pretty calm. Most of the children are sitting at tiny

140

tables eating pieces of fruit. I well up as I spot Sorrel, who appears to be trying to give a piece of his banana to the girl next to him. She takes the piece Aura carefully sliced, which is already starting to go brown, and crams it into her cute, chubby little face with an open palm. She then passes Sorrel a sticky-looking handful of raisins which he wolfs down with a grin. He loves raisins – Aura doesn't usually let him have them as she thinks they're too full of sugar.

Sorrel still hasn't seen me. I feel a twinge of panic. 'Where's Bay?' I ask the nursery worker who let me in and can't be much older than the kids I've been teaching all day.

'In the baby room. He's doing great – come on – let's go and get him.' I glance at Sorrel, who by now is sticking his tongue out to show the girl next to him his half-chewed raisins while she squeals in delight.

Bay is in a colourful room full of toys, sitting in a bouncy chair and happily kicking his heels as the girl sitting on the ground in front of him plays peekaboo with him. He adores peekaboo.

'Hey, Bay,' I say, unclipping him from the chair and lifting him up. 'Have you had a good day?'

'He's been grand,' says the peekaboo girl. 'We've had a great time, Bay, haven't we?'

She shows me a page in a book where she's noted nappy changes and how many bottles he had, and I nod and smile but I'm not listening – both the boys made it through the day happy and safe and that's all I care about right now.

'See you tomorrow, Bay!' the girl cries, adding, 'he's a lovely little chap,' as she squeezes his Babygro-clad foot.

I go back into the main room where Sorrel is now sitting

on the floor with the same girl he was with before, building something from Duplo. He looks like he's concentrating hard. I crouch down, somewhat awkwardly as I'm holding Bay. 'Hi, Sol. What are you building?'

He looks up and brandishes a brick at me, narrowly avoiding hitting me in the face. 'Bridge!' he shouts, delighted. He pushes the brick onto the top of the structure, which I can now see does look a little like a rudimentary bridge. It collapses under the force of his chubby hand.

His face falls. 'Oh dee. Bridge brukken,' he says.

'Oh dear,' I say. 'Never mind, mate. You can build a new one tomorrow. It's time to go home now.'

His face lights up. 'See Mummy?'

'Yeah. C'mon, let's go and see Mummy.' It galls that I am always a consolation prize to the kids, second-best to their mother, but I tell myself not to be so petty. Both Sorrel and I stand up and he hugs my legs, which is so sweet I feel like the worst person in the world for begrudging him asking after his mum a few seconds earlier.

I take his hand and we walk out to the car, with him chuntering continuously with his limited vocabulary about what he's been up to today and his new friend. All my reservations about putting the boys in nursery melt away – I think it's going to be amazing for them. Way better than being stuck at home all day with Aura ignoring them as much as she can and wishing she was somewhere else. And even though I wasn't sure this was all going to work out, suddenly I can see that it might be for the best after all. Maybe it will actually improve things between Aura and me. Maybe we'll start having sex again. Things are looking up.

# 26

Nick

The boys are fed, bathed and in their pyjamas by the time Aura gets home and we are watching CBeebies bedtime hour. It is my favourite time of day with the boys; they are clean, quiet and cuddly. It's very calming. In my imaginary, better life, after this I would take them upstairs to a small bedroom which would perhaps have some kind of Winnie the Pooh frieze and glow-in-the-dark stars on the ceiling. I would tuck them up into their little cots and read them a simple story. Their eyes would droop and before I'd finished they would have dropped off, Sol cuddling his squirrel and Bay making little sucky movements as his bottle drops from his lips.

In my real life, though, that isn't what happens at all. We put the boys to bed in our bed and one of us (usually me)

143

sits with them, stroking and patting them until they fall asleep. I then tiptoe out very quietly, praying that they will stay asleep long enough for us to at least have dinner in peace. But often as not Sorrel is up and down the stairs, wanting water, complaining about a nightmare or wanting a cuddle, or Bay will wake with a yelp, start crying and the whole process has to start again. It is exhausting.

But before all that, I can enjoy some calm time on the sofa with my boys while we all watch CBeebies and I'll sometimes have a sneaky beer or even a gin and tonic if I'm feeling particularly decadent.

So that is exactly what I'm doing when Aura comes in. She kisses each boy on the head (doesn't kiss me but I've stopped expecting that by now) and flops down in the armchair. Neither boy takes their eyes off the TV.

'How was your first day back?' I ask.

She stretches her arms backwards and turns her face up towards the ceiling.

'It was fine, I guess. I forgot how long the day is when you're in front of a computer all day though.'

Really? Before she said a day was never longer than when looking after a baby all day. Anyway. Whatever.

She rocks herself up out of the chair. 'And I missed these guys, of course,' she says, taking each boy's face in her hands in turn and kissing them on the lips this time, which always grosses me out a bit. 'I think I deserve a drink. Want anything?'

I raise my glass towards her. 'No – I'm sorted, thanks.'

My phone buzzes in my pocket and I take it out to read the text, shifting Bay as I do. He is already falling asleep.

Perhaps we can have a nice quiet dinner after all. Maybe we could get a takeaway – we've both had a long day and it might be a nice thing to do. Celebrate Aura's first day back at work, in a low-key way.

The text is from someone called Ed. I don't think I know anyone called Ed.

*Did you really not recognize me in class or were you just pretending? Not sure how offended to be . . .*

I start tapping in *Who is this??* when a memory of my recent night out clicks into place and suddenly I realize.

Oh God.

# 27

*January, London*

**Ella**

OMFG.

I recognized him as soon as I walked into the classroom.
The teacher. It was the guy from the club. I'd barely given
him a second thought until he walked in. God, I was so
drunk that night. So excited to have my friends down from
Manchester for the night. It's shit enough having to start a
new school in the middle of the year but being away from
my friends is even worse.

But Mum doesn't care about that – all she's bothered
about is her precious career. She's been angling to move to
London for years – basically since Dad left her. You'd have
thought she could have waited another year or two until I'd
finished school at least, but no, apparently not. She's been

offered head of features at a newspaper everyone loves to hate and according to her, she has to take it – now or never.

'I thought you'd be delighted about moving to London!' she gushed. 'Imagine all the great places you can go. The shops. And the people! Honestly, once we're there you won't look back.'

Mum is such a snob. She moved to Manchester with my half brother and sister not long before I was born to be with my dad, but she never liked it there. She was always banging on about how much better London was, even though Manchester is the only home I've ever known. But Dad's in Dubai now with his new wife who's not that much older than me and their baby, my brother's in Manchester but Mum wouldn't let me stay there with him (plus he lives in a crap house share anyway) and my sister's off travelling, so it's just me and Mum.

I don't know anyone at all here in London but Mum let me have Tash and Lily down to stay for a few nights and we had a great time shopping and going out. Manchester is really cool and I miss it and I wouldn't ever admit this to Mum but there are some pretty great places in London too. But that doesn't count for anything if you don't have anyone to go to them with, does it?

So that night with Tash and Lily. Mum was out at some event so we started off with a couple of vodka and tonics while we got ready and then we went to a bar in the high street for more of the same. We were going to go into the West End after that but then these guys started buying us drinks and Lily fancied one of them even though they were a bit old, and then they asked if we wanted to come to this club Mint with them so we thought we might as well (Tash and me that is – Lily was absolutely desperate to go).

Mint is about the naffest club we'd ever been in but it didn't matter because we were together and having a laugh. God, I miss my girls so much! And all Lily was bothered about was getting with this guy and he was clearly up for it too so she was happy. We barely saw her from when we went in to when we left.

Tash and I danced for a while and then the guys we came in with bought us some more drinks and we sat at a table with them and then some others came over that they knew as well. I got to that stage of being drunk where everything seems too loud and bright and I couldn't hear what anyone was saying over the music and it was an Eighties night so the music was pretty rubbish too. Everyone was talking to the person next to them and I was just staring into space, too tired and pissed to try to get back into the conversation over the music.

Then another guy stumbled over and joined us – I think he knew some of the others and he was quite fit. He started talking to me but I couldn't hear what he was saying and by now Tash had started getting with someone on the other side of the table and I suddenly felt really lonely at the thought that Tash and Lily were going back home tomorrow and I still couldn't hear what the guy was saying so I thought I might as well just get with him instead.

So we did that and then I asked for his number because, let's face it, I don't know anyone here so I thought I might as well. And he was fit and he seemed OK, or as far as I could tell because he was pretty drunk too. He put his number in my phone and then I texted him and he took his phone out and saved it so unless he's a very good actor it was his real number and he wasn't pretending.

But then in the morning I almost forgot about it and I was just sad about Tash and Lily going home and I thought about texting him but really, what would be the point? What would I say?

Until I walked into the classroom and saw that he was my teacher.

I don't know how to deal with that.

# 28

*January, London*

**Nick**

Shit. Fuck. Wank.

What the hell did I give her my number for? Did I even do that? I don't remember. Could she have got it from someone else? Who? Why?

ED. Not Ed at all. Ella Dooley. I guess I had the presence of mind to disguise her number in my phone, at least.

But shit! How can she be in my class? I feel sweat bead above my lip. Does this mean . . . is she . . .

I take a deep breath. No. She's in Year 12. She's must be at least sixteen. That doesn't make it OK but . . . I didn't know! And we didn't have sex anyway. Nothing like that. A drunken snog in a nightclub – that's all.

But . . . shit! If she tells anyone . . . if anyone saw . . .

oh God. I need to speak to her. Head this off. I'm about to reply to the text when Aura walks back in with an enormous gin and tonic and some Kettle Chips. I shove my phone back into my pocket as she takes a big slurp of her drink.

'Mmmm,' she says as she sits back down in the chair and starts fiddling with her phone, probably on Facebook or whatever as usual. 'How good does this taste? Sure you don't want one?'

I shake my head and down the rest of my drink. 'No. Thank you. I'm fine.' I'm so not fine. The bedtime music is playing on the TV now so I lift the remote and switch it off. 'Why don't you relax and I'll see if I can get the boys to bed?'

Aura puts her phone down, tips her head back so it's resting on the back of the chair and closes her eyes. 'That sounds blissful. Thank you.'

'Sol? You go up and choose a story, OK? I'm going to put Bay in his cot for now as he's already asleep so I don't wake him up while I'm reading to you.'

Shit. Fuck. Wank. I need to get through bedtime as quickly as possible and reply to that text. But what am I going to say? Is it already too late? How many people will she have told? Might she have reported me to anyone? Have I actually done anything wrong if I didn't even know?

Oh God oh God oh God. This is career-ending stuff. I feel myself start to sweat – it's always too hot in this house. I ease Bay down into his cot – he will wake up in about an hour screaming and Aura will probably tell me off for putting him here at all instead of in our bed, but I can deal with that later.

Bay snuffles and shifts as I gently pull my hand away from his back and he settles back to sleep. He's so adorable. Oh God. Why didn't I just stay in last night? What the hell have I done? I go into our room where Sol has tucked himself into his favourite place bang in the middle of the pillows, rubbing his squirrel gently against his face and holding a book.

''*Martest Giant*, Daddy,' he cries, waving the book at me. He already looks sleepy so hopefully this shouldn't take too long. 'Don't laugh when his trousers fall down,' he adds sombrely.

I take the book. 'Of course I won't, Sol,' I say, feeling a pang of love for him along with guilt that I'm feeling so desperate to get away from him to respond to a text from some random girl I snogged in a nightclub. Oh God. I take a deep breath and start to read, slowly. I will not rush. I owe my son that much, surely.

Sorrel is asleep even before the giant's trousers fall down. I tuck the duvet around his chin, kiss his forehead and then creep into our en suite, locking the door behind me. I close the lid of the loo and sit down to reread the text.

*Did you really not recognize me in class or were you just pretending? Not sure how offended to be . . .*

No emojis. No kisses at the end. Is she genuinely offended? Or is she joking? So difficult to tell. I feel like a teenager over-analysing a text from a girl I fancy. Which is not the case here. It isn't. Shit.

Is she angry with me? Or is the text mildly flirtatious? What's the best way to respond to shut this down?

Because that's what I need to do, obviously. Shut this

down. Perhaps I should ignore her. But then . . . if she is upset and I don't reply, she might tell someone. If she hasn't already.

My face grows hot. What if Aura finds out? What if the school finds out? I'm not sure which is worse.

I don't really remember anything about this girl. What did we talk about? Did we talk at all? I vaguely remember us snogging, her hand on my leg . . . oh God, what if someone saw us? Who was she with? Were they from school too? No. She's new. She doesn't know anyone here. Does she? Might she? Christ.

The words of her text swim in front of me. I need to reply. We need to talk. I need to make her see how important it is that this doesn't go any further.

What am I thinking? There is no 'this'. We had a drunken kiss. I'm a married father of two. She is my student. She is more than ten years younger than me. But I didn't know any of this. I haven't done anything wrong. As long as she understands that, it'll be fine.

I stare at the phone. I didn't recognize her at school. I was very drunk – so was she – I'm amazed she recognized me. But should I say that? Probably not. I'll avoid the question.

*Hey* I tap in, and then delete. Too informal. Bordering on flirty even. No. Stay professional.

*Ella.*

Much better.

*Sorry – it was a surprise to see you.*

Isn't that the truth.

*I think we should talk.*

But where? Nowhere we can be seen. I can't meet her anywhere outside school. Not a café or anything like that. Inappropriate. Here? Is that worse? Probably. Needs to be at school.

*Can you stay behind after lessons tomorrow?*

Yes. Bland. Unthreatening. Safe at school.

*Pretend you need to talk to me about where you're up to with your studies as you've just moved.*

Hmm. Should I be asking her to lie? I don't want her to feel that we're plotting together. I delete.

*We should speak about where you're at with your studies as you've just arrived.*

Better. I reread, my thumb hovering over the 'send' icon. I think it's OK. Bay starts wailing – that didn't take long. The message will have to do. I press send, stand up and go and get Bay.

# 29

**Ella**

Tash:   *OMFG I can't believe he didn't recognize you!!!!! Rude.*

Lily:   *LOL he's your teacher!!! No way!!! What a perv.*

Me:   *It's not like he knew!*

Lily:   *Whatever, it's wrong. You should tell someone.*

Should I? I don't think I want to do that. It's not his fault. Plus I'm new here – I don't want to forever be known as that girl that got with the teacher.

Tash:   *But he was hot!*

Yeah. He was. Is.

> Me:     *If he doesn't recognize me I might just leave*
> *it. It's not like anything's going to come of it.*
> Lily:    *That's so disrespectful though. He should at least*
> *acknowledge you. Say something. You can't be in*
> *his class all year and not say anything.*
> Tash:   *Plus he might be pretending.*
> Me:     *D'you think?*
> Tash:   *idk*

We go backwards and forwards like this for an hour or so until we come up with a text the girls think I should send.

Apart from anything else, sending it and waiting to see if he replies gives me something to think about. It's so boring being here on my own, not knowing anyone.

I send the text. I'm not sure what to expect, or even what I hope will happen. Maybe he'll ignore it. Almost immediately my phone pings.

> Tash:   *Did he reply????*

And again.

> Lily:    *So?? What did he say?*
> Me:     *Nothing. No reply. Mum's calling – speak later x*

Mum isn't calling – she's not even here. But to my surprise I feel a pang of disappointment at his lack of reply. I don't want to tell the girls that.

156

# 30

*January, London*

Nick

Bay is tearful when I drop him off at nursery this morning but Sol hardly looks back – he can't wait to get in and play with the Duplo again. He's barely stopped talking about it this morning. We don't have Duplo at home because Aura won't have plastic toys in the house. Sorrel slept better than usual last night – only woke up once – so maybe being at nursery rather than kicking round the house all day with Aura is helping to tire him out too.

I, on the other hand, barely slept at all. I deleted both Ella's text and the one I sent to her before I went back downstairs, but don't these things always exist in the cloud or something? Is it possible to ever delete anything entirely now? I wonder about asking the IT guy at school but then he might wonder why I want to know. Maybe I'll google it later. Does that leave a trace? I imagine it must do.

I hand Bay over with the minimum of fuss, even though he is still crying, and exit quickly. It feels easier today than yesterday – I'm not sure if it's because it's the second time I've done it or because I'm so distracted. I'm both dreading and can't wait to get to school – get this over with. It needs to be sorted.

I glance at Ella as I come in. She's at the back of the classroom where I suggested she sit yesterday, fiddling with her phone. Poor kid – it must be hard starting at a new school at her age when the cliques are already so established. Teenage girls can be so mean. Maybe when we have our chat after school I'll suggest some clubs she can join.

Though that is hardly the priority here. I don't look at her as I call her name in the register. I don't trust myself to keep my expression neutral, and also I'm a little scared of what I might see in hers. Mocking? Pity? Disgust? Hatred? I've really no idea.

Ella didn't reply to my text yesterday. I don't know if that's good or bad. But while I fretted about this all night I came to the conclusion that being as open as possible is probably the best thing, so at the end of the registration period I say in front of the entire class, 'Ella, please come and see me at the end of the day so we can have a catch-up about where you're up to work-wise, thank you,' as if everything is totally normal and I'm not potentially about to be added to the sex offenders register.

I look up at her but she isn't looking at me. Instead she just nods and, I think, blushes.

Oh God. Is that normal?

Yes, I tell myself. I've just drawn attention to her in front of everyone and she's new. She's bound to be feeling self-conscious.

The day drags by and I find it difficult to concentrate. Despite having planned out my conversation with Ella in my head, I can't stop going over and over it again and again, with different permutations and imaginary outcomes.

I make my way back to my classroom when the final bell of the day rings to find that Ella is already there. She's sitting on a desk at the front of the room, legs dangling.

'Ella,' I say, doing my best to sound brisk and professional as I close the door behind me, 'thank you for coming.' I sit down behind my desk to create space between us and to reinforce the idea that I am the teacher and she is the pupil but then my eyes are level with her knees and her skirt is short and it feels wrong. I indicate the chair behind the desk she is sitting on. 'Would you mind sitting down, please?' I ask.

She does the typical teenage eye-roll-and-slouch movement into the chair, drops her bag to the floor and looks at me. It's difficult to read her expression but if I had to put money on it, I'd say insolence.

'Thank you,' I say. 'I've had a look at the report from your previous school and, while there's nothing which leaps out at me as being a matter for concern, I wondered if there was anything you wanted to discuss or anything you felt you needed extra help with at the moment?'

She continues looking at me in silence. 'Ella?' I prompt.

159

She shakes her head. 'No, nothing I need to discuss about my work,' she says meaningfully.

We lapse back into silence. I guess it has to be down to me as the grown-up to bring up what happened, but she certainly isn't making it easy for me.

'Right. Well. I guess we both know what you mean by that. The other night.' I was determined not to, but I feel myself go red. 'Do you . . . have anything you wanted to say about that?'

She leans back in her chair with a small smile. I feel like she has the upper hand here. 'Nothing particular, *sir*,' she says, oozing sarcasm. 'Do you?'

I feel myself blush deeper. 'Well, yes, Ella, I do. As I'm sure we both know, what happened at Mint – that nightclub,' I say, trying to somehow distance myself from it, make it seem more formal, 'would never have happened had I known you were going to be my pupil. In my class. My school. Or had I known you were only sixteen. I had no idea. Obviously.'

She leans forward. 'Are you saying you regret what happened, sir?' she asks.

Oh God. How do I answer that? 'Ella, I'm sure you understand it's nothing personal. There can't be relations of any kind between teachers and pupils. We both know that.'

''Specially not married teachers, eh, sir?' she adds, glancing at the ring on my finger.

I snatch my hands away from the desk and rest them on my lap. 'Yes. There are many ways in which I didn't cover myself in glory that evening. I'm not going to make excuses for myself; my behaviour fell well under par on several counts.'

Something suddenly occurs to me – could she be recording this conversation? Should I have asked her for her phone? Have I gone about this all the wrong way? Should I have 'fessed up to the head immediately and done all this through official channels?'

Oh God. Oh God. It's so difficult to think straight when I never get any sleep.

'I fear I could lose my job over this,' I say quietly. 'I think we both know that what happened was a genuine mistake, and I would like to apologize profusely for my actions. Nothing similar will happen again, I assure you. If you could find it within you to accept my apology and let us put this incident in the past, it would be greatly appreciated.'

That sounded less formal and twatty when I rehearsed it in my head. Ella rolls her eyes.

'Fine,' she says, evenly. 'It was only a kiss, sir, no big deal. I'm not going to tell anyone, if that's what you're worried about.'

Relief washes over me and I allow myself a smile and then wonder if that's appropriate. I rearrange my face into a more sober expression.

'Thank you, Ella.' As planned, I then switch back into teacher mode. 'So tell me, how are you finding things so far? It must be very tricky starting a new school at this point in the year.'

I fully expect her not to want to engage any further so am not surprised when she replies with a curt; 'It's OK, I guess.'

I nod. 'I'm sure you'll feel more settled soon. In the meantime, if I can help in any way, as your teacher, then please don't hesitate.'

She pushes her chair back with a loud scraping noise. 'Is that it then? Can I go now?'

'Of course. Thank you very much for your time and . . . co-operation, Ella. Have a nice evening.'

She leaves the classroom without a word.

# 31

*January, London*

**Ella**

Fuck's sake.

What's wrong with me?

When I leave Mr Dorian I go straight into the loos and burst into tears.

I sit in the stinking cubicle stifling my sobs in case anyone else is still around.

I'm not crying about what he said. It was pretty much what I expected him to say, only he was nicer about it than I thought he might be.

But it makes me think about how it would have gone if this had happened back home. Tash and Lily would have been waiting for me outside and we'd have gone to Emma's

Café to have hot chocolate with whipped cream and flakes and pull apart what he said.

Instead I brush away my tears and send a Snap to them both: *You there?*

But neither replies. I try calling my sister, though God knows what time it is wherever she is, and my brother, but they don't answer either. I wouldn't tell them either of them about Mr Dorian but I just need to hear a friendly voice. Speak to someone who cares about me.

Fresh tears fall as I realize how alone I am.

# 32

*January, London*

**Nick**

I guess that went as well as could be expected.

As Ella is so new at school, and I barely remember anything about the night in the club, I don't know much about her personality, what she's like.

But she didn't call me a dirty fucker or a paedophile or anything like that, neither did she cry (not that I was really expecting that, but you never know). So that's all good.

I think she understood where I was coming from. The importance of keeping this quiet.

I feel a lot lighter picking up the boys than when I dropped them off. Sorrel is with the same little girl as yesterday, playing with Duplo again. He's obviously made a friend – so cute. Bay seems pretty happy too and, according to Kerry, one of the staff, there were no more tears today once he'd settled.

'Sorrel loves the Duplo,' she tells me, 'and he painted this picture for you too.' She thrusts a grey piece of paper at me which is daubed with various swirls of brightly coloured paint that have gone a murky brown at the points where the colours overlap.

'Is Mummy!' Sorrel beams. There are no discernible shapes at all, but I say, 'It's brilliant, Sol, she'll love it. We can put it on the fridge at home, can't we?'

Sol nods happily and sticks his finger in his mouth, reaching up to take my hand with his other hand.

'Will we see you tomorrow, Sorrel?' Kerry asks, ruffling his hair. 'You can carry on with that castle you were building earlier with Indy.' Sorrel nods solemnly as Kerry indicates a cluster of Duplo bricks seemingly randomly stuck together which is Sol's 'castle'.

'We're still missing some forms for the boys,' Kerry says. 'I emailed your wife again about it, but nothing's come through yet. Would you be able to give her a nudge for me? Perhaps you or she can get them completed and bring them along later this week?'

'Yes, of course – I assume Aura knows what's needed?' I ask as Kerry hands me Bay.

'Yep – it was all in the application pack and also the emails. See you tomorrow, Bay. Bye-bye!'

Bay grins and waves his chubby little hand. 'They're lovely little boys, Mr Dorian; you should be proud,' Kerry adds.

'Nick, please,' I say. 'And thank you, that's very kind.' I wonder if she says that to all the parents, and also if she'd say that if she had to be kicked awake by them every single night.

I sort the boys out a simple dinner of fish goujons and fresh peas (Aura won't let the boys have ordinary fishfingers, which is a shame because I love a fishfinger sandwich; organic goujons just somehow aren't the same) and have a couple of beers while I watch them eat. Considering how it could have gone with Ella, I think today went OK, and I want to celebrate.

The three of us are settled in front of CBeebies as usual when Aura comes home. The front door slams, harder than usual, and I hear her stomp into the kitchen without a word.

Oh dear.

The boys are transfixed by what's happening on the screen so I ease myself out from between them and put Bay in his bouncy chair, steeling myself for what I might find in the kitchen.

Aura is standing by the sink, pouring herself a massive glass of white wine.

'Darling?' I say gingerly. 'How was your day?'

She takes a huge slug of wine and slams the glass down. 'It was shit, but thank you for asking.'

'What happened?'

She turns to face me and rolls her eyes. 'Nothing *happened* as such, it's just that the work is so boring and I'm too old to be treated like some kind of teenage work-experience girl.'

'Who's treating you like that?'

She waves her hand in front of her face as she takes another gulp of wine. 'Everyone. Photocopy this, type up

167

that, file these, sort the post, all day long. I'm better than this.'

I want to say, *But it's an admin role – you knew that, and that's what admin tasks are*, but I know that isn't going to help.

'I know, darling, I'm sure it will get better. And look at it this way, because you're only working part-time it gives you the chance to study for the counselling, like you said you wanted to do.'

'Don't say "only",' she snaps. 'I'm working, bringing home the bacon, same as you. And now I need to go and get ready for class this evening, and then tomorrow I'm off, thank Christ. Boys OK?' she asks, pretty much as an afterthought.

'Yes, they're fine. Look, Sorrel did you a painting. It's on the fridge,' I add, pointing. 'It's a picture of you, apparently.' I see her face soften.

'Aww. That's sweet. I'll go and give them a kiss before I get changed, but then I'll have to dash out. You OK to do bedtime?'

I nod. 'Of course.' It is exhausting having to do tea and bedtime every evening after a day at work and I hope Aura is going to take up the slack on her share again at some point, but now is clearly not the time to bring it up.

She downs the rest of the wine and shoves the glass in the dishwasher. 'I'd probably get yourself something to eat as I won't be back till about nine thirty – I'll grab a takeaway for myself on the way home.'

I go to try to give her a hug but she ducks out of my way and rushes off into the living room. A few seconds later, I hear her run up the stairs and then after another ten minutes when I'm back with the boys on the sofa she shouts "Bye, see you later!' from the hall and I hear the front door slam.

Bedtime is the usual shitshow but eventually after three stories and lying in the dark in bed staring at the ceiling for about half an hour, both boys drop off. I ease myself up, careful not to move too quickly so as not to wake anyone, and go into the bathroom. I take my clothes off and get in the shower – I prefer to have a shower pretty much as soon as I get home from school but thanks to our new routine, these days there is usually no time. The water is hot and welcoming.

Squeezing shower gel into my hand, I also get started on my somewhat tragic routine more suited to a teenage boy of wanking while I shower. Since Aura decided the boys were going to sleep in our bed every night, it's been pretty much my only release. I run through my usual favourite mental images of actresses, pop stars and ex-girlfriends I could have ended up with had my life turned out differently but am surprised and somewhat ashamed to find that it's Ella's face in my head when I come.

# 33

*January, London*

**Ella**

Three weeks on since my arrival in London, things are not that much better. They're all so up themselves here. I usually tag along with Molly, who I sit next to in class, because it's better than hanging round on my own the whole time. Everyone is already in their cliques and not interested in a newcomer like me.

Molly's OK, I guess, though I get the impression she's a bit desperate for a friend and my arrival is something of a relief for her. Even so, I can kind of imagine us being proper friends, in time. It's not like being with Tash and Lily, but I've known them since I was about five so it's just never going to be, is it?

Sometimes Molly and I hang out after school in a café or

go shopping. I like it when we do that – Mum is often late at work and even if she is home, she spends half the night on her laptop or phone. And while I still talk to Tash and Lily on Snap most days, it's not the same when I haven't been to the party they'll be talking about or don't know what the boy who works in Nando's that everyone fancies looks like. My brother is busy with his job and new girlfriend and my sister is in a totally different time zone which makes it almost impossible to speak to either of them. I miss them all so much. Having someone to spend time with after school does make it easier, even if she's not my BFF.

Molly and I are in Latte Da complaining about the amount of homework given by our English teacher when Ethan, her twin brother, and his mate Jack join us.

Molly kicks my leg under the table and I kick her back. She keeps saying Jack really fancies me, but I'm not so sure. He joins us for lunch sometimes at school and he lives fairly near me so we've walked back from school together a few times, but I don't get the impression that he's interested in me in that way. Molly is convinced though, and goes on about it to the point where it sometimes gets a bit annoying.

The four of us chat and laugh and I realize that their company is kind of starting to feel normal, even if a lot of the boys' chat is boring stuff like whether Maseratis or Ferraris are better and whether or not backing stuff up to the cloud makes you more likely to be hacked. Two more boys, Max and Tom, arrive and we all slide along the benches to let them in. It's quite squashed now and Jack's thigh is pressed up against mine. Is he doing it on purpose? I'm not sure.

'You going on the skiing trip?' Tom asks the table in a general way.

'Yep,' Jack says. 'Can't wait.'

'I'm going too,' Molly pipes up, and blushes. She really likes Tom and got with him at a party before Christmas, but she's not sure if he remembers as he was really drunk and she doesn't know whether to say anything or not. I give her a sympathetic smile and she smirks.

'Ella? You should come too,' Ethan says. 'It'll be really fun.'

Part of me is excited and happy about being asked, but the other part is in a panic because I don't really know these people. Wouldn't it be weird? 'Oh, I don't know . . . I've never skied. I'm not sure it would be my thing.'

'You should definitely come,' Ethan continues. 'None of us has skied either. Except posh-boy Jack here, that is.'

Jack gives Ethan a good-natured shove. Ethan shoves Jack back, pushing him against me. He straightens himself up and then pats my leg, saying, 'Sorry about my imbecilic friend here.'

I blush as Molly kicks my ankle again and gives me a knowing look.

'Anyway, as I was saying before I was so rudely interrupted by this bellend, you should come with us,' Ethan says. 'It would be fun. We're not as bad as we seem, honestly. At least, I'm not.'

'Maybe. I'll need to ask Mum – I'm not sure if she's got any plans for the holidays.'

I don't particularly care if Mum has any plans or not – I can't imagine she does anyway as she'll no doubt be working.

But up until now I was hoping to go back to Manchester and stay with Tash or Lily this holiday, see everyone, go to our usual places.

But suddenly I feel like maybe I *would* like to spend more time with these people. They are actually kind of OK. Going on the trip might even make me feel like I fit in a bit better too. I'm stuck here for almost two years at least, after all. It's probably worth making the effort.

'I'll see what she says,' I add, making up my mind that I do want to go. Although I'm pretty sure Mum will say yes – anything that gets me out of her hair is good news for her, and she'll also be pleased that I'm trying to fit in at school.

As I leave the café my phone pings with a text.

*Sorry am going to be late. Not much food in – can you get yourself something? Will pay you back. Love Mum xxx*

I duck into Sainsbury's Local to get myself a Charlie Bigham fish pie and a bag of prepacked salad – not for the first time this week. While I'm picking out a chocolate bar as I wait in the queue for a self-service till I notice that Mr Dorian is standing next to me, staring blankly at the racks of chocolate. He catches my eye.

I might have imagined it, but it looked like he blushed. 'Ella. Hello. Do you, ah, live near here?'

'Yep – All Saints Road. And you?'

'Oh, not too far, just . . . round the corner.'

He obviously doesn't want to tell me where he lives. Not sure if that's normal for any teacher because they don't want kids throwing eggs at their doors, or if he's worried I'm going to start turning up and stalking him.

'I'm just getting some bits for the boys' dinner before I pick them up from nursery,' he says, brandishing his basket at me. I glance at it – organic carrot sticks, apples, cucumber, hummus, beetroot crisps. Yuk. No chocolate or little treats. Poor children.

'I'm getting my dinner too,' I say, holding out my pie and salad. 'Mum's out this evening.'

He smiles nervously. 'That looks lovely. I wish . . . well. Anyway. I hope you have a nice evening, Ella, and I'll see you at school tomorrow.'

He moves away as a till comes free. I am standing behind him as I wait for a till and can see that his neck is bright red as he scans his food through.

# 34

*January, London*

Nick

Oh God.

It's always weird bumping into kids from school out of hours. They somehow don't expect you to have a real life outside of lessons and neither I nor they ever seem to know how to react.

But I'm never usually as bad as that. I see Ella every day at school and had pretty much managed to push what happened out of my mind. Beyond registration, we don't have to interact that much.

But when I saw her in the supermarket like that all I could suddenly think about was that time in the shower and what I was doing while thinking about her so I could barely get my words out. And then I nearly told her I wish my wife would let me eat ready meals like she had in her basket, as if I'm some downtrodden house-husband – which I guess these days I pretty much am.

For fuck's sake. I will not think about her. I will not.

# 35

*January, London*

Ella

Molly's invited me to a party. My initial instinct is to say no but then I realize that, if I don't go, all I'll be doing is sitting at home sending Snaps to Tash and Lily, who will probably be out doing something fun and I won't be there and I'll only get jealous and pissed off about being stuck in London. As usual.

Ethan, Tom and Jack are going to the party too. They're fine, I like them and everything, but like all boys of my age, they seem pretty immature.

After I bumped into Mr Dorian in the supermarket I was thinking about that time in the club. How hot it was. I bet it's not the first time he's done that to his wife. I don't reckon it would take all that much to make it happen again. It would kind of be fun to have a thing going with a teacher, wouldn't it? Give me something else to think about other than being taken away from my friends. I don't care that he's married, it's not like I'd want to be with him forever or anything, and I wouldn't want to tell his wife or anything like that. It would just be a bit of a laugh, something to tell Tash and Lily. Make them remember who I am.

But about tonight – this party. It's at Max's place – Molly says it's an enormous house by Clapham Common and his parents are out of town.

Molly and I have a few drinks while we get ready at mine, just like I used to back in Manchester. It isn't nearly as much fun as with my girls, but it feels like weeks since I last did something like this. Which I guess it is. Since that night I went out and got with Mr Dorian. Molly is sweet, seems almost overexcited this evening. Like she's really pleased to be round at mine, to be going out, to be doing all these things which are actually very normal. Maybe she's not that used to drinking, I don't know.

I have more drinks before we leave than I normally would because I'm a bit nervous. I'm not sure why – it's not like I really care what these people think of me; I guess it's just that I don't know anyone down here. And by the time we get to the party my head is already spinning. I hope there's some food – I need to eat something. My phone chirrups just as we're going in. It's my brother – no doubt calling me back after I left a message having a go at him for never answering his phone. But I shove it back in my bag – I can't talk to him now.

We can hear the music from the corner of the road and

178

the front door is open. The rumours were right, the house is enormous, with at least four storeys, and the downstairs rooms are heaving. We push through to the kitchen and help ourselves to vodka and tonics. Outside in the garden the trees are lit with fairy lights even though it's too cold to want to spend much time out there – though there are a few smokers on the patio, and I can see the tips of two cigarettes or joints glowing further down the garden in the darkness. There is a huge bowl of ice in the kitchen so I chuck a couple of cubes in my drink and eat one of the slices of pizza from the boxes on the table. It makes me feel better almost instantly.

The party is fun. We drink, and dance, and drink some more. Molly was right about Jack fancying me; he barely leaves my side. By the end of the evening when we end up snogging in an armchair in a dark corner because I am drunk and a little bit horny and it's comforting to be touched that way and feel like someone is really into me – it's been so long.

At the end of the evening Jack asks if we can do something next week but I'm sort of out of it by then so I'm only half paying attention. It's 2 a.m. and the police are here because the neighbours have complained about the noise so the party is breaking up.

Molly links her arm through mine as we walk back to my house – we're both staying at mine because it's closer and that way we can keep both our mums happy as neither of us will be walking home alone.

'So, you and Jack, hey?' Molly slurs. 'Told you he likes you.'

'Yeah. Was just a kiss though. I don't think anything will come of it.'

'You don't like him? He's fit.'

Bloody hell – why is she so keen for us to get together? 'He's OK. I'm just not . . . really in a place for anything like that at the moment.'

She stops and turns to face me, her eyes widening as she wobbles slightly. 'You've got a boyfriend back in Manchester!' she cries. 'You didn't tell me!'

I laugh. 'No! Nothing like that.'

'So you've met someone since you've been here?'

'NO!'

She narrows her eyes. 'There's someone. My spidey sense is telling me.'

'There isn't,' I say, but feel myself blush.

She grabs my arm. 'There so is. C'mon, you have to tell me. I won't tell, I promise. So you're telling me there's no one in Manchester and there's been no one since you arrived in London?'

I smirk – I can't help it.

'There is!' she cries. 'Who is it? Someone at school?'

'Kind of,' I blurt. I have had too much to drink. I shouldn't say anything. 'But look, it was really nothing. Just a drunken snog. We're not, like, together or anything.'

'Tell me!'

Her eyes are shining and it feels so nice to have a friend who is interested in my life and the things happening to me and I am so drunk that I can't resist. It's exhausting keeping it to myself, especially as I find myself thinking about him more and more. I tell Tash and Lily about him but sometimes

180

I think they're not all that interested – it's not like they know him like Molly does. I can't tell my brother – I know he'd disapprove, and my sister still sees me as basically a baby. Neither of them would want to know.

'OK,' I agree. 'But you have to promise not to say anything. To anyone.'

Her eyes widen further. 'He's with someone else?'

'Yes.'

'Is it Ben? Ooh! No, I know, I bet it's Noah! It's Noah, isn't it?'

'No.' I pause for dramatic effect. 'It was Mr Dorian.' Argh. I regret telling her almost as soon as the words are out of my mouth.

She stops stock-still and her hand flies to her mouth. Oh God. I knew I shouldn't have said anything.

'Just a thing in a club,' I clarify. 'One night. Before I started at St Benedict's. He didn't know I was going to be at school there. I didn't know he was a teacher. It was right after I'd moved. We'd never met before.'

Her eyes are like saucers. 'Mr Dorian! No way!'

'Yes way,' I say. Shit. I shouldn't have told her. 'But it was nothing, and nothing will come of it. And it has nothing to do with me not being that into Jack, he's just not my type,' I babble.

Molly still hasn't moved but she finally takes her hand away from her mouth. 'OMG. You like him though. Mr Dorian, I mean. I can tell.'

'No I don't,' I counter. But I'm lying.

181

# 36

*February, London*

**Nick**

I thought the idea was that Aura going back to work and training as a counsellor was supposed to mean she would be happier and more fulfilled, which would benefit us all as a family.

Nothing could be further from the truth. She's working a few hours, three days a week. From what she says, she spends her time answering the phone, filing and photocopying, but apparently it is 'utterly exhausting'. Then she complains that on top of this she has her course – in other words, a couple of nights a week at an evening class for bored housewives and maybe a bit of homework in between. For fuck's sake, how hard can it be?

But more to the point, no one is making her do any of

this. It was her choice. She gave up sitting around at home watching children's TV, fiddling around on Facebook half the day and hanging out in the park drinking coffee to do some boring office job and pointless course, but that was her choice. I'd give my right arm to give up my job and spend all day at home with the boys, but we simply can't afford for me to do that.

And because she's so 'busy' and exhausted, I now pick up pretty much all the slack with the boys, which in some ways is fine because they're such fun to spend time with. But I hate that they still have to sleep in our bed all the time and I hate that Aura and I never have sex. Surely there has to be some correlation between the two? If the boys weren't in our bed, there would definitely be more chance of some intimacy.

While there has been the odd slip-up fidelity-wise in our marriage on my side over the years, I do the best I can. And, to my knowledge, Aura's never found out. Before Ella, it hadn't happened for absolutely ages. But now I can barely stop thinking about her.

Ella hasn't made it easy for me. She lives near school and I keep bumping into her in the supermarket. The first time was unbearably awkward but now that it's happened a few times it feels more natural and we usually have a chat. Nothing inappropriate – we stay on safe topics: homework, holidays, that sort of thing. I try not to picture us together in the club and I try not to think about her while I'm in the shower, but often I fail.

Half term is coming up and Aura has taken a week's holiday from work. We considered going somewhere, maybe

183

renting a cottage in Cornwall or something, but in the end we figured that taking the boys on a trip would end up being more disruptive and less restful than staying at home. Plus we're not exactly flush now that we're paying full-on nursery fees until Sorrel's free hours kick in (which is much longer away than Aura led me to believe), so in the end we decided against it.

The prospect of a cold and rainy half term likely to be spent largely in a stinky, noisy soft play centre with the kids is looming heavily over me when the school rings and asks if there is any way I can accompany the school ski trip over half term.

'I know it's short notice,' Gillian the sports teacher says. 'But Greg, who was due to accompany, has been taken ill. I wondered if you'd be able to come? Or do you have plans for the holiday? I know you have young children, but I've already asked several people and so far haven't found anyone – they all have stuff booked. It would be such a blessing if you were able to help out, and I know Mike would be especially grateful.'

Mike – the head teacher. Cunning of Gillian to mention him – she knows I want to go for head of department. But I'm not going to go on the trip just because of that. No, I'm going to go if I possibly can because I deserve a holiday, I want to get away from home on my own for more than about five minutes for the first time since Sorrel was born. And besides, this trip is free. It's win-win.

'Should be fine,' I say. 'Let me run it by my wife and I'll get back to you tomorrow.' I wince. Could I possibly sound any more pussy-whipped? I decide in that moment that one way or another, I'm going. I deserve it. I'm not going to let Aura stop me.

'What?' Aura cries. 'But I took that week off so we could spend it together!'

This isn't what she said when she booked the annual leave – once we decided we couldn't afford a week away she said she'd take the time off anyway to concentrate on her coursework and would be expecting me to take charge of the children. Also, she hates her job and wants a break from it. But now is clearly not the time to bring any of this up.

'I don't think I can say no,' I lie. 'You want me to get that promotion, don't you? If I get it, there'll be more money coming in and maybe then you could cut down your working days – spend more time on your coursework.'

Her face softens at this. 'That would be nice,' she concedes. 'I am really enjoying my course – it would be good to have more time to study. Then maybe I could do the next level up too.'

'Exactly,' I say. 'And I also thought that, with me away, the boys at nursery and you off work, you'd have plenty of time to get on with it. You could even treat yourself to a massage or something too. Spend the week concentrating on you. Wouldn't that be nice?'

She hesitates before she replies, but I can tell she's coming round to the idea. 'Mmmm. I guess so. But the boys will be quite hard work on my own for an entire week,' she counters.

*They'll be at nursery most of the time for fuck's sake*, I think to myself, fighting not to let my feelings show on my face, trying to conjure up a sympathetic expression as I take her hand. 'I know. But you can do it. Maybe you could book the boys in to nursery for an extra couple of days – some families will be away so there'll probably be space. And it'll be lovely for you to have some bonding time alone with the boys. They barely see you these days and they miss you. Every day when I pick them up from nursery the first thing Sorrel asks is when he's going to see you.'

I can see that my last statement, which was, to be fair, true, was a winning one. Aura's expression softens.

'Really?' she asks.

'Yep. And I tell you what, how about when we get back, we go away for a night somewhere not too far away, just you and me? Maybe send the boys to my parents? They're always asking to have them.'

As I suspected it would, a panicky look crosses her face – I know she'll never agree to that. But objectively it is a nice offer, she can't deny that, even if it's one I know she won't take me up on. 'Hmm. Not sure I'm ready for that,' she says, as I knew she would. 'But OK. You go on the ski trip. And then next time, it's my turn, OK?'

I'm not sure what she means by that and I don't much care; right now I'll agree to anything if it means a week away from home on my own.

I kiss her forehead. 'Of course. You're the best, Aura.'

Back of the net.

# 37

*February, French Alps*

**Ella**

'Ooh yay, this is so exciting!!!!' Molly trills. 'A whole week away from home! No parents!'

She lugs her enormous suitcase over to the edge of the coach and dumps it with the rest of the pile. 'Come on, hurry up!' she adds impatiently. 'If we're going to be on this thing for an entire day or whatever it is, I want to make sure we get a decent seat.'

'I was kind of hoping Ella would sit with me,' Jack interrupts.

A warm feeling rises through me, alongside a vague one of unease. It's nice that Jack likes me so much. I'm trying hard to like him back, in *that* way. We've been out a few times since the party, though mainly as part of a group. And he's come over to mine some evenings when Mum's been out and we've had a bit of a session because, well, why not? It's fun and it feels nice. And it's not like I've got anything else to do. But we haven't gone all the way; I haven't wanted to. I like his company and he's very sweet to me, but I don't feel that rush of adrenaline when I see him, like I do every time I see Mr Dorian, even though it's only at school or in the supermarket.

Molly tuts and rolls her eyes. 'Fine!' she says. 'Looks like you're stuck with me then, brother dear,' she says to Ethan, who carries on fiddling with the straps on his enormous rucksack and ignores her. 'I'll get on and save us some seats. Ella, you come with me so we can sit close together at least.'

'See you on the bus, Jack,' I say, following Molly, who is already racing up the steps of the coach.

'I hope Jack isn't going to try and monopolize you this holiday,' Molly grumbles, expertly scanning the coach and selecting the best seats with extra legroom next to the coffee machine. 'I was hoping we could have some fun together while we're away.'

I sit down behind Molly and Jack slides in next to me, immediately taking my hand. It feels too public and I fight the urge to pull it away.

'Excited?' he asks.

I nod.

'Me too.' He pauses. 'I wish we could share a room,' he whispers.

I laugh, feeling myself blush. We're *way* off anything like that. Aren't we? We only got together a few weeks ago. I

still see us more as friends with not-going-all-the-way bene-
fits rather than actually as a couple.

'St Benedict's might like to think it's liberal, but I don't
think it's *that* liberal,' I say, skilfully avoiding having to agree
that I wish we could share too.

He puts his hand on my thigh. 'Shame, that.'

I don't know what to say, so I say nothing and put my
hand on top of his and give it a gentle squeeze.

'Right – is everybody here?' Miss Fielder shouts from the
front of the coach.

'I'm not!' someone calls from the back.

She ignores the call and walks slowly to the back of the
bus, counting heads under her breath as she goes, and then
walks to the front again.

'Forty. Plus myself, Mr Woods, Miss Oliver and Mr Dorian.
Good. Looks like we're ready to go then.'

My stomach lurches and suddenly my face feels like it
is burning. Molly turns round and gives me a knowing
look.

'I didn't know *Mr Dorian* was coming,' she says, putting
far too much emphasis on his name. 'Did you?'

A bizarre, panicky feeling rises through me – I can't work
out if this is the best or worst thing that could possibly
happen. I daren't look at Jack.

'I thought Mr Baxter was coming with us,' Molly shouts
towards the front of the bus.

'He was,' Miss Fielder replies, 'but he has just had an
emergency appendectomy and so is unable to come. Mr
Dorian has stepped in at the last minute, for which we should
all be very grateful.'

On cue, Mr Dorian climbs on to the bus. He is wearing a black ski jacket and beanie hat and looks much hotter than he usually does in his boring school shirt and chinos combo. I feel something I shouldn't low down as I think about us kissing in the nightclub and my face is burning like it's on fire.

I sneak a look at Jack. It's a relief to see he's busy fiddling with his phone and AirPods and seems thankfully oblivious to my turmoil.

'Good old Mr Dorian,' Molly sings. 'Where would we be without him?'

Oh God.

By the time we're about half an hour into the journey I'm veering between feeling calmer and almost out of control. Mr Dorian coming on this trip is no big deal, right? Molly seems to have pretty much left the subject alone since I accidentally told her about what happened after the party – she's been more interested in hearing about what is (or isn't) going on between me and Jack. And it's not like anything could *happen* between me and Mr Dorian, is it? Not on a trip like this. Not with everyone else here. Being on this trip is pretty much the same as being at school. But then why is he coming? Why doesn't he go skiing with his family? Maybe he wants a chance to . . .

'Chewing gum?' Jack asks, offering me the packet.

I smile. 'No thanks, I'm fine.'

He smiles back and carries on nodding along to whatever he's listening to and I go back to staring out of the window. It's lucky Jack's a boy – he doesn't seem to have noticed that since Mr Dorian got on the bus I can barely sit still. I bet Molly has, even though she's sitting behind me.

And then . . . Mr Dorian walks past. I catch a whiff of his aftershave which takes me right back to that night at the club. So hot. He tells some boys at the back to quieten down and then walks back to the front of the bus.

He doesn't catch my eye, but then, why would he?

I close my eyes and pretend to be asleep.

# 38

*February, French Alps*

**Ella**

'This feels weird, being in a room, just you and me, without anyone to tell us what to do,' Molly says, taking stuff out of her suitcase and flinging it into a deep shelf in a cupboard. 'So it's lucky I managed to smuggle this in!' she trills, picking up a clear bottle and waving it around.

'Vodka?' I ask, pulling a top from my case and folding it neatly onto another shelf. Molly might intend to live like a pig this week, but I don't. 'Where'd you get that from?'

'Nicked it from the cupboard at home. No one'll notice and, even if they do, I'll just blame Ethan. I thought maybe we could play some drinking games.'

'Cool,' I say, feeling my stomach clench slightly. Drinking games aren't really my thing, but there's no point trying to tell Molly that. 'What're you going to wear this evening?' I ask, not because I particularly want to know, but because I want to change the subject.

'This . . . and this,' she says, reaching into her scrunched-up bundle of clothes and pulling out a pair of jeans and a standard-issue hoodie seemingly at random. 'No one I want to impress here. Well, except Tom, I guess, but he's going out with Sadie now, so nothing's going to happen there. At least for now. You?'

'Oh, um, I hadn't really thought about it,' I lie, picturing the skimpy top I was planning to wear with my favourite vintage Levi's jeans but suddenly realizing that it probably isn't particularly snow-appropriate as an outfit.

'How are things going with you and Jack?' she asks bluntly, apropos of nothing.

'OK,' I say. 'But like I've told you before, we're just friends who get together sometimes. It's no big.'

'D'you reckon that while you're here, you might . . .'

'Might what?' I ask, playing for time as I know exactly what she means.

'You know . . . I could always get out of your way and bunk in with Ethan if you wanted to—'

I blush furiously and continue pointedly with unpacking, not looking at her. 'No, I don't think so,' I interrupt tersely. 'It's not like that. I don't think we're ready to anyway . . . after all, we've only just met.'

Molly snorts. 'YOU might not be ready! I bet he is though!'

I look up at her. 'What do you mean? What has he said?'

She waves her hand. 'Nothing. But he's a *boy*, isn't he?'

'Has he said something to Ethan?'

She shrugs. 'Dunno. Even if he had, Ethan wouldn't tell me.' Hmm. I guess my brother probably wouldn't tell me anything like that, but we never talk about sex stuff anyway. I think my sister would tell me though. And twins are closer, aren't they? I wonder if Ethan *has* said something about what Jack's said and she just doesn't want to let on?

I turn my back and get on with my unpacking, but Molly won't leave it alone. 'I'm just surprised that you, that you're still . . . I mean,' she continues, 'would it be your first time?'

'None of your business,' I snap. I should never have told her about the whole Mr Dorian thing. Suddenly Molly seems to think we need to know everything about each other and I really don't feel that way. It's not like she's Tash or Lily. I mean, we've only just met. Why is she so nosy and needy?

Molly holds up her hands. 'Fine. Sorry. I bet if Jack were . . .' she tails off.

'If he were what?' I ask impatiently. She's overstepping the line. I don't want to talk to her about this.

'Nothing. Forget it,' she says airily. 'You'll only go off on one.'

I go back to unpacking, acting as if I don't know what she was going to say.

But I do. And she's right. If Jack were Mr Dorian, I would feel differently.

Once we've unpacked we all go off to get our ski stuff. In the end I settle for wearing a purple cashmere jumper (a reasonably clingy one with my best boob-enhancing bra

194

though) rather than the little top I was planning on and I'm glad I did because it is *freezing* outside. The hotel is really, really heated, triple-glazed and super-insulated, so it's easy to forget that as soon as you step outside it's something mad like minus ten degrees.

It might be cold here but it is very, very pretty. There are foot-long icicles hanging off the roofs and our footsteps make a kind of muffled, squeaky sound as we walk the hundred or so metres to the ski shop. I stick my hand out to catch some falling snowflakes on the back of my black ski glove and examine them. They're like tiny, mini versions of those snowflakes we used to cut out from paper when we were at primary school at Christmas – you can actually see their delicate, intricate pattern and it's true what they say – every one is different.

'Look how pretty they are,' I squeal, holding up my glove to Jack's face for him to inspect the flakes.

He smiles at me. 'Do you know what I like best about you?'

I frown. 'My inside-out knowledge of *Modern Family*?'

He laughs. 'I have to admit that is *pretty* appealing, but what I was going to say is that you seem to have no idea of how gorgeous you are.'

I lean over to kiss his cheek. I wish I could make myself like him more, in the way I like Mr Dorian. 'That's such a nice thing to say.'

He shrugs. 'I'm only saying it because it's true.'

I don't know what to say to that but luckily we are at the ski shop and Miss Fielder is shouting stuff about needing to decide now whether to ski or snowboard and making

195

sure we are signed up to the right lessons, so I start asking Jack about ski lengths and bindings and things like that I really don't care about at all, and our conversation quickly moves on to safer ground.

About an hour later we are finally kitted out with our ski stuff. I am dreading having to carry it all back to the hotel – it's so heavy and unwieldy – but it turns out we can leave it in the ski shop and pick it up in the morning.

It's snowing even harder on the way back. 'Powder'll be amazing tomorrow,' Jack says.

'Powder?'

'That's what you call fresh snow.'

'Oh, I see. Lots to learn.'

Jack links his arm through mine. 'It's a shame we won't be in the same group during the day.'

I laugh. 'I think you'd be pretty bored, skiing with me. I'll probably spend the whole day on my arse.'

'Such a nice arse, though,' he says, pinching my bum. 'I suppose you'll be with Molly? And Ethan, as they're beginners too?'

'Think so.'

There is a pause.

'Can Mr Dorian ski?' Jack asks, out of nowhere, his voice somehow artificially light.

My stomach lurches. 'Um – no idea. Why d'you ask?' I say, equally lightly. Why is he asking about Mr Dorian?

Jack waves his free hand. 'No reason. Just wondered if he might be with me.' Pause. 'Or with you.'

'Oh – um – I really don't know. I guess he might just ski

by himself? I'm not sure if they'd make him join a lesson, would they?' *Can we please stop talking about him.*

'Maybe not,' Jack muses. I sneak a look at him but I can't read his expression. He looks back at me and smiles. Back to normal.

'I wonder what's for dinner?' he says.

# 39

*February, French Alps*

**Ella**

'Seven thirty! Up you get!' Miss Fielder shouts, banging on our door before it is even light. 'Got to be in reception all kitted out and breakfasted by nine o'clock at the very latest! *Vite, vite, vite!*'

'Whose idea was it to come on this trip?' Molly groans, switching on the bedside light and rolling out of bed.

'Um – yours?' I say. 'Or actually I think it was Ethan who first suggested I come.'

'Pffft. Bloody Ethan. I'll blame him, then,' she grumbles, padding over to the tiny bathroom and closing the door behind her.

Guess that'll be Molly having first shower then. I force myself out of bed and over to the cupboard. I fish out my pants, ski socks, thermals, neck warmer, inner and outer gloves, jumper, wildly unflattering salopettes, goggles, sunglasses, brand-new ski jacket from TK Maxx and the bag of Mini Mars Bars Mum insisted I bring to put in my pockets. That's the other thing about skiing, apart from the early mornings – there seems to be so much *gear* to deal with.

The bathroom door opens and Molly comes out wrapped in a towel. 'Bathroom's free!' she sings. 'I don't know about you, but now I'm properly awake I'm actually quite excited about today.'

By the time we get down to breakfast it's five to nine, so we only have time to cram in a croissant and have a quick slurp was                ite before Miss Fielder is shouting at us all to                assemble in reception. As we start walking to to                o pick up our stuff, I suddenly feel quite nervous. ver        ugh, is bouncing around, totally excited in a way u        seen him before. 'Look at that blue sky!' he says. going to be amazing!'

ile. 'I'm a bit scared,' I admit.

'Don't be,' Jack says. 'Honestly, by the end of the day I bet you'll wonder what you were worrying about. You'll love it.'

I stand with the gathering group of beginners, watching the door of the ski shop from where the stragglers are still appearing. I'm trying to look like I'm just staring into space but really, I'm looking out for Mr Dorian. I haven't yet seen him this morning and I know it's ridiculous but there is a part of me that misses him. As if I just need to see him, even if we don't speak.

Another, smaller part of me wishes he hadn't come on this holiday at all. Maybe if he wasn't here, I would be able to stop thinking about him every waking minute. Maybe then I could concentrate properly on Jack. Maybe then I'd actually want to . . .

And suddenly, there he is. He looks so hot in his black beanie and I instantly feel self-conscious in my hideous rented helmet which is probably giving me nits. I drag my eyes away from him and look at my reflection in the shop window. I don't know if it's the angle of the glass or the padding in my clothes but I feel like I've never looked less sexy.

And then he's walking towards our group. He looks so at ease carrying his skis over his shoulder, so assured and comfortable in this beautiful but alien environment. I convinced he'd be with the advanced skiers, with Jack.

I was feeling nervous before but now it's all I can do stop myself trembling. He catches my eye as he comes and smiles. I smile back, shyly, glancing at Jack but he's chatting with his instructor and doesn't even notice me.

'You with us, then, Mr Dorian?' Molly asks. I feel my blush.

'Yup. I'm a total ski virgin,' he says, and I feel myself blush deeper.

I want to say something. I want him to think I'm witty and funny, natural and easy to be with.

But I can't think of anything at all, so instead I crouch down and needlessly adjust the buckles on my boots while Molly witters on seemingly about whatever comes into her head.

'Beginners' group, *oui?*' asks a deeply tanned man in a

red ski suit, who seems to have appeared out of nowhere, but then I guess I had been studiously looking at the ground. 'I am Romain, your *moniteur* – teacher – for the week.' He does a head count. 'Ten. *Impeccable*. All here. Good! Then we go! Follow me!'

'Whoa, he's gorgeous!' Molly says, predictably, as we clump after Romain towards the cable car.

'Careful,' Ethan grumbles, 'you nearly whacked me with your pole.'

'Sorr-ee! Got your period or something?' Molly says.

'Leave me alone,' Ethan mutters, increasing his pace to get past us.

Molly tuts and rolls her eyes. 'I don't know what's wrong with him, he's been in a bad mood since we left London.'

The entrance to the lift is surrounded by a huge throng of people queuing but Romain pushes through a little gate at the side and we go straight to the front. 'When you are with me, you are a VIP,' he quips.

Molly chatters away on the way up, flirting with Romain. I turn to face the outside and simply watch as we rise up into the mountains. It is so beautiful. The sky is a clear blue, the trees are all covered in snow and there's something floating in the air – I'm not sure what – which actually glistens.

'It's amazing,' I breathe to no one in particular.

'Isn't it?' says Mr Dorian.

My stomach lurches. I'd been so engrossed in the view I hadn't noticed he was standing right next to me. His gloved hand is on the window next to mine, almost touching. My breath catches in my throat. *Stay calm*, I tell myself. *Talk sensibly. Be interesting.*

I take a surreptitious deep breath. 'Have you ever seen anything so beautiful?' I ask.

He glances at me, and then out at the view. 'Almost never,' he replies. 'I've certainly never seen a landscape like this in real life. It's my first time skiing.'

'And mine,' I say.

'A first . . . for both of us then.' He pauses. 'All of us probably, I mean. All of us here.'

I smile and he smiles back briefly before turning to look out the window again and we ride the rest of the short journey in silence.

# 40

*February, French Alps*

**Ella**

The morning is tiring but fun as we find our feet and learn something called a snow plough – going up a conveyor belt and then putting the tips of our skis together so we can slowly weave our way down the nursery slope. After that, Romain announces we are ready for something called the *tire-fesse* – 'I think, *en anglais*, a drag lift,' Romain adds. He shows us how to use it, making it look easy and graceful, and then we follow.

Ethan is at the front of the queue and shuffles forward. He takes the pole and puts it between his legs. I watch him brace himself in a way which Romain didn't but a couple of seconds later Ethan is gliding calmly up the slope too.

'Yay!' I call, clapping my hands. 'Go, Ethan!' He is hanging onto the bar with both hands and doesn't look round, but then, I probably wouldn't either in his position.

'Well, if my silly little brother can do it, I'm sure I can,' says Molly, pushing forward and taking the bar. One by one they all go up the hill, not looking quite as relaxed as Romain, but making it look pretty easy even so.

And then it's my turn. I take the pole as the man hands it to me and place it between my legs. I bend my knees and hold on tight. I almost feel like closing my eyes, but I don't imagine that would help. I tense and wait, there is a little tug and I start moving. I'm moving! I'm going up the hill!

'It's working!' I call out to no one in particular. 'I'm doing it!'

Something to my left catches my eye – maybe a snow-boarder moving very fast – and I turn my head to look.

Big mistake. My skis cross and suddenly I am falling forward. The *tire-fesse* pulls away from me and I desperately try to hang onto it but I am falling, falling . . . and I'm on the ground. But I'm OK – I'm not hurt.

And then someone is shouting. 'Move, Ella, move, move!' It's Mr Dorian. He's on the lift behind me and approaching fast. I try to shuffle out of the way on my bum but with the skis still attached to my legs it's impossible.

'Nooooo,' I call as his skis crash into mine and he falls on top of me. I duck my head to avoid the swinging pole and notice the lift has stopped.

'God, Ella, sorry – are you OK?' he asks breathlessly as he levers himself off me. Our skis are tangled up together. I try to pull mine away from his but I can't. My goggles are covered in snow so I push them up onto my helmet.

I nod. 'I'm fine. It was my fault. I fell off the lift. Are you OK?'

'Yep – nothing broken.' He leans forward and pushes the back of the bindings down – both his and mine – so that our boots click out of the skis. He stumbles to his feet and pushes our skis out of the way. 'There. No harm done.' I am still on the ground and he holds out his hand to pull me up. I take it and haul myself up. A little thrill runs through me as I do so. He feels so strong. I wobble slightly as I stand and he steadies my elbow.

'You sure you're OK?' he asks. He has pushed his goggles up onto his helmet and is looking straight into my eyes. Those lovely, deep brown eyes. 'You didn't bang your head or anything?'

We are standing so close I can feel his breath on my face.

'Ella?' he prompts, and I realize I am still staring at him and haven't said anything. I look down at his mouth and then back into his eyes. He is still holding my elbow. I could stay like this forever.

'I'm . . . I'm fine,' I stutter. 'Just fine. Sorry.'

He looks at me for a couple of moments longer and then suddenly smiles awkwardly and steps backwards.

'Good. Good. So we're both fine. Nothing broken. Guess we'd better put our skis back on and try that again then?'

Unbelievably, by the end of the day we *do* actually ski all the way down to the bottom of the mountain. Admittedly it takes our group most of the afternoon and I don't think my thighs have ever screamed so much or I've ever felt quite so bruised and battered from so many falls. But I've also never felt quite so *exhilarated*.

'So, a good day, yes?' Romain asks as we arrive back in front of the ski shop.

'It's been *amazing*!' I squeak, as if I am five years old and have just spent the day at Disneyland. Molly loops her arm round Romain's neck, a little awkwardly as they are both still wearing their skis, and kisses him on the cheek. 'It's been *brilliant*,' she coos. Normally I would think this was typical flirtatious Molly but this time I can see how she feels – I almost feel like kissing him myself but I'm not going to do anything like that in front of Mr Dorian.

Romain laughs. 'I always thought you *anglais* were so reserved. Perhaps it is not so.'

Mr Dorian shakes his hand. 'I think I speak for all of us when I say we've really enjoyed today. Thank you for all your help.'

'*De rien*. I wish you a *bonne soirée* and that your legs do not ache too bad. *A demain!*'

And with that he pushes off and kind of skates away, leaving me, Molly and the other girls dreamily watching his retreating back and perfect bum.

Mr Dorian claps his hands together. 'Right – good work today! You've got a few hours now to get changed and . . . do whatever you want to do and then dinner's at seven thirty downstairs followed by . . . bowling, I think?' He presses his poles down on to the backs of his bindings in turn, clicks his skis off and hoists them on to his shoulder. He nods briefly. 'See you all later. In the meantime, behave yourselves.'

# 41

*February, French Alps*

Nick

Today was a great day. I'm really glad I came. The kids were on good form and fun to be with. One day, I will come back to the Alps with my family and teach Sorrel and Bay to ski. I bet they'll love it. But right now, although I feel a little guilty about it, I'm rather enjoying their absence.

Much as I love my boys, I haven't had an entire day away from them since they were born. Every morning I've had to sort their breakfast, every day after school I've had to rush to collect them from nursery or help out with bath time and I literally haven't had an unbroken night's sleep since Sorrel was born.

Conversely, this evening once we'd finished skiing for the day I got to have a beer with the other teachers, without having

207

to keep an eye on the time like I do if I go out with a mate after work, and without worrying about the bollocking I'd get from Aura for coming home slightly later than I said I would.

Instead, when I was ready, and when I decided, I came back to the tiny, basic hotel room and had a leisurely shower without fretting that I needed to get out as soon as possible in case one of my boys choked on a marble or fell down the stairs while I was doing something as simple as having a wash.

And while I'm not expecting much from the all-inclusive buffet dinner we'll be having this evening, I won't have to cook organic fish goujons or pasta and pesto for anyone who will likely refuse it or throw half of it on the floor, neither will I have to wash up afterwards, so I can't wait. Best of all, I can sleep all night. Unless there's an emergency with one of these kids who are pretty much adults, no one will wake me up.

Lounging on my bed in my towel with a cold beer, I realize with, I have to admit, some reluctance, that I should probably check in with Aura. I hope she's in a good mood. She'll have had a day to herself to get on with her coursework like she wanted, and hopefully by now the boys will have eaten and be quietly watching CBeebies. They should be soft and calm and smell of their madly expensive organic lavender baby bubble bath Aura insists on. I feel a pang of love for them. Even though I am enjoying the time to myself, I do miss them. Though I am still also hugely looking forward to my unbroken night's sleep.

Aura answers on the second ring.

'Nick?' she says. Oh God. She sounds stressed.

I pretend not to notice. 'Hi, Aura. How was your day?'

'Started well, ended horribly. I don't think Sorrel's well.'

208

I feel a lurch of alarm. 'Not well? What's up with him?'

She sighs. 'I don't know. Probably just a cold or something. He's tired and grumpy, a bit of a runny nose and a cough.'

'OK. That doesn't sound so bad?'

'No, I don't think it is. I could do without it right now though.'

'What's he up to at the moment?'

'He's watching CBeebies – he didn't eat much and he's not really himself. Floppy. Listless. He hasn't thrown up or anything. It's a bit hard to describe.'

'OK. Hopefully he'll feel better in the morning. Kids get little bugs all the time, don't they? Especially now they're at nursery and mixing with other children more – bound to. Did you get some work done while they were out?'

Even at a distance and over the phone I hear her voice brighten. 'Yes, I did, actually. Honestly, the course is so interesting. I'm really enjoying it, especially because I can devote myself entirely to it this week and not have to go in to my boring job. I wish I'd done it ages ago. Did you know that . . .'

I tune out as Aura starts to regale me with various facts and figures she's learnt today. She hasn't asked how my day was, but I think about it anyway. The scenery, the crisp air, my fall on the drag lift. Ella's wonder at the scenery in the lift and the ice crystals in her hair as we untangled our skis.

I realize I've absent-mindedly let my hand wander under my towel to my crotch and snatch it back. I will not do this. I will not.

'And they think women are much more likely than men to seek counselling, not necessarily because they are more sensitive or prone to depression but simply because they're less likely to see it as a weakness to seek help. Isn't that fascinating?' Aura is saying.

'Isn't it?' I agree, even though I haven't been listening.

'What are you up to this evening?' Aura asks.

'Not sure – probably stodgy dinner, making sure the kids aren't trying to sneak out to bars, I think maybe we've got a bowling session, that kind of thing,' I say, deliberately trying to make it sound as uninteresting as possible. 'And you? You got anything good lined up to watch on TV now that you have full control of the remote?' I joke. In fact Aura always has control of the remote as it makes my life easier if she gets to watch what she likes, but it seems like the right kind of thing to say.

'Yeah, I'm catching up on *Married at First Sight*. Looking forward to it, actually! I only hope the boys stay asleep long enough to let me get through a few episodes. Speaking of which, Sorrel's fallen asleep and is drooling on my lap, so I'd better get him to bed.'

'Aww. That's a shame. I wanted to say hi.'

'Next time.'

'Do you think you'll send him to nursery tomorrow? If he's not well?'

She sighs. 'Not sure. I guess I'll have to see how he is in the morning. But if it seems like it's only a cold, that's OK if he goes, isn't it? I'd really like another full day at my coursework.'

'Think so. Hopefully he'll be OK after a good night's sleep. Miss you,' I say, because even though I haven't thought about Aura all day, right at that moment I do miss her. And the boys.

'Miss you too,' she replies. 'Let's speak soon.'

210

# 42

*February, French Alps*

**Ella**

I'm lying on my bed wrapped in a towel almost dozing off when there is a knock at the door. 'Come in?' I call sleepily, sitting up.

The door opens – it's Jack. His hair is wet – I guess he's just got out of the shower too.

He grins. 'Hey! I just came to see how your first proper day skiing went. Exhausting, by the look of you.'

I rub my face. 'Do I really look that bad?'

He sits down on the edge of the bed next to me and kisses me full on the lips. 'No. You look gorgeous. But you also look like you've just woken up and I can see that here . . .' he traces his finger along my thigh, 'you've got some bruises coming.'

He continues to trace his finger up and down my thigh over the nascent bruises, which sends a tingle through me. 'It was amazing,' I say. 'I fell loads – I even fell off the drag lift . . .' I pause as I remember how Mr Dorian and I looked at each other then but force the image from my mind, 'but I totally loved the skiing. And guess what? We went all the way down from the top of the lift to the bottom!'

'Yay! That's amazing, Ells. You mean from the lift by the nursery slope? If you've done that already, you'll probably go up higher tomorrow.'

He leans in and kisses me again, pushing his tongue in this time. I kiss him back. It's nice. I feel his hand creep up the inside of my thigh and suddenly I'm very aware that I'm wearing nothing except a towel which makes me feel a bit freaked out.

'Jack,' I whisper warningly, but he ignores me, kissing me hungrily. His hand keeps moving up my thigh. A panicky feeling rises in my chest. I don't want him to go any further when I'm practically naked like this. But I don't want to tell him that either. 'Jack, we can't . . .' I say, a little louder. 'Molly's in the bathroom.'

He moans softly. 'I don't care, she won't care . . .' With his left hand still inching up my thigh, he moves his other hand up to my boobs, pawing at me a little roughly for my liking, which makes the towel fall away.

I leap up as if someone had electrocuted me, grabbing at the towel and wrapping it around my naked body. 'Sorry, but *I* care,' I say, this coming out much more primly than I had intended. 'I mean, I don't want Molly barging in when you and me, when we're . . .' I continue, helplessly. I don't

212

really know what I mean. After all, he's right, Molly wouldn't care at all if she walked in on a bit of groping, which I'm sure was all Jack meant to do. Wasn't it? In fact she'd probably be actively pleased, the way she's been going on about me and Jack.

Jack looks up at me from the bed. His expression is difficult to read. Hurt? Annoyed? Angry, even? I'm not sure.

He stands up. 'Fine,' he says crisply. 'I'll see you at dinner then.'

'Jack, don't be like that!' I say, sounding more whiney than I expected to. 'I just . . . with Molly there . . .' I tail off.

He looks at me. 'You and me. You know how much I like you. I've made that clear. And I thought you were into the idea of *us*. But then sometimes . . . sometimes it seems like . . .'

'Like what?' I ask hoarsely.

He pauses. 'Nothing. Look, I'm not that good at this kind of thing, I really like you, Ells, but it seems as though you, you . . .' He stops. 'I'm going to go now before I say something I regret. I'll see you later.'

'But . . . we're OK?'

He sighs, looks at the ceiling, and then back at me. His face is suddenly colder. 'I don't know. You tell me.'

He turns on his heel, opens the door and slams it behind him.

Exactly one beat later, Molly flings open the bathroom door with a crash.

'Bloody hell! What was all that about then?'

'Nothing,' I mutter. 'I don't want to talk about it.'

# 43

*February, French Alps*

**Ella**

'Today – a new challenge,' Romain announces, 'but I know you are ready. *Le telesiège*! The chair lift!'

'How come it doesn't bang you in the back of the legs when you get on?' I ask. 'And what if it knocks you over?'

'Ah, Ella,' says Romain. 'It is magic! *On y va*. You sit down, lower the bar and, *voilà*! It is very easy – you will see. Compared to the *tire-fesse*, a chair lift is a piece of bread.'

'Cake. Piece of cake,' Mr Dorian corrects.

'*Merci, monsieur*. A piece of cake, *c'est ca. Allons-y*. I will go at the last in case anyone gets knocked over.' He gives me a wink.

'We'll go first,' Molly pipes up, pulling at my arm, killing any hope I had of being able to share the lift with Mr Dorian. I follow her forward, through the little gates and shuffle into position. 'Here it comes!' Molly calls. The lift man catches the chair as it comes round. 'Sit down!' Molly yells. We sit into the chair and it swings up and away. We pull the safety bar down and lift our feet on to the footrest.

'That was easier than it looks,' I grin. We rise up and suddenly there are no more trees, just snow, interrupted by the occasional mountain restaurant and more mountains behind. 'Isn't this amazing?' I enthuse.

'Yeah,' says Molly, uninterestedly. 'Amazing. Listen . . . I want you to tell me about what's going on with you and Jack.'

I frown. 'What d'you mean?'

'You *know* what. You say you're into him but I heard what happened last night. If you'd have had a shitty stick, you'd have been beating him off with it. And he didn't sound too happy about how things are going either.'

I feel myself go red. Hopefully Molly won't notice under my helmet and goggles. 'Well, you being in the bathroom, obviously listening as it turns out, kind of killed the mood,' I say lightly.

Molly pushes her goggles up on to her helmet and stares at me, narrowing her eyes. 'I don't think that was it. I've been thinking about it.'

'Perv,' I joke, but she's having none of it.

'Don't try and avoid the issue. You don't want to do that kind of stuff with Jack, and I think I know why.'

'Do you now?' I say, more snippily than I mean to.

'Yes. You're all hung up on Mr Dorian.'

215

The chair goes over a pylon which makes it rock around. I reach out to grab the safety bar. 'Whoa, wobbly,' I say, as if I haven't heard her.

But she isn't going to be side tracked. 'So? Are you going to admit it?'

'Admit what?' I ask, playing for time.

'The Mr Dorian thing!'

'No! I told you ages ago, I've moved on. It's not going to happen. And even if it was – which it isn't – I'm not interested anymore. Neither is he.'

She nods slowly and sarcastically. 'Riiiiiiiiight. So what was that thing that went on between you on the drag lift?'

'The drag lift? What are you on about? I fell off and he crashed into me! Even *you* can't read anything into that!'

'When he picked you up. You stood there for ages. I saw how you looked at each other. It was like the dictionary definition of sexual tension. There's stuff you're not telling me.'

'I'm not telling you anything because there's nothing going on!' I practically shout. For fuck's sake. Why won't she just leave it?

She sighs. 'You do realize I don't actually *care* if there's anything between you and him or not? In fact, that's not true, I do care. I hope there is, as you're obviously gagging for him, whatever you say. But it makes me sad that you're not telling me. I thought we were friends. I thought we told each other everything. So that upsets me.'

She turns her head away from me to face forward again. She bites her lip. She's not going to cry, is she? Why is this such a big deal to her?

We haven't known each other that long. I've barely even spoken to Tash and Lily about this. Or anyone else. Why does she have to be so full-on about it? 'Molly, of course we're friends but there's nothing to tell,' I say tightly. A blue sign with a picture indicating that we are coming to the top of the chairlift comes into view on the next pylon. 'Quick – we have to lift the bar!' I shout, panicking and trying to yank it upwards. It doesn't move.

'You need to take your feet off the footrest,' Molly says coolly. I move my feet to one side and the bar rises. As the ground comes up to meet our skis we stand and push away from the chair.

'I wish you'd tell me,' Molly says.

I roll my eyes. 'I would. But there's nothing to tell.'

# 44

*February, French Alps*

Nick

Many of my friends have made jokes about my 'freebie holidays' on the few occasions when I've accompanied school trips before. If they had any idea how exhausting and full-on it is, they would think differently. So far we've had a broken leg, kids sneaking out at night and getting drunk, several lost phone dramas and one poor boy who had to leave early when his mother was diagnosed with cancer. Every day we're up early, ski all day, and then supervise an evening activity of some type or another, as well as making arrangements for medical visits and sorting out new travel arrangements and insurance claims needed around the various dramas as they arise. So while I have usually (though not every night) enjoyed the unbroken sleep I craved, there has barely been a spare moment and, bar a few texts, I haven't heard from Aura for a couple of days.

On Thursday the weather isn't good and we call it a day early. My legs are aching and I have a little more time in the early evening than usual before my presence is next required for teen-wrangling so I decide to treat myself to a bath.

I call Aura. I know from her texts that she kept Sorrel off nursery yesterday as he seemed very tired but she still thinks it's only a cold, so I'm not too worried.

'Hello?' she whispers, answering on the first ring.

'Aura? You OK? You sound weird.'

'I'm fine. Sorrel's fallen asleep on my lap – I don't want to wake him.'

I imagine him sucking his finger in his sleep, his squirrel pressed against his cheek, and in that moment I miss him so much it almost physically hurts.

'How is he?' I ask. 'Any better?'

'No, I don't think so. I'm going to take him to the doctor's tomorrow. I've given him some pulsatilla but he's still got a temperature.'

I sigh. 'Aura, we've been through this before. If he's got a temperature, you need to give him some Calpol. Not that homeopathic . . . stuff,' I say, biting back the word 'nonsense' to avoid a row. 'It's only fair to him, it'll make him more comfortable.'

She pauses. 'If he's not better in the morning, I will. You know I don't like putting that rubbish in their bodies.'

I clench my hand into a fist so hard that my nails dig into my palm. The thought of poor Sorrel burning up makes me feel sick. But trying to tell Aura what to do while she's in charge of the kids and I'm off on a 'jolly' as she sees it isn't going to end well.

'What's his temperature?'

'Thirty-eight. So it's only up a little bit.'

'And has he been sick or anything?'

'Nothing like that. I think it's just a bad cold.'

'OK. But you promise you'll take him to the doctor's in the morning if his temperature's still up?'

'Yes!' she snaps. 'I already said I would. If you know so much better how to look after them than I do, you shouldn't have gone off skiing, should you?'

I scoot myself lower down into the water, rolling my eyes. 'You know I'm not saying that, Aura,' I say. 'I'm worried about him, that's all. The thought of his little hot body makes me sad.'

She sighs. 'Kids get ill, Nick, especially when they're at nursery. It's fine, it's normal, it's good for their immune system. But I'll take him to the doctor's if need be. Then you can enjoy your little holiday with a clearer conscience,' she adds snidely.

# 45

*February, French Alps*

**Ella**

After Molly having a go about me and Mr Dorian again, I deliberately stay out of his way for the next few days. I'm really regretting telling Molly about it all and wish she'd just drop it.

I make a real effort with Molly, pulling her up when she falls down, trying to sit next to her on the lifts, and she doesn't ignore me as such, but she stays fairly frosty. She, Ethan, Jack and I hang out together as usual, but things are different. Molly and I talk, but only about stupid stuff which means nothing. Ethan is grumpy and offhand with me; I don't know why. I hope Molly hasn't told him about what happened with Mr Dorian. Surely she wouldn't?

And Jack. After that time in the bedroom, he barely touches

me. We hold hands now and again, but it feels like we're going through the motions. I'm not sure if he's gone off me, if he's simply trying to give me some space, trying not to pressure me, or if he just can't face me saying no to him again. I have to admit, a large part of me is relieved.

# 46

*February, French Alps*

Nick

My phone keeps buzzing in my pocket all morning but I am one of the slowest skiers (probably what comes of also being the oldest, I guess), so there is never time to get it out before the group moves off again. I am terrified of dropping it off one of the lifts as at least two kids have already done this week so I can't look at it then. It's lunchtime by the time I manage to actually get it out of my pocket and see that I have five missed calls from Aura as well as several texts from her in capital letters and with increasing numbers of exclamation marks demanding *CALL ME URGENTLY!!!!!!!*

Shit. Shit. I go outside the *hors sac* picnic room and call. She answers before I even hear it ring.

'Aura? What is it?' I ask. Oh God. It's Sorrel. I know it

is. Please let him be OK. Why didn't she take him to the doctor earlier? Not meningitis, please. Please no.

'It's Sorrel,' she says, and a wave of nausea rushes through me. 'He's got measles.'

My first feeling is relief – not meningitis or anything like that – and then bewilderment.

'What do you mean, measles? Are you sure? No one gets measles anymore, do they? Is he OK?' It's not meningitis. He's going to be all right. Isn't he?

'That's not serious, is it then?' I continue. 'I think I had it when I was a child. Or maybe it was chickenpox – I can't remember.'

She sighs. 'No, it's not serious, and he should be fine, but I got a massive telling off from the doctor and she said I had to tell the nursery, so that was embarrassing. And now neither he or Bay can go back for ages, and chances are Bay will get it too because it's really contagious, so I've got that to look forward to as well.'

'But . . . how did he get it?'

She sighs again. 'I'm tired, Nick, and don't massively want to have this conversation now, but according to the doctor, he got it because he hasn't had the right injections. I'd guess probably from that dreadful soft play you take them to – there've been a few cases in the area, apparently, and it has now been shut down for a deep clean. It's an awful place anyway.'

I'm still confused. Aura's always been obsessive about the children's health and keeping them safe – she always took charge of medical appointments as she was at home and I was at school.

224

'But you . . . were always so careful with their health,' I say, keeping my voice steady, pleased with myself for phrasing it as a compliment rather than a criticism. 'I don't understand how you would have missed anything.'

But it doesn't work. 'If you felt so strongly about their health, you could have helped!' she snaps. 'I spent hours doing my research about what was best for them; you were always at work or busy with "marking" and never showed the slightest interest.'

'Aura, of course I was interested,' I counter, 'I just trusted you with it.' I try and fail to keep the edge out of my voice.

'They didn't have MMR jabs – it's too many illnesses all at once for their little bodies to cope with. Barbaric. I read the vaccine inserts and I discussed it on Facebook with other mums, and I came to the conclusion that there were too many risks. It's not a decision I took lightly and I'm still convinced it was the best one. There was no way I was letting anyone put that poison inside their little bodies.'

Poison? What is she on about? She decided this after talking to random Facebook mums? My face grows hot. She is still talking.

'I saw a homeopath instead and both boys had homeopathic vaccinations. Much safer, according to my research.'

'Homeopathic vaccinations? What? How is that even a thing?'

'Of course it's a thing!' Her voice is shrill and hysterical now. 'There are no needles or chemicals, so not vaccination in that sense, but it's usually very effective. Sorrel was just unlucky.'

What the fuck? How can Aura think she knows better

than science? But this is not the time for a row – while she is home with my sick son and I'm stuck here in the Alps. I shouldn't have come. It was selfish of me. But she should have made sure our sons were properly protected. In retrospect, so should I. But I thought I could trust her with something as important as this.

I swallow my anger down. 'I see,' I say, as evenly as I can. 'And how is he? What do we need to . . . do for him?'

'He's fine. He's got a rash and a temperature. I bought the Calpol and have given it to him, even though I hate it. I'm giving him pulsatilla too, which I'm sure is helping much more.'

'And . . . it's not dangerous, is it? Measles?' I feel tears well and brush them away. I'll never live it down if the kids see me crying.

'Not really,' she says. 'Well, the doctor told me about all these possible complications, but I think they only say that stuff to scare you. Back in our parents' day, everyone caught measles, didn't they? It's only since Big Pharma realized they could make some money from their vaccinations in spite of the risks they've started making out these illnesses are more dangerous than they really are. The doctor said to keep him home, keep him comfy, give him the Calpol and call if I have any concerns. Which I don't.'

'Thank God. OK. Thank God I'm leaving tomorrow anyway. Or do you want me to try and fly home tonight?' I cross my fingers that she'll say no. Much as I want to be home with poor little Sorrel, there are rules around adult to child ratios on school trips and I'm not sure how easy an early departure would be to organize for many reasons, or indeed if I could get back any earlier than if I left early tomorrow as planned anyway. It's a long way to the airport and I haven't a clue how I'd get there.

'No. It's fine. Like I said, it's not a serious illness and I've got it all under control. He's sleeping most of the time anyway – to be honest, in most ways he's easier to handle than normal.'

'If you're sure. Give him a kiss from me and I'll see you all tomorrow evening.'

Homeopathic jabs, for fuck's sake. Why didn't she make sure they were properly protected? If anything happens to Sorrel because of this, I'll never forgive her.

# 47

*February, French Alps*

## Ella

And then . . . on the final night of the holiday, Molly seems
to call a truce. After we are back from our final day's skiing,
showered and dressed, she gets the vodka out of the cupboard.

'I thought we should celebrate our final night in style –
what do you think?'

I smile. I've got a headache and I'm not really bothered
about drinking tonight, but I want Molly and me to be
friends again – she's my only real girlfriend in London after
all, so I say: 'Sounds fun. What did you have in mind?'

'Nothing special – I invited the boys to come down before
dinner and I thought we could play cards or something. I
bought some Coke to go with the vodka, and also some crisps
and stuff. I thought it would be nice, just the four of us.'

'That sounds lovely.' And it does.

She looks at the floor. 'And I wanted to say sorry for . . . being a bitch this week. I've been thinking about it, and I'm not going to hassle you. If you don't want to tell me about Jack or . . . whatever else, then that's up to you. It's not for me to force you. I know I can come on a bit strong sometimes but . . . you've been a real breath of fresh air for me. I haven't really had a friend like you before.'

Tears come to my eyes and I hug her. 'Oh, I'm so relieved! I thought you were really angry with me.'

She pulls away and I see her wipe a tear from her eye too. 'I was.'

'But that's silly,' I say. 'There's nothing to tell. With Jack, I like him, but I just want to take it slow. You were right when you said that I'm . . . that I've never . . . y'know. And the whole Mr Dorian thing – it's never going to happen and I've accepted that. It was just something in the club – a mistake.' For him at least.

She hugs me again, and then lets me go, holding me at arm's length and looking at me. 'It's OK. I know now that nothing's going on with you and Mr Dorian. I've been keeping an eye the last few days, and I believe you.'

Brilliant, I think. Nothing like taking me at my word, is there? But then I remember that I'm not being entirely honest with Molly, so I don't say anything.

'But you have to PROMISE me that if anything does, you'll tell me?' she continues. 'Straight away?'

I hug her again. 'I promise,' I say. And as nothing is going to happen, it doesn't matter if I don't mean it.

\*    \*    \*

By the time we go down to dinner, we're a bit drunk. But we're clearly not the only ones who have been having our own pre-dinner party – just about everyone seems rowdier than they would normally be.

As it's the last night, the hotel has put on a 'disco' for us – there's no proper dance floor as such but they have got an ancient-looking DJ who is playing the kind of songs my mum always embarrasses me by dancing to at weddings. A bit like the ones at the club the night I met Mr Dorian.

I thought eating would make me feel less drunk but after dinner I actually feel more spinny – I don't know if it's a delayed reaction to what I drank before or whether Molly has been surreptitiously topping us all up with vodka. Perhaps both. By now I'm just up for a good night and I don't really care if Molly's been spiking my drinks all evening.

The music couldn't be worse but I see why they play this dire stuff at weddings – it gets everyone dancing.

I dance for ages with Molly, with Jack, with Ethan and with just about everyone else, even Mr Dorian, but only because Molly dances with him too, so I think I can probably get away with it. Then, suddenly, I feel really hot and a tiny bit sick.

'I'm just going to stop and cool down!' I shout at Molly over the music, who nods and carries on twirling round and round. I shimmy over to the door, yank it open and a welcome blast of cold air hits me as I stumble outside.

I lean against the wall, enjoying the coolness along my back. I can still hear the music – another awful Eighties track I inexplicably know all the words to – and sing along gently to myself. The bitingly cold air is blissful. The sky is clear and I tip my head back to look up at the stars. It's beautiful. All so beautiful.

'Ella? Are you OK?'

I turn my head too quickly and for a second the ground seems to move and then rights itself.

It's Mr Dorian. But instead of the usual panic and fluster I feel when he speaks to me, all I feel is happy. Gotta love vodka.

I smile, move towards him and gently touch his arm, like I might if he was Jack, or Molly, like I'd never normally dare to do with him. I expect him to pull away from me, but he doesn't. 'I'm fine! Fine, fine, fine,' I cry. 'Couldn't be finer. Why d'you ask?'

He smiles back. 'I noticed that you and some of the others are . . . a little worse for wear this evening, and when I saw you come out here I wanted to check you weren't out here chucking your guts up or falling asleep in the snow or something.'

Ha! He's been watching me. Noticing me. He does like me, after all. I knew it.

I shake my head, which makes everything wobble again. I stumble, and he takes my arm to steady me. 'I don't know *what* you mean!' I cry, over-enunciating each syllable in an effort not to slur.

He laughs. 'Ella, it's fine. You're not in trouble. You're sixteen, you're on holiday with your mates, away from your parents. It would almost be more of a worry if you guys *hadn't* smuggled any booze in.'

'Booze? What is this booze of which you speak?' I tip my head to one side and look at him.

He laughs again. 'OK. Have it your way.' There is a pause. 'It wasn't that long ago I was on school holidays myself. I'm not going to spoil your fun. I only wanted to check you were OK. I care . . .'

He stops abruptly.

My heart starts beating faster.

'What did you say?' I ask.

I heard what he said. But maybe he meant something else.

'Nothing.' He lets go of my elbow, looks up at the sky and exhales loudly. 'God, Ella, I wish I wasn't your teacher,' he mutters. 'Sometimes I even wish I wasn't married.'

The ground sways and I stumble again. He takes my arm again to steady me.

I look into his eyes.

It's now or never.

I lean in and upwards and kiss him on the lips.

He tastes of coffee and whisky.

I feel his tongue push between my lips as he pulls me closer.

# 48

*February, French Alps*

**Ella**

A few seconds later, he abruptly pulls away.

'Christ! Jesus! Sorry, Ella. Fuck! I shouldn't have done that, that shouldn't have happened . . .'

He runs his hands through his hair and looks around wildly. For a second I think I see movement out of the corner of my eye, but when I look around, no one is there.

'It was probably my fault,' I say teasingly, reaching out to touch his arm again. He jumps back as if he's been electrocuted.

'But you . . . But I . . . God! No one saw us, did they?' He looks around again.

I shake my head. 'I don't think so. There's only you and me out here,' I add flirtatiously.

'This isn't a joke, Ella!' he fumes. I feel a lurch of alarm as I realize that the mood has totally changed. 'If anyone found out about this, I could . . . oh God!' he is saying, kicking at a piece of snow on the ground violently. 'Stupid, stupid, stupid!'

'I'm . . . um . . . I'm sorry,' I offer, not knowing what else to say.

He smacks his forehead with the heel of his hand. 'It's not your fault,' he says, but tightly as if he doesn't mean it. 'I shouldn't have . . . I'm the adult here, I'm the one who . . . Jesus! What was I thinking!'

'I'm sixteen,' I say quietly. 'Kind of an adult.'

'That's not the point!' he says, sounding as if someone is strangling him.

Mr Dorian casts around again and then turns towards me. He takes hold of my shoulders and puts his face close to mine. 'Listen, Ella,' he says in a low, voice, 'I know you're pretty wasted at the moment, but you have to take this seriously. You must NOT tell ANYONE about this! Do you understand! No one. Not Molly, not your mum, definitely not your boyfriend. No one. Got it?'

His face is twisted somehow. He looks totally different to how he usually does. Angry? Scared? I'm not sure.

'Jack isn't my boyfriend,' I say pointlessly, because he obviously doesn't give a shit whether he is or not. 'I understand. I won't tell anyone. I promise.'

'And if anyone asks – we both deny it. No one can prove anything. If anyone asks us what we were doing out here, you felt sick, I came to check on you. OK?'

'Umm . . .' I've never heard him sound so aggressive before, and it throws me.

'OK????' he repeats, even more firmly.

'Yes, OK,' I reply. I just want to get away from him now. He's scaring me a bit.

'So say it,' he continues.

'Say what?' I don't know what he means. My head is spinning and I want to go back inside. I'm too drunk for this.

He rolls his eyes and squeezes my shoulders tighter, giving me a little shake. 'What we were doing out here! If anyone asks.'

'I felt sick and you came to check on me,' I say in a small voice.

He lets go of my shoulders. 'Good. Fine. No one saw us so we should be . . . fine. You do understand you mustn't tell anyone?' His voice is now almost pleading. Less aggressive. More like he is normally. Like he is when I picture how he would be with me if we were alone together as a couple.

I nod. 'Yes. I understand.'

He smiles weakly. 'Good girl. And Ella, I can only apologize for my behaviour. I've had a bad day, my son's not well but . . . that doesn't make it OK. What I did was inexcusable.'

I shake my head. I'm not going to let him say that. I wanted him to kiss me. 'No it wasn't. Inexcusable, I mean.'

He pauses. 'Yes, it was. You need to understand that. You go back in now. I'll be in in a minute.'

'OK.'

I stumble back over to the door and yank it open.

I can't believe it.

Mr Dorian kissed me. He actually kissed me.

'There you are!' Molly yells, suddenly in my face before I've had time to fully process what happened outside. 'I've been looking for you. Where'd you go?'

'I, um, I felt sick, so I went outside,' I babble, confused. Do I have to say that to everyone? I don't want to get Mr Dorian into trouble.

Molly lurches forward and gives me a hug. 'Awww. Poor baby. Probably too much voddie. You OK now? You didn't vom?'

I nod and then shake my head, unsure of which question to answer first. 'Yes I'm fine. No I didn't vom. I think I was just a bit too hot.'

She nods. 'Good. But you're all right now? Come and dance then!'

I follow her back onto the makeshift dance floor and try to throw myself back into it.

I keep looking out for Mr Dorian, but I don't see him for the rest of the evening.

# 49

*February, French Alps/London*

**Ella**

It is a ridiculously early start the next morning, and I sleep pretty much the whole way back on the coach. I sit with Molly instead of Jack – I make some excuse about us both listening to the same podcast but I'm not surprised when he doesn't object. I think he knows it's over between us (was it ever a thing, really?) but even so, I've realized something. I need to make it crystal clear that he and I are not a couple – it's only fair to him. That kiss with Mr Dorian was how a kiss should feel. Like it's the only thing in the world that matters. Like nothing else exists except me and him. Like I would do anything at all for him. Anything.

I like Jack, but however hard I try, I don't feel that for him. I will tell him, definitely. But I can't do it today. Not with all these people here. And I'm so tired. It can wait till we get back.

I can see Mr Dorian sitting at the front of the coach with Miss Fielder.

We haven't spoken since we kissed.

I wonder if he's thinking about me?

'Ella!' Mum grabs me in a bear hug as I get down from the coach. She's not usually so demonstrative. Maybe she missed me, though I find it hard to believe, as most of the time she barely seems to notice if I'm there or not. 'Did you have an amazing time?' she asks, speaking into my neck because she hasn't let go of me yet.

I nod. 'It was brilliant.' *In so many ways*, I think to myself.

'I'll get your bag, shall I?' she says brightly.

I smile. 'Thanks, Mum. I'll go and say 'bye to Molly and . . . everyone.'

Mum bustles off to where the driver is unloading the cases. My breath catches in my throat as I notice Mr Dorian is there, helping to haul the cases off, and feel a little thrill as I see him grab my hot pink case and swing it out from the bus and onto the ground.

I want to go and say goodbye to him, but I can't.

# 50

*February, French Alps/London*

Nick

The coach journey is interminable and is not helped by the 5 a.m. start or that I, pretty much all the other teachers and a good number of the students too are extremely hungover. We've had to stop the coach twice before breakfast time to let kids off to throw up but at least they managed not to do it in the coach. Doesn't bear thinking about.

I drank far too much last night, stressed out by my conversation with Aura, worried sick about Sorrel and also full of guilt, both for being away and for not realizing that Aura had deliberately not got the boys' jabs done and didn't even feel she needed to discuss it with me. Why hadn't I paid more attention when they were small? Why had I left it all to her?

I should have stuck to beer last night; once I moved on to whisky it made me maudlin, as it so often does. But when I followed Ella outside I had nothing on my mind other than checking she was OK – she and her entourage were among the most drunk last night. Obviously the kids aren't meant to drink, but Christ knows how their parents and the authorities think we're meant to police it. These kids – especially the girls – simply don't look like children. If they want to buy a bottle of vodka at the supermarket or order a drink at almost any bar, then they will. God, if Ella actually looked like a child rather than a fully grown woman, then I wouldn't be in this mess. That night in the club in London wouldn't have happened. I had no idea she was so young. It's not like I'm some kind of pervert.

And then, last night . . . if I hadn't had the whisky, if I hadn't been so stressed all day, if she hadn't been so drunk, if she hadn't come on to me like that, then it wouldn't have happened. It was wrong, I know that. But it all came from her. When a girl, a woman, offers herself to you like that when everything at home is so shit then . . . argh. No. It was wrong. Wrong, wrong, wrong. But I think Ella understands that and I trust her not to tell anyone. All I need to concentrate on now is getting home to Sorrel and looking after him.

I text Aura, *How is Sol today?* but there's no reply.

When we finally arrive in London, instead of hanging around saying my goodbyes I get busy hauling the cases off, grab mine and head straight for home. I find Aura sitting on the sofa with the two boys draped over her, watching CBeebies.

'Hey,' I say, picking Sorrel up and giving him a cuddle. He lays his head on my shoulder. He has a rash and his eyes look weird. Tears spring to my eyes when I feel his little body so hot and floppy in my arms. He is too little to be ill. 'How're you doing, little man?'

He puts his finger in his mouth and drifts back off to sleep without a word. Aura gives me a half-smile and strokes Bay's head, which is in her lap.

'He's OK. I think Bay's coming down with it too though, poor thing.'

I lie Sorrel on the sofa and touch Bay's head, which is also hot.

'Poor Bay. Have you been giving them their Calpol?'

Aura rolls her eyes. 'Yes!' she snaps, clearly annoyed at the question, but I don't know whether to believe her. I decide I'm going to take charge of their meds from now on.

Sorrel wakes up and gives a little wail. I pick him up. 'Hey, Bud, what's up?'

'Ear hurt,' he says, tugging at it. I give it a kiss.

'Oh dear. How about I give you and Bay a nice bath now I'm home and we can see if it makes it feel better?'

He nods solemnly and grips me tightly when I try to put him down. 'Aura, can you bring Bay, please?' I ask.

She gets up without a word and follows me up the stairs, carrying Bay. Sorrel lets me sit him down on the closed loo seat as I run the boys a bath.

'I'm sorry I was away when this happened,' I say to Aura, and I am, though not as sorry that she didn't check they'd had all their proper medical procedures, I think to myself. But that conversation will have to wait.

241

'Yep, well, never mind, you're here now,' she says, laying Bay down on the bathroom floor. 'I'll leave you to get on with the bath and I'll phone for a takeaway, I think. I'm exhausted. Chinese, Indian or pizza?'

# 51

*February, London*

## Ella

It's a huge relief to finally be back in my roor
again. It's the first chance I've had to think
happened without Molly being there, or Ja
else. And it's kind of nice to be on my own. B
people absolutely all the time can be pretty

I flop back on my bed and squeeze my ey
my lips, trying to remember how Mr Dor

It's a little hazy though. I wish I'd bee
so I could savour it fully. But if I had t
dared kiss him.

Because however vague my memor
the kiss. I remember that well.

And if I hadn't, what would hav

have kissed me? Or would we have simply gone back inside, and carried on dancing, everything just the same?

And then the biggest question of all.

What happens now?

The next day, almost as soon as I walk through the school gate, I know that something is up. A Year 9 girl stage-whispers 'That's her!' to her little group of friends, who instantly collapse into fits of giggles as I pass. A boy whose name I don't know from the year above wolf-whistles and says: 'Ella Dooley. Wouldn't have thought you had it in you.'

I scuttle past, ignoring him but feeling my face burning. There are only two possible scenarios I can think of. Either Jack has been bragging about stuff we haven't even done – which doesn't seem like his style but then again, you never really know with boys; they don't like to lose face in front of their mates. The, other, worse option, is that people have found out about Mr Dorian. I feel sick.

I walk into my classroom just as the bell rings for registration. Everyone seems to be huddled in little clusters on their phones, sitting on their desks. They look round at me almost in unison when I come in, before turning back to their screens.

Molly is sitting at her desk alone, staring at her phone. I into my seat next to hers. 'What's going on?' I ask ously.

looks up at me with an expression which is verging ntempt. 'You don't know?'

holds her phone out to me to look at. She's got am open.

I peer at the screen, at the picture which is filling it. It's a shot of the entire group on the ski trip, taken by a waiter. I remember Miss Fielder getting us all together for it, the night I kissed Mr Dorian. I lean in closer to read the text below.

*@Molly2003 Who definitely wasn't left out in the cold by Ella Dooley on the 6th form ski trip? Find out tomorrow!*

My hand flies to my mouth. 'What does that mean?' I shriek, trying to sound innocent. 'Who sent you this?'

She shrugs. 'Someone called skisneak. And not just to me – everyone who follows the school's Instagram account has had it.'

'Everyone?'

She shrugs. 'Dunno, seems like it. Everyone at school, at least – don't know about parents and teachers.' She pauses. 'Everyone except you, that is.'

I stare at the screen, my eyes filling with tears. 'But why would they . . . what do they . . . '

'Anything you want to tell me?' she snaps.

'No! I don't know what this is about, what it means . . . do they mean Jack?' I babble.

She snorts. 'Hardly! You're not exactly working your way through the Kama Sutra, you two, are you? I think I know *exactly* what it means.'

'Do you?' I say, more sarcastically than I meant to.

'Yes.' She narrows her eyes. 'I think you lied to me. I think there *is* something going on with you and Mr Dorian.'

'Well, you can think what you like. There isn't,' I say, trying and failing to keep my voice steady.

There is a pause. 'So you're not worried about anything

this skisneak might post tomorrow then?' she continues.

'I . . . well I don't want people posting any stuff about me to the whole school, so yes I'm worried about that, but not because I did anything . . .' I tail off.

Oh God. This is such a disaster. I'm still holding Molly's phone and click to look at skisneak's profile. It simply says, 'Truth teller', and this has been their one and only post, made at 8.23 p.m. last night. Along with private messages to make sure everyone sees it, it would seem.

'Who would do this?' I whisper. 'Who is skisneak? Is there any way of finding out?'

'Dunno. I guess if you're really techy you might be able to find out where they were when they posted – but my guess would be a burner phone with the location turned off, if they've got any sense. All I know is that, whoever skisneak is, they know more about you than I do these days.'

'Molly, that's not true!' I protest but just then Mr Dorian comes in. For a couple of seconds I actually think I might throw up as I realize that he must have seen the post. Mustn't he? Did it get sent to teachers and parents? Even if it didn't, he must have heard about it. I feel suddenly cold and shaky, and Molly rolls her eyes. 'Yeah right. Nothing going on. Looks like it too.'

Molly snatches back her phone and turns away from me in disgust.

'OK, guys, at your desks please, simmer down,' Mr Dorian says, sitting down at his desk and preparing to take the register. He looks the same as he does any other day. Is it possible he doesn't know? Or is he just putting on a cool front?

He doesn't look up as he calls the register, not at me, not at any of the others either though.

'Right – I have to rush off for a meeting now, but please gather up your books and make your way to your first class quietly. I'll see you at afternoon registration.'

He swings his bag up and is gone. I stare after him and hear Molly tut. A wave of disappointment washes over me. I don't really know why. I don't know what I was expecting. That he'd make some excuse to keep me behind? Surely he must want to talk about the Instagram post?

Maybe skisneak doesn't know what happened. Maybe it's just someone playing a stupid joke on me. People do things like that all the time, don't they? Maybe it's total coincidence. Nothing to do with Mr Dorian. Just someone who wants to wind me up for some reason. God knows why though.

## 52

*February, London*

**Ella**

The rest of the day is a total nightmare. By mid-morning even those who haven't seen the Insta post have heard about it and so everyone knows. Wherever I go, people are making stupid comments, or giggling and pointing. Molly ignores me the entire day and makes a point of not sitting next to me in class.

At lunchtime I am on my own, trying to plough through a barely edible shepherd's pie when Jack arrives. He sits down at the table across from me, but he doesn't have any food with him.

'Hey,' he says, giving me a brief, strained smile.

'Hey,' I reply, barely able even to smile back.

'What's this Insta thing about then?' he asks tersely. 'People haven't shut up about it all day. It's making me look like a right tool.'

'Oh well I'm so sorry if it's spoilt *your* day,' I snap sarcastically and then instantly add: 'I'm sorry, Jack. I didn't mean that. I don't know what it's about, but it's stressing me out.'

I reach over the table to try to take his hand but he pulls it away. 'Did you get with someone else on the ski trip?' he asks bluntly.

My instinct is to say no, like I would to Molly, or to anyone else who asked that question, but I hesitate. This is all too much. I can't deal with it. I should have already made it clear to him that we're not an item. I stare at him dumbstruck for a few beats too long like a rabbit caught in headlights before I start to stutter: 'I, um, there isn't, I didn't, I was . . .' I tail off.

He nods. 'Right. I think that tells me all I need to know. And I guess that explains why you never wanted to . . . whatever.' He stands up. 'I thought you were better than this, Ella,' he says coldly. 'I really liked you. You know that. I thought we could have something good. You could have at least been honest with me. Even that would have been something.'

I try to reach for his hand again but he snatches it back. Tears well in my eyes. 'Jack, please! It's not like that! I'm not seeing anyone!' That much is true. 'It's probably someone's idea of a stupid joke.'

He looks at me, unsure for a moment. 'So why couldn't you tell me straight away that there wasn't anyone else just now when I asked? Why did you hesitate like that?'

'Because I . . . I don't know.'

'I should have listened to Ethan. He said you were hiding something from me. I thought he was jealous. But he's my best mate. I was stupid to trust you over him. I should have known better. I won't make that mistake again.'

That stings. I thought Ethan was my friend. Why would he say something like that to Jack? 'Jack, please, let's talk about this . . .' I say.

'No. I'm done with talking. It's all you ever seemed to want to do, and even then it turned out you weren't telling the truth. I think we're finished here – I only wish you'd had the decency to let me know you weren't interested instead of stringing me along.'

'Jack, I . . .' I protest, but he flings up his hand and walks away.

# 53

*February, London*

**Ella**

I contemplate bunking off school the next day, but eventually decide not going in will make things worse. I'm on edge all day. At the end of every lesson I check Insta on my phone but nothing changes.

At lunchtime I leave school and walk around aimlessly – we're not allowed out without good reason and I'd be in trouble if I got caught – but I can't face being in the school grounds with Molly and Jack ignoring me and almost everyone else whispering about me. My stomach rumbles. I haven't eaten. I check Insta almost every fifteen minutes. Nothing.

My spirits start to lift a little. Maybe it's all a bluff. Maybe it's someone trying to get information out of me. Another thought hits me. Could skisneak be Molly? Doing that classic double bluff of pretending she knows about something she doesn't to find out if anything actually *was* going on?

No. She might be annoyed with me now, but she's still my friend. She wouldn't do that. Would she? But perhaps it's someone else winding me up. Could be anyone. Although if that's the case, I don't know why they picked me. There are plenty of other people with loads more dirt on them.

Just as I enter the school gates, I hear a shout.

'Wooraggggh!!!! Lucky old Mr Dorian!!!!!'

Oh God.

I don't look anywhere except at the ground as I run the rest of the way to the classroom. I ignore all the shouts, whoops and catcalls. I force myself not to turn and run away. I hold back the tears. I need to do this. I need to stay at school. I need to stay strong for Mr Dorian. Deny everything. Nothing happened. I will do it for him.

I walk with as much dignity as I can muster (not much) through the classroom to my desk. I pull out my phone and, holding it in my lap so no one can see, pull up Insta.

Skisneak has posted a story. It's a picture of me and Mr Dorian. We are not actually kissing, but he's touching my arm and we're looking at each other. The picture is surrounded with animated pink heart stickers and little Cupids.

Tears come to my eyes and I bite my lip.

Molly flings herself down in the chair next to me, glancing at me contemptuously. 'You still denying it, then?' she asks.

I nod. 'Nothing happened!' I wail, looking straight at her even though there are tears running down my face now. I wipe them away but I know everyone will have already seen. 'We didn't do anything! He came outside to check if I was OK!'

Her expression flickers to almost sympathetic, but then almost instantly returns to a look of hard contempt.

'Sorry, but I don't believe you.'

The door opens and I look up, expecting to see Mr Dorian. But it's Mr Woods. I feel myself pale. A low murmur starts up around the room. 'OK, quieten down class 12A, I'm doing your register today. And Ella Dooley,' he looks towards me, but not quite at me, 'the headmaster wants to see you in his office now.'

# 54

*February, London*

**Nick**

A hush falls over the staffroom as soon as I enter and imme-diately, I know. I've known this was coming since I got wind of what the kids were all smirking about and saw the pictures. But if I stick to my story, if Ella does too, I think it can be explained away.

But will they believe me? Is this it? Is this my career over? Quite possibly my marriage, too, or what's left of it?

No one will meet my eye. Some of the younger staff are trying to hide smirks. A couple of the women glance at me in disgust and one, who has never liked me much anyway, audibly tuts.

'Nick,' Greg says. 'There you are. Mike has asked if you will go and see him immediately, please.'

Has Ella said something? Why would she do that? I thought we had an understanding. Is this revenge for me saying it could never happen again? Might she have embellished what happened? Might she have said I forced her? Or that we had sex? How would I be able to prove that we hadn't?

I swallow down my panic and try to compose myself, praying silently that Ella has kept to the story we agreed.

# 55

*February, London*

**Ella**

I try to ignore the giggles and smirks as I stand up. I don't look at Molly. Suddenly, I wish I had told her what really happened. I need someone to help me through this. I wish I knew that someone would be rooting for me, supporting me. I haven't told anyone the full story. I feel so alone. But it's too late now.

I hold my head up high, walk to the front of the class and out of the door. I feel like I'm walking to the gallows. I walk as slowly as I can, getting my story straight in my head. I felt sick. I went outside. Mr Dorian came to check on me. I felt better. I went back in. Nothing happened.

That's all.

# 56

## Nick

'Nick, thank you for coming,' Mike says, indicating the seat opposite his desk. 'Please sit down. Emma Lovelace is here as our designated safeguarding officer. I hope we can have a chat now and sort all this out, but if you'd rather reschedule for a time when a representative from your union can be here, that is your right and we can do that. However, should you take that route, as you probably know, you would need to be suspended in the meantime in a case like this.'

'No, no need for a union rep,' I reply, trying to keep my voice steady. 'This is all a misunderstanding and I'd rather get it sorted and out in the open right away.'

Mike nods. 'Good. I hoped you'd say that. Have you seen the picture which has been posted on Instagram today by an account called skisneak? It would appear the account is already being followed by most of the school population, and the picture has also been sent by private message to many others too.'

I try to ward off the rising panic, reminding myself to stay calm. 'Yes. I saw the picture. I followed the account after the allusions he – or she – the account holder made yesterday. I wanted to keep an eye on what they were alleging.'

'So you'll have seen that the picture appears to show yourself and Year 12 student Ella Dooley in what can only be described as an embrace, alone in the snow.'

I draw my hand across my face. Stay calm. Stay calm. 'It wasn't an embrace. Despite the best efforts of myself and my colleagues to prevent the students drinking alcohol, several of them were obviously inebriated that night, Ella Dooley in particular. I noticed her go outside by herself and I wanted to check she was OK. That she wasn't feeling ill, or going off somewhere on her own in the snow. She was a student in my care, after all.'

Mike nods and writes something on his pad. 'I see. And you were touching her because . . .'

'She was drunk and unsteady. She stumbled. That picture . . . it's a lucky camera angle, that's all. Someone messing about. Maybe even her boyfriend, perhaps they'd had a row. I don't know.'

I feel panic rising and sweat beading on my upper lip. I wipe it away and take a deep breath before I continue: 'If anything untoward happened between Ella and me, or indeed between myself and any student, I would expect a formal lly expect to be punished.

complaint to be mad... lemished record as a
I think you'll agr... apply for the
teacher, and it is ... man with
department he... ongness
two young ...
of any li... uld
risk b...
like...

...nt course of action we...
to return to the staffroom

secretary's door and she calls me
...apers around her desk and a flicker
...sment? Outrage maybe? – crosses
...'Ah, Ella, thank you for coming.
...twood is with Mr Dorian at the
...n't be long.'
...a couple of chairs and I sit down.
...questioned separately. To see if we
...uess.
...ords in my head.

### February, London

### Ella

I knock on Mr Atwood's
in. She is shuffling some p
of something – embarras
her face when I come in
Sit down, please, Mr A
moment. I'm sure he wo
   She waves vaguely at
Looks like we're being
say the same things, I g
   I go over the same w
   I felt sick.
   I went outside.
   He checked on me.

I was fine.

I went back in.

Nothing happened.

The door to Mr Atwood's door opens and Mr Dorian comes out, closing the door behind him.

He runs his fingers through his hair and glances at me. I smile at him but he doesn't smile back. He walks out without a word, shutting the door behind him in a way that suggests he is being careful not to slam it.

I glance at the secretary, who is staring at me but looks away and starts shuffling her papers again as soon as she catches my eye.

Her phone buzzes. It's on speakerphone and I hear Mr Atwood say, 'Can you send Ella in now, please?'

I get up, smooth my skirt down and open the door.

'Ella, come in, sit down,' Mr Atwood says, pointing to a chair on the other side of his huge desk next to Miss Lovelace, the school counsellor.

I sit down. 'Why is Miss Lovelace here?' I ask.

He clears his throat. 'She is our safeguarding officer. It's procedure. Plus it is better . . . in the circumstances . . . that we have someone else here. In case there are things you . . . want to say which have to be followed up later.'

'You mean like a witness?' I ask, horrified.

He smiles tightly. 'Not really. More to make sure that procedure is followed and that you are protected.'

I nod. Stay calm, I tell myself. 'OK. But I don't think it's necessary. This is all a lot of fuss about nothing.'

'That's as may be. Now then, I assume you are aware of

261

the picture on Instagram? Posted by the person calling themselves skisneak? Concerning yourself?'

I nod. 'I am.'

'And . . . can you tell me what was happening when that picture was taken? I can't think of a way to put this delicately so I'm just going to come straight out with it: did anything of a sexual nature happen between you and Mr Dorian on the ski trip?' When he says 'sexual nature' I notice the tips of his ears go pink.

'No,' I say as firmly as I can, shaking my head.

'Or at any other time?' Miss Lovelace interjects. I look at her. I bet she's loving this. Usually she doesn't get to deal with anything more interesting than some kid upset about their parents getting divorced, or 'mediating' between two boys caught fighting in the playground.

'Of course not,' I reply steadily. 'He's my teacher.'

Mr Atwood and Miss Lovelace glance at each other. 'So can you think of any reason why someone would post a picture to deliberately spread a rumour of this nature?' he asks.

I shrug. 'For a joke? I've got no idea. You'd need to ask skisneak, I guess.'

'Do you know who skisneak is?' Mr Atwood presses.

I shake my head. 'No, I don't.'

'No ideas?'

I pause. It can't be Molly, surely? And even if it is, there's no way I'd want to drop her in it. Things are already bad enough between us.

I shake my head again. 'No idea. None. I'm new here. I don't even know that many people.'

'OK.' There is a pause before Mr Atwood continues: 'Let me ask you this. Was there ever a time during the ski holiday when you and Mr Dorian were alone? That could have led to someone surmising that something improper might be going on?'

'No,' I say automatically, but my mind whirrs. Obviously they have seen the picture and we agreed the story about him coming out to check on me.

'You're sure?' Mr Atwood presses.

'Oh, wait. I guess . . .' I add, my heart starting to hammer in my chest as I silently pray that this is the right thing to do, 'the picture you're talking about was taken on the last night when we had the party. There was a point when I wasn't feeling that well – I was a bit hot.'

I see Miss Lovelace roll her eyes, I guess meaning that she knows or at least supposes that I was drunk. Maybe Mr Dorian told her I was. Hopefully that means I'm doing the right thing.

'So I went outside to get some fresh air. Mr Dorian came out to check I was OK. He said he was worried I was going to fall asleep in the snow or something. I was feeling a little dizzy at first, but once I'd been outside for a minute or two I felt a lot better so I told him I was fine and went back inside. That's what the picture shows. I slipped on some ice, he steadied me. He was checking I was OK. Nothing else. So I guess we were alone, briefly, but not *alone* alone. If you see what I mean. And we weren't actually alone even then, because someone took the picture. Some of the other students may have been outside too,' I embellish, improvising now. 'I can't remember. Obviously, you can't see them in the picture, but that doesn't mean they weren't there.'

'I see,' says Mr Atwood. 'So you weren't alone together at any time? Other than for a few minutes when this picture was taken, for the reasons you have already explained. Am I understanding correctly?'

'Yes.'

He scribbles something in a pad.

Miss Lovelace reaches over to me and puts her hand on my arm. 'Ella, if Mr Dorian – or anyone else for that matter – asked you to do anything you didn't want to do, it's very important that you tell us. Even if you didn't do anything. We need to know. You wouldn't be in trouble, I promise.'

She stares into my eyes and I have an almost uncontrollable urge to laugh but manage to fight it down. 'No. He didn't. No one did. Nothing happened. This whole thing is just a picture of something which looks like something else and someone's lame idea of a joke.'

Miss Lovelace gives my arm a little squeeze and then lets go.

'OK,' she says.

'Can I go now?' I ask.

Mr Atwood nods. 'Yes, you can. Thank you for coming. If there's really nothing else you want to tell us, I think we can draw a line under this and hope it's the end of the matter.'

I feel relief wash through me. 'You mean nothing is going to happen?'

He gives me a quizzical look. 'I meant I hope this skisneak isn't thinking about kicking any more hornets' nests.'

'Yes, that's what I meant too,' I babble, and as I barge out through the door I feel like I am walking out into the sun. I think he believed me.

By the time I get back to my classroom everyone's gone, so I grab my books to head to my next class. I wonder what they asked Mr Dorian, and what he said. I wonder if he will teach his afternoon classes, or if he'll have been told to take the day off.

Will he have been suspended? Sacked, even?

Surely not. They have no proof. Mr Atwood seemed to believe me. And as long as I don't tell anyone, no one can be sure what happened. Can they?

Unless there are more pictures, of course.

I text Mr Dorian several times that evening to ask what Mr Atwood said to him and what was going to happen now, but he doesn't reply. Oh God. Oh God. I've ruined his life. I literally don't sleep a wink.

# 58

*February, London*

**Ella**

The next morning I leave it until the last minute to go to the classroom. I pretend to be rummaging for something in my bag so that I don't have to see everyone giving me pointed looks and also so I don't stare at the door. I now understand the term sick with nerves – I actually feel like I might throw up for worrying if Mr Dorian is going to be coming back, or if I've wrecked everything for him forever because of one drunken kiss.

'OK, class, simmer down,' he says. It's Mr Dorian. He's still here. Thank God.

I straighten up, looking directly at him, avoiding catching the eye of any of my classmates. He's fiddling with some papers on his desk, deliberately looking down. I look away, grab a pen and start writing something in my rough book. Anything. Nothing. My face grows hot as I sense people staring at me.

I hear Mr Dorian clear his throat. 'Right, before I take the register, I've got an announcement to make.'

Oh God. He's going to tell us he's been sacked. That this is his last day. That we're never going to see him again. That his career is over. My eyes fill with tears. Luckily by now everyone has turned to look at Mr Dorian.

'As I'm sure you are all aware, there has been a picture on Instagram of myself and one of your classmates, Ella Dooley.'

The entire class turns to look at me again. I stare at my fingernails as I blink the tears away, hoping no one can see.

'The picture is entirely innocent. Ella wasn't feeling well that night on the ski trip, and I was checking that she was OK. Ella and myself have both spoken at length to Mr Atwood and Miss Lovelace about the matter. A note is to go out to reassure all your parents as a precaution in case any of them have seen or heard any rumours, which again, I stress, are entirely unfounded.'

Oh God. Mum's going to know.

'Any follow-up pictures or remarks alluding to the rumours will result in instant detention as a minimum. Is that understood? I would also recommend that if any of you knows who skisneak is, you tell them to shut down the account immediately, otherwise the school will be forced to take action.'

'Yes, sir,' mumbles the class.

'Good. Right then,' Mr Dorian says briskly, opening the register. 'Jason Addison?'

Mr Dorian doesn't look at me once.

# 59

*February, London*

**Ella**

I'm surprised to see Ethan waiting for me at the school gate at the end of the day. I look around for Molly or Jack, but they're not there – he seems to be waiting for me.

'Hey,' he says.

I smile back. 'Hey.'

'OK if I walk with you?'

'Of course,' I say, almost formally. He falls into step beside me and for a few seconds we walk side by side in silence. Ethan's very loyal to Jack and, in his way, to Molly too, so I wonder what he wants from me. I haven't spoken to any of them properly for days. Does he want to join Jack and Molly in telling me what a bitch I've been?

A few moments later, just as the silence is starting to

become awkward, Ethan breaks it, saying: 'Jack's pretty cut up about all the Mr Dorian stuff, you know.'

I sigh. 'Yeah. I know. But nothing happened, so it's not as if I can do anything about it.' I pause. 'I wish he'd believe me.'

'Molly's upset too,' he adds. 'She thinks you're keeping stuff from her. But I could have a word with her, if you like. She listens to me, even if she pretends not to.'

I turn to him and smile. 'Thanks, Ethan, I'd really appreciate that. This whole thing's been a nightmare. I feel terrible that they're upset about it. I wish I could make them see it's not my fault.'

He shrugs. 'I think, deep down, Molly knows that. She'd never say it, but it's obvious she misses hanging out with you -- she's been moping around at home in a right mood. Jack, though . . . I'm not so sure about him. He might be trickier.' He pauses. 'He really likes you, you know.'

'I know. I like him a lot too, but—' I stop dead. I can't say 'but not in that way' to Ethan, he's Jack's best friend and will probably tell him. 'I just think a relationship of any kind for me is tricky at the moment with all this stuff going on. I need a bit of time and space, for now at least.'

'But do you think you might get back together in time?' he presses.

I stop walking. Has Jack asked him to ask me this? 'I don't know, Ethan. Can we talk about something else?'

He shrugs again. 'Sure. You going to the après-ski party on Saturday?' he asks.

With all that's been going on this week, I'd pretty much forgotten about the party, or maybe simply put it out of my head as none of my friends was speaking to me. But I should probably go. Act as if nothing's happened. Maybe people will have forgotten about all this by then anyway.

I nod. 'Should think so. You?'

'Planning to.'

'Great. And Jack and Molly?'

'Hope so. I'll talk to them both. See if they can call a truce with you. Put us all back on the right track. After all, we had fun together, didn't we, the four of us? I miss that.'

He looks down at the ground and blushes. I kiss him on the cheek and we start walking again. 'Thanks, Ethan. That would be great.'

# 60

*February, London*

Nick

My conversation with Mike went way better than I expected. I felt like he was on my side, that he wanted to believe me, that he didn't want the allegations to be true. In fact, he seemed to have so much faith in me that I almost felt bad lying to him. But really, the whole thing is a storm in a teacup. It was a consensual kiss between adults when we were both too drunk to know better. I'm not some kind of predator and Ella is in no way traumatized by what happened. Both times, in fact, she initiated the kiss. I understand that I shouldn't have succumbed, given my position but . . . well. It's not the end of the world – no real harm done. But I need to make sure I distance myself fully from her now, to avoid any more rumours. Ella texted me but I didn't reply and also deleted her number. I need to tell her, gently, not to contact me.

But my conversation with Mike is likely to be child's play compared to the one I'm going to have to have with Aura. As the parents are going to be told about the skisneak thing, there's no way I can risk trying to keep this from her – she's almost bound to find out at some point.

If we were a normal couple, I would book a babysitter, take her to a nice restaurant where she would be less likely to make a scene than at home and tell her there. But we never go out together without the children, so we don't know any babysitters. Even if we did, Aura would be so on edge about leaving the boys it would defeat the objective.

Instead, I buy clams, parsley and a couple of decent bottles of white wine on the way home. I'll get the boys settled nice and early and hope they stay asleep for a few hours for a change. I'll make spaghetti vongole, one of Aura's favourite meals, and tell her what's happened then.

Neither of the boys can go to nursery at the moment because of their measles, so Aura is staying at home with them. After a day with both of them, not even able to go out to the park or whatever, she's not going to be in the best of moods. Sorrel still has a rash but seems a bit better in himself, while Bay's rash is just coming out. So having to break the news that there's a rumour going round school that I've got something going on with one of the sixth formers could hardly have come at a worse time – plus I'm still not entirely forgiven for going on the ski trip.

But all is quiet when I open the door. 'Aura?' I call quietly, not wanting to wake the boys if by some miracle they're already asleep. But as I go along the short hallway I hear CBeebies on low in the living room. I stick my head round the door and see that Sol is staring at the screen and sucking his finger, transfixed, and Bay has dozed off in his bouncy chair. 'Hey, Sol,' I say, 'how're you feeling?'

''Beebies!' he says brightly, giving me a quick glance before turning back to the screen. He's obviously on the mend. 'Where's Mummy?' I ask.

'Stairs,' he says, not looking at me. Upstairs. OK.

I go up to our room where I find Aura flinging things into a suitcase.

Oh God. 'Aura? What's going on?' I ask, though it's fairly obvious.

She stops throwing clothes and stands up, staring at me angrily. 'As if you don't know,' she says scornfully.

'Is this the thing at school?' I ask, though all the while I'm thinking, *How the fuck does she know?*

She goes back to rifling through drawers, seemingly picking things out at random and throwing them towards the case. I catch her wrists and gently pull her towards me, but she turns her head away.

'Aura, look at me, please.' She doesn't move. 'It's nothing, honestly,' I continue. 'I've already spoken to the head about it; he's also spoken to the girl in question and he's happy that there's nothing in it. And there isn't. I promise.'

'What do you mean?' she hisses, finally turning towards me and wrenching her wrists away from my hands. She is dry-eyed and shoots me a look of pure hatred. 'It doesn't look like "nothing" in that picture. Someone at work sent it to me. Their daughter goes to your school. My colleague said she thought I'd want to know, but obviously they'll all be having a good laugh at my expense now. So thanks for that too.'

She stamps over to the wardrobe, pulls out a handful of clothes and flings them in the case.

'Aura, please, listen.' I wheedle. 'It's all a misunderstanding – someone messing about. I'd just gone outside to see if Ella – the girl – was OK. A lot of the kids were drunk that night, I saw she'd gone out by herself and wanted to check she wasn't going to choke on her own vomit or lie down in the snow and go to sleep or anything. Honestly, kids of that age are a liability. They're worse than toddlers in some ways. What sort of person would I be if I hadn't checked she was OK? Imagine if it was Bay or Sorrel when they're bigger. You'd want someone to check on them in the same situation, wouldn't you?'

She picks up her phone and the screen comes to life. I can see she has the photo open and is examining it closely.

She looks up from the phone at me. 'Why you, though? Why did it need to be *you* to check on her?'

'It didn't need to be me.' I look her directly in the eye. 'I just happened to see her go. Really, it was nothing – we were out there about a minute, if that. She assured me she was OK, stumbled a little, which is when God knows who must have taken that picture, and then we both went back inside. It was totally unremarkable.'

She looks at the phone and then back at me. Tears fill her eyes. 'I want to believe you, Nick, I do, but . . . I'm just not sure.'

'I'm telling the truth,' I say softly.

She swipes at her face, brushing away a tear. 'I need to think. I'm going to go away for a couple of nights. Against my better judgement, I've called your mum because I couldn't think of anyone else, and she says she'll come and babysit. She's already had measles so she says she's happy to do it.'

'Did you . . . tell her?' I ask, a wave of nausea washing through me.

She gives me a look of contempt. 'No. I'll leave that up to you.' She continues flinging things into her case.

'Please don't go, Aura,' I plead. 'Stay here. We need to talk. I want you to stay. I want us to be together here, as a family.'

She shoots me a look of pure hostility. 'What you want doesn't come into this right now, Nick.'

# 61

*February, London*

Ella

Over the next couple of days, Molly seems to forgive me. I wonder if Ethan did have a word with her like he promised. Even though they act like they don't like each other much, I guess as twins they must have a bond. Same as I do with my brother and sister, only more so. Or maybe Molly eventually took me at my word that nothing happened with Mr Dorian and my promises that I would have told her if it had. I've said it dozens of times now, and each time I feel less guilty. Nothing much did happen, after all. It was a crush. A drunken kiss. I'm over it now. Everyone needs to move on.

The school hall is totally unrecognizable. The party committee has spent the whole day turning the usual drab room into a winter wonderland. The huge windows are frosted and giant snowflakes have been stuck all over the walls. Silvery-blue shiny draping everywhere looks like frozen streams and there is silver glitter all over the floor.

'Isn't it beautiful?!' Molly shrieks as we walk in.

'It's fabulous!' I'm really looking forward to this evening. It's the first time since we've got back from skiing that everything has felt almost OK. Molly and I are friends again. Mr Dorian can just about look me in the eye now on a good day, and it seems like we got away with what happened without any real fallout. Jack isn't exactly seeking out my company but when we're all together as a foursome, things are OK. Even Mum was calmer about the Insta thing than I expected her to be, and, amazingly, believed me when I told her nothing had happened. Skisneak hasn't posted anything more, though I keep checking and the account is still live, but everyone seems to have pretty much forgotten about it. The whole thing feels like it happened ages ago. It's amazing how quickly things can move on.

Molly is on the party committee. As she's had so much involvement in setting up the evening she wanted to wear an outfit that would create a stir, and persuaded me that I should too. 'You must!' she cried. 'Show everyone that you don't care what they say! That you're not paying attention to the stupid rumours! That you're too fabulous for the likes of Mr Dorian anyway!' I think it's partly to show me that I'm forgiven too, that we are friends again, and what happened (or didn't, as far as she knows) is all behind us.

We've got matching snow-queen outfits from a weird little costume hire shop on the high street and I have to admit, they're pretty amazing. We're wearing fitted strapless silver bodices which give even me a bit of a cleavage, with big netted fairy skirts covered with silver glitter. We also have silver boleros and tiaras. Earlier we spent ages putting on body glitter, silver eye-shadow and nail varnish and sparkly lipstick while messing about in my bedroom and having a few V & Ts. It was lovely – the way things used to be.

'Wow – you two look amazing!' Jack says, heading over as he sees us come in. I'm surprised when he hugs me for the first time since the ski trip, but it feels nice. A friendly hug. Maybe Ethan managed to talk him around too.

Jack's eyes look glazed as he pulls back. Maybe that was the reason for the hug – he's pissed.

'Looks like you already started on the drinks?' Molly asks.

'Yeah, me and Ethan had a few before we came.' He turns to me. 'Dance with me?'

I nod. Hopefully we can be friends after all. We go over to the already-packed dance floor.

'It's great that you and Molly are mates again,' he shouts over the music. 'Ethan said she was really upset about it all.'

'Yeah – I was too. I'm glad we made up.'

He moves in closer and puts his hands on my waist.

'I'm glad we did too,' he murmurs, leaning in so close that his breath feels hot on my ear. 'Sorry I gave you a hard time the other day. I was being a dickhead.' He pulls me closer. 'Maybe now that all that Insta stuff has blown over we could . . . y'know . . . think about getting back together. Properly.'

Oh God. I thought he understood that that wasn't going

278

to happen. But I don't want to get into this now. I don't want to spoil the evening. 'Maybe,' I say vaguely.

He nods and lets go of my waist. 'Fine,' he says curtly, his demeanour totally changing. 'I'll leave you to do things in your own time. I've had enough of this song – let's go and get a drink.' He turns and walks away and I follow him towards the drinks table, where Mr Woods is serving some bizarre-looking silver non-alcoholic punch.

We each take a plastic cup and take a sip.

I pull a face. 'Ewwww. It takes like melted sherbet.'

Jack takes another sip. 'I quite like it.'

We look out at the dance floor. I see Molly's skirt swishing about – it's hard to miss it as it's so enormous – and notice with a lurch that she's dancing with Mr Dorian.

Mr Dorian looks faintly embarrassed and is clearly being careful to keep his distance from Molly. He catches my eye and I smile, but he looks away. I'm surprised he came along tonight, but I guess he felt he should make a show of normality. Just like me.

I watch them for a while. I know Molly would never try it on with Mr Dorian, but even so, I feel a pang of jealousy. I thought I was over this. Guess I'm not.

Then she starts heading towards me and – oh God – she is dragging Mr Dorian behind her. He looks mortified. 'I'm exhausted!' she breathes as she comes close. 'Ella – you dance with Mr Dorian.'

I've no idea if she is doing this out of naughtiness, because she wants to show me that she totally believes now that nothing went on, or because she hasn't thought it through. Whatever the reason, it would be far too awkward to protest so neither of us has any choice but to head out to the dance floor together. We jig about chastely opposite each other, both being careful not to touch each other at all. I glance around but no one is paying us any attention. Thank God. Since that rumour started that Mr Robbins is leaving school to go on *Love Island*, we're now yesterday's news.

'I'm sorry about Molly doing that,' I shout over the music.

He nods. 'You haven't said anything?' He looks incredibly tense.

I shake my head. 'No. And I'm not going to. I promise.'

'You understand that you could finish me off if you do?'

'I do.' I do a little twirl. 'But it'll be OK. I'm pretty sure most people have already forgotten about it.'

He smiles tightly. 'I hope so.'

'Did it go all right with Mr Atwood?'

'Guess so. I'm still here, after all. My wife might take more persuading. Things are still a bit tricky at home.' He takes my hand gingerly to spin me round, carefully keeping his distance from any other part of my body. 'As long as you never tell anyone, and skisneak stays in the shadows, we should be OK, school-wise at least.'

We carry on dancing for a little while longer, and suddenly I feel like everything is going to turn out just fine.

### Thirty minutes later

Sirens, so many sirens.

It's so cold. The gravel of the courtyard is scratching my face. I can't move.

'Is she breathing?'

'Stand back from her, let me through! Don't move her.'

280

'What happened?'

'She must have fallen from the window. What was she doing all the way up there? Ella? Can you hear me?'

I try to reply but no sound comes out. Everything hurts. It hurts so much.

'Did anyone see what happened? Was anyone with her?'

'Oh God her pulse is really weak. Ella! Stay with us, help is on the way. Don't try to speak.'

I try to say something, tell him what happened. Who did this to me. But there is too much shouting and they can't hear. Or maybe my words aren't coming out – I'm not sure.

'Thank Christ, the paramedics are here. Ella, they're going to help you. Do you understand?'

I have a blurry impression of people in green and I try to nod. But I am too tired, and I fall asleep.

*They say that time heals all wounds. That over time, you learn to live with grief. That it becomes easier to bear. But it's not true. It doesn't. You just get angrier.*

# PART THREE

# 62

*November, Mozène*

**Aura**

I wasn't sure what to expect from a funeral in France, but it certainly wasn't this. The blocky, anonymous-looking crematorium is on an industrial estate at the edge of our nearest town. We all mill about nervously in the bland atrium with screwed-down metal chairs and a simple coffee-vending machine, before shuffling through into the main room where the service, such as it is, will be held. And instead of the coffin arriving in a traditional hearse, the funeral vehicle looks more like a delivery van, only black and clean.

I've left Sorrel and Bay at home with Helen. They're too young to be exposed to death in this way. Also, it would be very hard to keep them quiet. There is no good reason for them to be here. Seb and Chloe have come along though

– they were told they could film as long as they were discreet.

Frank's son Andrew is the first to speak. He looks like a younger, thinner version of his father. He's probably about the same age as me but he's already going bald, poor guy.

'I hadn't seen my dad for five years before he died,' he starts. 'And obviously, this is now a great regret for me. We fell out over something that, in retrospect, was none of my business. And because he lived here in France while I live in the UK, we somehow never got round to getting together for a pint, talking things over and making up. He tried, I didn't.' He looks towards the large mahogany coffin, standing on its plinth. 'Dad, I apologize.'

He pauses to wipe away a tear. I wonder, inappropriately, what the row was about.

'And you people here,' he continues, 'both the local expat community and his French friends, have been much more his family than we have since his move and for that, I want to thank you all.'

He glances around and there are gentle murmurs and nods. The small room is full and there are even a few people standing at the back. Frank had a lot of friends here. Or at least a lot of people interested enough in him to turn up for the gossip and some free sandwiches, I think to myself, less charitably.

'Even though I haven't been in touch with Dad much since he moved, I have had the great pleasure of meeting some of you over the last few days. I only wish it had been in happier circumstances. I've learnt how you welcomed him into your lives, invited him to dinner, to parties and more. He, in turn, as I understand, paid back your generosity by looking after newer arrivals, taking time to help them find their way around, navigate the famously tricky French bureaucracy,' a murmur of agreement goes around the room, 'and many more tasks besides.'

I feel a pang of guilt – Frank helped me a lot and I didn't appreciate it enough. After what Tiggy had said, I was actually trying to distance myself from him. And I haven't paid my respects to the family yet. I make a mental note to do so properly at the wake.

'In the various letters and emails he's sent to me over the last few years, in an attempt to reconcile our differences, he would tell me a bit about his life here and the things he was doing,' Andrew continues 'To my shame, while I read his letters, I never replied. But it was clear from what he wrote that he was happy here. He felt he fitted in. That he was liked. Appreciated. Accepted. Certainly welcomed.'

There is a pause while Andrew wipes his eyes and glances at the coffin again. 'And given all that, it is almost incomprehensible that someone within this small and, as I understand, supportive and tight-knit community, decided, for reasons we don't have the first idea about, that they wanted to kill my dad at a Halloween party. Quite possibly one of you here. As you all know, someone literally stabbed him in the back.'

He pauses again. The room is totally silent.

'My dad wasn't perfect. None of us is. But since his move to France, his life centred around you people here. He made every effort to help you as much as he could. And to think that it all ended like this makes me sadder than I can begin to express.'

287

He picks up his notes and stamps away from the pulpit without so much as a glance at the congregation. The young, English-speaking vicar announces that there will be a hymn, 'Dear Lord and Father of Mankind' followed by a few short prayers.

I pick up the order of service sheet which includes the words to the hymn. On the front is a picture of Frank, clearly taken a good few years ago, along with his dates of birth and death. I quickly work out that he was fifty-five. No age at all really. He must have had his children young, like me and Nick. I barely knew him, and am surprised to feel tears come to my eyes. I wipe them away surreptitiously as Nick continues to stare straight ahead. He is annoyed I made him come along today – he said he wanted to get on with ripping out another one of the old bathrooms rather than 'wasting half a day on someone I didn't know or like', as he put it. But I managed to persuade him it would look weird if he didn't come. And when there is already so much gossip going around about who killed Frank and why, that's the last thing I can be bothered with.

After the prayers, a curtain goes around the coffin and there is a whirr as the conveyor belt starts up. There are a few stifled sobs and I take Nick's hand. He glances at me and squeezes it, before letting go and looking straight ahead again. The vicar walks to the back of the room and opens the doors, so we all get up and follow him out, past the next group of mourners who are in the atrium waiting to come in. It is all over in less than thirty minutes.

# 63

*November, Mozène*

**Aura**

The wake, organized by Frank's family, is held at his house.
Though he'd been over to ours loads of times, I've never
been to his and so am not sure what to expect. It turns out
to be a small, terraced house without a garden in the middle
of a medieval village, La Bastide de Mozène. There are two
reception rooms and a galley kitchen downstairs and it's not
really big enough to fit everyone in – it's too cramped. I
wonder if the family were being tight in not renting a func-
tion room somewhere; if they felt they didn't want to spend
their money on him. Then again, maybe they didn't expect
this many people to turn up.

There are a lot of photographs on the wall. Somewhat
heartbreakingly, given that he clearly didn't have much

contact with them, they seem to be mainly of kids who I assume must be his grandchildren. Everything is neat, tidy and well-kept. I feel a pang of grief for this man I didn't know very well, who helped me a lot and whom I could perhaps have made more time for. Somehow, coming to his house has made me see how lonely he must have been.

His three sons and the woman who I guess must be his ex-wife have prepared an extraordinary amount of sandwiches and are handing them round, along with glasses of wine. It's not long before the noise level and the heat start to rise, and people drift out on to the pedestrianized square outside to escape the small, stuffy rooms.

After an hour or so I figure I should be getting back to the boys but remember I had promised myself I would go and speak to the sons before I left. With this in mind, I head outside into the cobbled street. The freshness of the air is a huge relief. I can see the son who made the speech talking to Tiggy, and head over to them.

'Aura!' she says. 'Great timing. I was just telling Andrew here about you. How you were Frank's latest . . . protégée? Not sure that's quite the right word. I mean that he'd been helping you out since you arrived.'

'Andrew, lovely to meet you,' I say, sticking out my hand, which he takes with a soft smile. 'I'm so sorry for your loss. We're all terribly shocked by what happened – as you said at the crematorium, it's inconceivable that anyone would want to hurt Frank. Have the police got any idea . . .'

He shakes his head and bites his lip. I wonder if he's going to cry. I hope not, I don't think I can bear it.

'Frank was incredibly kind to me,' I gush to fill the silence.

'We've only recently arrived, and he was so obliging with helping me to set things up and find my way around. I don't know what I'd have done without him.'

'Did you come out alone, or do you have a family?' he asks. I get the feeling he's keen to steer the subject away from his father. I guess it's all too raw, or he feels guilty about never reconciling after their falling out.

'I came to France with my husband – he's inside some-where – and two small sons, Sorrel and Bay.'

He looks at me and frowns. 'Sorrel, you say?'

'Yes. I know it's quite an unusual name but as soon as he was born it just seemed to fit.' I get so bored of having to justify their names. Not everyone wants to call their kids Oliver or James, do they?

'No, it's not that. It's a great name. It's just . . . something weird we found on Dad's phone.'

I feel a lurch of nausea. Oh God. That time when he babysat. Sorrel's nightmares. Did Frank . . . did he . . .

'What kind of thing?' I squeak. 'Pictures?'

His face drops. 'Oh gosh, no, sorry, nothing like that.' He touches my arm. 'No, absolutely not. Dad had his faults but there's no way he'd ever hurt a child. He loves kids. Loved. Sorry. I didn't mean to scare you like that. Please don't worry.'

I let out a long breath that I hadn't realized I'd been holding. 'Thank Christ for that,' I say. 'So what was it you found on his phone?'

'You said your son was Sorrel – is your email something like SorrelsMummy?'

'Yes,' I say, blushing. It seemed cute when I set it up as a second email for some of the mummy forums but over time it's slowly become my main email and it's started to feel a bit embarrassing to define myself by my child.

'It's an email account on his phone but we couldn't work out whose, until now.'

I frown. 'Why would he have my account on his phone?' I am suddenly very aware of Seb filming over my shoulder. Why does he always manage to appear at the worst possible time?

'Didn't you say he helped you with your internet set up?' Tiggy asks. 'Could he have had it for that?'

'Yes!' I cry, relieved. 'That will have been it. I probably gave it to him at some point. I'm never as careful with my passwords and the like as I should be. I think it was something to do with that Astrid gadget, he needed it for that.'

'Rather you than me,' Tiggy says. 'I hate those things. Harvest your data. Frank loved them, though. He was always trying to persuade me to get one, but I said there was no way I was having one in my house.'

There is a pause. 'Well, I'm glad we sorted that out,' Andrew says.

'What are your plans now?' Tiggy asks. 'Are you staying around for a while or heading straight back to the UK?'

'The other three are heading back tomorrow. I'm the most flexible because I'm freelance, so I'm staying on for a week or so to sort out the house, get it on the market and take care of all the various formalities. I haven't booked a flight back yet as I'm not sure how long it will all take.'

Tiggy reaches into her bag and pulls out a card which she hands to him. 'Don't hesitate to call if you need a hand with anything. Frank was so helpful to me over the years and I'm more than happy to repay the favour. If you're not familiar with the French way of doing things, you may need some help finding your way around the paperwork, apart from anything else.'

He takes the card and I see his eyes fill with tears. 'Thank you,' he says hoarsely. 'That's so kind. I may well take you up on that.'

'I'm happy to help too,' I add, 'though I barely know my way around myself yet! I don't have a card but – actually – tell you what – why don't you come for dinner while you're here? I can't help with anything practical, but at least I can feed you and offer some company. Here' – I hand over my phone – 'put your number in and I'll give you a call. If you'd like to, of course,' I add hastily.

He taps his number into my phone and hands it back. 'Thank you. I would like that very much. Now, if you'll excuse me, I should probably circulate.'

As Andrew leaves, I notice Seb switch off his camera. 'You know, if Frank had your email account details on his phone, he could have operated your Astrid?' he says.

'What?' I've had a couple of glasses of wine, not enough food and my head is already slightly fuzzy. 'Why would he want to do that?'

He shrugs. 'No idea. But you know those times when it sounded like someone dropped in to it? Or when that music went off in the middle of the night? That could have been him.'

'He could do that remotely? I mean without even being in the house?'

'Yup.'

I shake my head. 'No. I don't think so.' I still think Seb set the music off himself to give them something else to film. 'It doesn't make sense,' I continue. 'I don't see why he'd want to do that. He just had my account on his phone because he helped set up the internet and the Astrid thing for us – I remember now,' I lie.

I don't remember giving him my account details. But that must be it, surely?

# 64

*November, Mozène*

**Aura**

Back at home the boys have had a great afternoon with Helen making a fort in their bedroom by stringing old sheets up all over the place. Tiggy and Bertie come in for a cup of tea on their way home.

'Well, that was a strange day,' Tiggy says as we sit quietly at the table. Helen has taken the boys outside. 'I can't believe we just buried Frank. He was such a part of the furniture here. Hard to believe he's gone.'

'And terrible that they still don't know who killed him,' I say, shuddering. 'Do they really think it was someone at the party? Doesn't everyone know everyone else here? Why would anyone do a thing like that?'

The wine from earlier is wearing off and I feel a pang of

alarm. It had never occurred to me until now that I was bringing my precious boys into a community where we don't know a single soul. Who anyone is. Where they've come from. What they're like. There could be hardened criminals here and I wouldn't have the slightest idea. Or paedophiles. Do they have a sex offenders register in France?

'They've no idea why anyone would kill Frank, as far as I know,' Tiggy says, interrupting my catastrophizing. 'I suppose it could have been a random person who wandered into the party. But it seems unlikely, given the location, doesn't it? Why would they?'

'Failed robbery?' I suggest helplessly. 'Isn't that what the police usually put it down to when there's no clear motive? Perhaps they were after his wallet?' I'd rather tell myself it was a stranger who did this than someone the boys or I might be mixing with.

'Poor sod,' Bertie booms. 'No one deserves an end like that. But the police are looking into it and life must go on. Let's talk about something else – take our minds off things. Any plans for the weekend?'

'The usual – sorting, demolishing, painting, moving broken crap about,' Nick replies with an air of resignation.

Bertie waves his hand as if swatting a fly. 'That can all wait. Why don't you join me on *la chasse* – the hunt? Great way of getting some fresh air and meeting a few of the locals.'

'Oh no we don't agree with—' I start, but Bertie interrupts me before I can finish my sentence.

'Don't give me that bleeding heart rubbish!' he barks. 'You're in rural France now! Hunting here isn't just sport

– it's a necessity. It keeps the boar population down – if the numbers aren't kept under control the buggers kill sheep and local farmers lose their livelihood, as well as the beasts writing off cars by running out in front of them. Everything that is killed during the hunt is eaten – and this being France, I mean literally everything: bollocks, brains, innards, the lot – nothing goes to waste. It's very hard to have an ethical objection to it if you actually know what you're talking about.'

'But . . .' I start, and then realize I don't know what to say. I feel myself go red. I'm not going to argue as there is clearly no point, but really, could he be any more patronizing? Poor Tiggy. No wonder she gets her kicks with Celia whenever she gets the chance.

'So what do you think, Nick?' Bertie persists. 'Fancy it?'

'Yep, sounds great,' Nick says, to my absolute horror. 'It'd be good to meet some of the real locals – we don't want to end up living in an expat bubble, do we, Aura?' he adds, slyly parroting something I'd said repeatedly before we came out to France.

For fuck's sake. He doesn't have to kill innocent animals to meet locals, does he? But I'm not going to start a row, especially not now with everyone here and Seb filming.

'You're your own man, I can't make your decisions for you,' I say tightly. An embarrassed silence falls over the table.

Bertie pushes back his chair, stands up and claps his hand on Nick's shoulder. 'Great! That's settled then. I'll bring all the fluorescent gear you need to wear, and I'll see you outside the boulangerie at 6 a.m. on Sunday.'

'Six?' Nick says incredulously.

'Yup. Start early, a few *pastis*, all over by twelve, then time for a few more drinks and lunch. Great fun. You'll love it!' Bertie looks at his watch. 'Right, we should be on our way now and leave you good people to it, but I'll look forward to seeing you then.'

'Any chance I could come?' Seb asks. 'I used to shoot at uni and I've got a licence – a UK one, but I'm pretty sure it's valid here. Would love another go. It would be amazing if they'd let us film too – nice picture of local life and all that?'

'Of course!' Bertie cries. 'The more the merrier. I'm sure they'll be fine with the filming too. Send me a copy of your paperwork and I'll get the stuff sorted at my end.'

I keep my face in a fixed smile as we do the *bise* and say our goodbyes, but as soon as they are out of the door, I turn to face my husband. I don't even care that Seb is still there.

'What the fuck, Nick?' I shout. 'Hunting? *Really?* You know how I feel about that!'

He looks at me coldly. 'You heard what he said – it's nothing like the fox hunts in the UK. If you think about it, it's actually right up your street. Free-range meat, ethically sourced from animals living happy lives in their natural environment. And aside from anything else, you're entitled to feel how you like about it, but so am I. And I am keen to go along, meet some new people who aren't expats and get out of this fucking house for something other than going to a DIY shop. Now, if you'll excuse me, I'm going to get on with stripping wallpaper. Again.'

# 65

*November, Mozène*

**Aura**

I invite Andrew for dinner the next day. He seems like a nice guy and I feel sorry for him, stuck in that house all on his own, knowing no one and probably dealing with the guilt of having fallen out with his father before he died. I also invite Tiggy to make up the numbers – Bertie has gone back to the UK until the weekend.

Andrew arrives with a bottle of wine and a bunch of flowers, and I serve the local crémant with crème de cassis as an aperitif – it's like Kir Royale except less than half the price. Tiggy has brought free-range eggs and some flowers from her garden. I gave Helen most of the day off today and asked her instead to take charge of the boys if they wake up this evening – which they no doubt will. Even though I'm keeping things pretty informal tonight, this is the first kind-of dinner party I've hosted since we arrived in France and I don't want to be running up and down the stairs all evening tending to the boys' needs. They know Helen well now – they won't mind her babysitting.

'So, how are things going over at Frank's house?' I ask, as we start with home-made butternut squash velouté with a swirl of crème fraiche and black pepper. I am quite proud of it – it looks like something I'd be happy to be served in a restaurant.

Andrew sighs. 'OK-ish. Slowly. It's a small house and Dad kept things pretty tidy, but there's still loads of stuff to sort out. Deciding what needs to be kept, what needs to be junked, what should go to the charity shop, as well as getting his house and the rental ones put on the market, and dealing with the notaire about probate and all that. It's all taking ages.'

I wonder who Frank has left everything to, given that the family had fallen out, but obviously I don't ask.

'It would be easier if I'd known more about him, I think. There are some things which are . . . a little strange – I don't really understand why he has them, and so I don't know what I should do with them.'

'Like what?' I ask, as I clear away the plates and bring the slow-cooked shoulder of lamb with garlic and rosemary to the table, with a warmed bowl of sweet potato mash and some buttered winter greens from the market. Even if I say so myself, dinner looks fantastic.

'Well, there's a box of things which look like keepsakes,

perhaps from women he's had relationships with since he and Mum split up, but I don't know who they belonged to or what they represent. I feel bad throwing them away, but also don't know what to do with them. For example, there are a number of women's scarves, but some more personal items – little boxes and trinkets, books, even a couple of, um, I don't know if I should say this, but even a couple of pairs of knickers.'

I see Nick stifle a chuckle.

'So I feel weird going through this stuff,' he continues, 'like I'm prying, but at the same time, someone has to do it.' He turns to Tiggy. 'You've been here some time, haven't you, Tiggy? Do you know of any women he's been involved with? I feel that whoever these things belonged to, perhaps I should offer them back?'

Tiggy shakes her head. 'No. To my knowledge he hasn't been in a relationship here at all, or at least not one he's let anyone know about. He has a lot of female friends – had, sorry – he always seemed more drawn to women than to men. I'd be happy to come over and help you though, as I said before. Maybe as I'm not . . . family it might feel less intrusive? Going through his things?'

Andrew visibly relaxes. 'That would be a huge help, thank you,' he says.

'Not a problem,' Tiggy replies. 'Shall I come over tomorrow afternoon?'

'I'll help too if you like,' I say. 'I could do with getting out of the house. And what about the investigation? Have you heard from the police?'

He sighs. 'Yes, they've been round to see me a few times.

And if what I hear on the grapevine is true, Thea is not at all happy about them swarming around her chateau. All they seem to know so far is that he was stabbed in the back, probably going out to use the loos at the front of the chateau while the fireworks were on. The knife was a brand-new standard-issue one that could have been bought anywhere. No prints on it, so the killer must have worn gloves. And with so many people at the house that night, there's little hope of anything useful to be found DNA-wise. They're questioning everyone who was at the party, but so far, no one has seen anything relevant. I imagine you'll hear from them eventually too.'

I'm not sure I want to be questioned by the police, but I guess I don't get a say in it. I don't want to be treated like a criminal and it might be unsettling for the boys. And my French isn't very good either – what if I say something I don't actually mean and it makes me look guilty? Or Nick does?

I hope they don't come here.

That night the music goes off again. The boys scream, Nick runs downstairs and unplugs the Astrid and Seb, as before, appears on the landing, showing off his musical knowledge uninvited like the last time.

'O Fortuna,' he announces smugly as he points the camera at me, no doubt revelling in my dishevelled look. 'A great piece of music, if a little over-played these days. You might recognize it from *The X Factor*.'

'I don't watch the bloody *X Factor*!' I snap. 'Get out of my way.' This time, despite the dramatic nature of the music, it is annoying rather than scary. I'm almost sure Seb is behind this. I now totally see why the production company insist the camera crew stay with us in the house while they are filming; eventually, that way, they are bound to see us at our worst.

'Are you doing this?' I hiss. I know I will regret it, but I'm tired and irritable and can't think straight. He puts his camera to one side and frowns. 'Of course not. Why would I want to do that? It's probably one of the pool workmen messing about.'

I remember what Seb said before about it being possible to control the Astrid from outside the house. But even if Frank had been doing that, which seems unlikely, he's dead and I can't see any reason why Andrew, who now has his father's phone, would bother with a prank like this.

'Perhaps you'd do it to get yourself some more interesting footage?' I suggest.

He pulls a face. 'I'm quite offended by that, Aura, if you don't mind me saying so. That really wouldn't be my style at all.'

Nick appears next to me at the top of the stairs. 'Let's chuck that thing out,' I say. 'Now that Frank's gone, I don't feel we have to pretend to like it anymore.'

# 66

*November, Mozène*

**Aura**

We meet Andrew in a café near Frank's house and have a simple lunch of confit de canard and sautéed potatoes with a carafe of rough red wine, which all costs next to nothing. This is what we came to France for, I remind myself. Because here it's considered normal for me to sit at a table in a restaurant and have a good, leisurely lunch of three courses and wine instead of a rushed soggy sandwich at my desk or gulped down in between trying to get the boys from one place to another.

After lunch we go to Frank's house. Now that it's empty of people, it feels dark and rather depressing. Andrew has clearly made good progress: the bookshelves have been emptied and pictures taken down from the walls, and there are large cardboard boxes scattered all over the floor.

'I'm pretty much done down here,' Andrew says, 'but if you were able to give me a hand with Dad's bedroom, that would be a real help.'

We go up the narrow stairs into the room at the front of the house, which overlooks the square. The double bed is immaculately made and there is still a glass of water, a box of tissues and a paperback on the bedside table. There is something tragic about it and I feel a stab of pity for this lonely man, estranged from his family.

Andrew opens the wardrobe and I see shirts, trousers and T-shirts arranged on hangers, all carefully ironed. 'Let me show you this box I was talking about,' he says, removing a wooden chest from the bottom, 'perhaps you can identify who I might return the things to.'

He puts the box on the bed and opens the lid. At first glance it looks like a jumble of colourful scraps of fabric and I can't imagine anyone will be bothered about getting them back, but it seems rude to say so when he is making such an effort.

Tiggy picks up a handful of patterned silk and frowns. 'This red scarf looks familiar . . .' she says, and then drops it on the bed as if it's stung her. 'Shit! It's mine. I bought it when we were on holiday in Dubai years ago. Why would he . . .'

I cast another glance at the box and suddenly my knees feel wobbly. 'This is mine,' I say, picking out an aquamarine scarf. Angry now, I rummage in the box and – for fuck's sake! 'These are my knickers!' I explode. They're bog-standard M&S, so I haven't missed them but . . . What the fuck!?

Andrew looks at me in horror. 'Oh my God. I'm so sorry. I can only apologize. I didn't think but . . . shit, I probably should have guessed.'

305

Tiggy is still rummaging in the box and pulls out a couple more scarves. 'Hermès. These have to be Thea's.' She holds them out to Andrew. 'These are very expensive – I think she might like them back.'

He slumps down to sit on the bed and puts his head in his hands. 'For fuck's sake,' he mutters, and then looks up at us. 'The reason Mum and Dad split up, the reason we all fell out with him, was because he would regularly become obsessed with local women. As far as I know, he never took it further than light stalking – in fact I've never talked about it fully with Mum but I suspect he may have become impotent. The police had to get involved when a couple of the women complained. I didn't know that he . . . took things, though. I didn't think he'd sink that low, or I'd never have asked you over here to . . . let him show me up like this. Christ.'

There is an embarrassed silence. 'Do we need to . . . tell anyone about this?' I ask.

Andrew throws his hands in the air. 'I don't know. I'll leave it up to you. Apart from the scarves you mentioned I don't think these items look valuable, but if you want to tell the police, I'm not going to stop you. That's it for me. I've had it with him. I can't believe he can embarrass me even from beyond the grave.'

He looks like he is about to cry. Tiggy puts her hand on his shoulder. 'I don't think we need to tell anyone official,' she says softly. 'I can't see that would achieve anything. Would you like me to return the scarves to Thea, though?'

He nods. 'That would be very kind, thank you. I don't think I can face having to explain what he did, but please pass on my apologies.'

# 67

*November, Mozène*

**Aura**

'Wow, that was weird,' I say, as Tiggy drives us home. 'I feel sick at the thought that I left the boys with him. He must have taken my stuff then.'

I see her grip the steering wheel tighter. 'Yeah. I know what you mean. But I honestly don't think he'd have ever touched the children. I think he was just lonely.'

'And a bit of a perv?'

She laughs. 'Looks that way. It seems we've both been his imaginary girlfriends, as well as Thea. And probably some others too.'

'I don't want to think too much about that box of tissues by his bed.'

'Ewww. Yep. And he may well have been listening to you

on that Astrid thing like Seb suggested, you know, as he had your account on his phone. I'm so relieved I wouldn't let him persuade me to have one of those things.'

'Oh yes! I hadn't thought of that.' Something else occurs to me. 'I didn't tell you about this, but that must be why he warned me off trusting you – he'd have heard us talking about him through it. But thank God our Astrid was only in the kitchen and not the bedroom!' Not that much goes on there anyway these days, I think with a pang of regret. 'Though I've thrown it out now anyway,' I continue. 'There was scary music from it again last night.'

Tiggy frowns. 'Well, it can't have been Frank this time. Even when he was still here, I can't imagine him doing that, can you? Doesn't seem to have been his style. Why would he want to scare you?'

'I don't think it was him either,' I agree. 'I think it was Seb, though he denies it. Or maybe it was just a glitch. Either way, we've chucked it away now, so the music thing can't happen again.'

With the Astrid gone, there is no midnight music that night. However, our bedroom ceiling lights come on by themselves at two o'clock, four o'clock, and half-past five. 'I can't take this anymore, Nick!' I yell, the third time it happens. 'I'm calling an electrician in the morning. Dodgy wiring or not, there must be something they can do.'

As I fling myself back under the covers with Nick mumbling something incoherent, it occurs to me that calling an electrician is the kind of thing I'd have asked Frank to do, given that I don't speak any French and have no idea who to call anyway. Perv or not, I will miss him.

# 68

*November, Mozène*

**Aura**

The police are continuing to question everyone at the party,
according to Tiggy, but they haven't got round to us yet.
Knowing it might happen at any time is making me feel so
on edge that I'm having to take extra homeopathic arsenicum
album, but even that is barely helping. And on top of
worrying about the prospect of being questioned by the
police, all week I'm annoyed about Nick having agreed to
go hunting. He refuses to back down.

I feel like the new breath of life which coming to France
was starting to give our relationship is being suffocated. I
try to get Helen on my side about the hunting, but she is
non-committal and refuses to be drawn, saying annoying
things like, 'Obviously it has to be a personal choice, but in

the countryside boar do need to be controlled.' Seb is loving it and seems to magically appear with his camera every time I try to have a word with Nick about it. He's had Chloe researching the documents they need to be able to go along too to film the action, which is also pissing me off. He reckons the hunt will be the perfect opener to the episodes about us. God knows why – I wonder if he's doing it deliberately to wind me up to give them more good footage for their programme. Sometimes I wish I hadn't agreed to this thing.

# 69

*November, Mozène*

Nick

'Pretty early morning, eh, Nick?' Seb says.

I yawn. 'Yep. God knows why they have to start when it's barely light.'

'Totally worth it – you'll see. I love it. I started hunting when I went to uni, had a friend there who was into it. Great fun. Your wife didn't seem very interested in hearing about it, though.'

I laugh, although it sounds false even to my ears. Aura has barely shut up about the hunt for days and there's now absolutely no chance of us having sex again any time soon. 'I'm in a lot of trouble for coming along today,' I agree.

'That's understating it,' Chloe adds. 'On and on and on. So much nagging. I don't know how you stand it.'

I open my mouth to say something, feeling like Chloe shouldn't be quite so rude about my wife, but I change my mind. She's right, after all. Frankly I'm relieved to get away from Aura for a morning, in spite of the early hour.

'Chloe's in charge of the filming today,' Seb says. 'The experience will do her good and I think she's ready for it.'

'So fucking patronizing,' Chloe says, rolling her eyes. 'What you actually mean is you want to go shooting innocent animals with the boys and fancied the day off.'

As early as it is, the bakery is open and a group of around twelve Frenchmen, plus Bertie and, I'm surprised to see, Tiggy, are drinking coffee and eating croissants outside when we pull up. I imagined the shoot would be men only, but it looks as if I was wrong.

'So glad you could make it!' Bertie booms as Seb parks the van and we get out. 'Thought there might be a chance your good lady wife might force you to stay at home. Glad to see it's you that wears the trousers after all.'

'I'm very much the trouser-wearer in our house,' I say, and I notice Chloe smirk and roll her eyes. I hope she didn't catch that frankly ridiculous comment on camera.

Bertie introduces Seb, me and Chloe to the hunters and there is a round of discreet nods, handshakes and bonjours. Seb exchanges a few words with the group in impressively rapid French. I have no idea what he is talking about and resolve, not for the first time, to sign up for some language lessons.

Everyone looks up as the gravel crunches and a Tesla pulls up to the bakery. Thea gets out of the passenger seat and the car rolls away, as silently as it arrived. She is wearing skin-tight camo pants and an expensive-looking hunting jacket. Her auburn hair hangs just so around her shoulders and she is fully made-up. All the men, who range in age from about eighteen to eighty, stop talking and turn their attention towards Thea. Chloe tuts and I look down, pretending to be fiddling with my phone.

Thea is truly hot though, no one can deny that. I think back to that party at hers and what might have happened if Aura hadn't flipped out and made us leave. Would we have all swapped partners? I feel a stirring in my pants and distract myself by remembering Aura's expression of disapproval and contempt as I left the house this morning, and it quickly goes away.

Fluorescent hats and tabards are handed out to everyone and there is a briefing about where we will be going and who will stand where. Bertie translates for me – my role is to stand silently behind him unless directed to act as a beater. Apparently I'll be able to have a go at shooting if Bertie feels it's safe, but I remain Bertie's responsibility. I suddenly feel nervous – do I actually want to shoot something or not? Yes, yes I do, I tell myself. I'm a man, not a mouse. It doesn't matter what Aura thinks. I'm going to be the trouser-wearer I claimed to be earlier, at least today.

Thea seems to have taken a liking to Seb and has not-very-subtly made sure that they will be standing close to each other. It occurs to me that she is the reason he wanted to come along today. He's younger than her, sure, but then so was Hervé and that clearly didn't bother either of them. I certainly wouldn't say no to Thea. Seb is leaning in towards

313

her, too close, as they talk about something, God knows what. She touches his arm lightly and laughs and I feel a surge of jealousy.

The dogs in the trailers are already frantically barking. Everyone leaves in vans to take up their initial positions.

# 70

*November, Mozène*

**Nick**

To start with, there is a whole lot of nothing. I stand behind Bertie, feeling stupid in my manky orange hat. It's cold, misty and starting to drizzle. My legs ache from standing still for so long and – not that I want to admit it to myself – I'm starting to regret coming. Chloe has stopped filming because there is nothing to see and is sitting in the van fiddling with her phone. I wish I could sit in there too, in the warm and out of the wet, but I can't imagine it would go down well with Bertie. So I carry on standing where I am, wet, bored and freezing cold.

Now and again I hear the dogs barking in the distance but Bertie has explained that if there is any reason to move, someone will call and we'll jump in the van to go to where the action is. But the longer I've been standing here, the less and less convinced I've become that I want to see a boar killed. I've never seen anything killed before, and have no idea what it would be like. What if the animal is injured but not dead and I have to watch it squealing in agony? Doesn't bear thinking about.

And then, just as my feet are going numb and I've given up on anything happening ever, Bertie's phone rings. '*Oui, oui*,' he says, nodding as he speaks to whoever it is that I can faintly hear jabbering away in French at the other end of the line.

'Right,' he says, as he hangs up. 'The woods. They've found a boar. We need to jump in the van and get over there ASAP.' He pronounces it *aysap*.

On the short drive over, I feel nervous and sick, not helped by the narrow roads, the pastis that I thought would be rude to refuse when offered from a hip flask this morning alongside the coffee, not to mention Bertie's too-fast driving. Why did I want to come today? I can't remember now. Chloe is sitting in the back, filming over our shoulders. Isn't the windy road making her feel sick too? Doesn't seem to be.

'Right, here we are,' Bertie says, pulling over to the side of the road behind a couple of white vans. 'This is where the action is.' He gets out and takes his gun from the boot, slamming it closed so hard it makes me jump. 'You just follow me, for now,' Bertie says. 'Stay behind me unless I tell you otherwise, OK?'

'Yup,' I say, trying to keep my voice steady as I feel a slight tremble in my knees and again, regret coming along. I think of Aura, cosily at home with the boys and wonder

316

what they are doing. Perhaps they are baking, or sitting by the fire playing a game. I mentally shake myself – much more likely she's fobbed them off on Helen again and is faffing around upcycling something pointless or fannying around with that 'counselling' website of hers. As usual.

'You too, Chloe,' Bertie continues. 'You stay behind me. And put your orange hat back on – safety and being seen is more important than whether or not it messes up your hair,' he guffaws. 'I know what you girls are like.'

Chloe rolls her eyes and puts the unflattering orange baseball cap back on, pulling a face. 'Yuk. Wonder how many people have worn this before me,' she says.

'Right, off we go, stay close,' Bertie booms. It's starting to drizzle again. 'Stay close, and quiet as possible.' He starts marching across the damp field at a considerable lick, considering his portliness. Chloe and I scurry behind him, struggling to keep up in the slippery grass. As we near the trees, the orange hats of the other hunters come into view. They have guns raised, pointing into the trees. Bertie slows his pace.

'Right,' he whispers, 'I'm going to take my place between Pierre and Jean-Marc there,' he says, pointing. 'It looks like the entire group is now here, in position.'

'Then what?' I ask.

'Then, we wait,' he says.

We wait. And wait. And wait. It's still drizzling and misty. I don't think I've ever been so bored in my life. I'm also now regretting all the coffee I drank at the boulangerie that morning in an effort to wake myself up as my bladder feels almost rock solid. I need to go soon or I'll wet myself. Plus it will give me an excuse to stretch my legs, ease the boredom a little.

'I'm going for a slash,' I tell Bertie, 'won't be a sec.'

Bertie nods, but I get the impression he's not listening; his eye remains trained down the barrel of his rifle. I wonder how he can keep his arms raised for so long – don't they ache?

My legs are stiff from standing in the same position as I walk fifty metres or so to find a suitable bush for a pee. Since we arrived in France I've noticed that many men here seem to think nothing of having a sneaky roadside wee in full view of whoever might be passing, but I don't want to do that, especially not in front of a young girl like Chloe. That would be uncouth, and disrespectful.

Opening my flies, I breathe a sigh of relief as the pressure on my bladder lessens. Just then, the dogs start barking frantically, there's a rustling sound in the long grass behind me and what looks like a giant pig thunders past. Christ – that's a boar? I hadn't expected it to be so huge. I was imagining something more like the micropigs at the city farm I used to take Sol and Bay to sometimes.

The barking grows more frantic and louder as the dogs get closer and I desperately try to stop the stream of piss so I can get my flies done up – I don't want to go back with a wee stain on my trousers any more than I want to be caught with my cock hanging out. But it's easier said than done, come on, come on . . .

The dogs race past me in pursuit of the boar in a blur of yelps – they pay me no attention, thank Christ – they're terrifying all together in a pack like that. I hear the footsteps of the hunters running towards me and suddenly I am scared – what happens now? Am I going to see the boar killed? I don't think I'm ready.

One of the men shouts something incomprehensible and there is a flurry of shots. A hot, white pain sears through my chest and I collapse to the ground, my hands falling away from my still-undone flies. There is more shouting, the thunder of footsteps and a scream, and then it all fades to nothing.

# 71

*November, Mozène*

**Aura**

'Thank you,' I say, automatically, as Helen puts yet another steaming hot mug of tea laden with sugar in front of me.

'Is there anything else I can get you?' Helen asks softly. 'You really should try to eat something.'

I shake my head. I can't eat. It's been two days since Nick's death and I've barely eaten a thing.

Sorrel keeps asking where Daddy is and I don't know how much more of it I can take. I'm not using words like heaven with the boys and I've explained as gently as I can that Daddy won't be coming back. But Sorrel just doesn't get it. Bay, of course, is oblivious, babbling away in his usual, happy way, but even that is upsetting. I'm mainly leaving Helen to deal with them and, as usual, she's been a saint.

The film crew have gone, for the time being at least. Even Seb, with his mantra of 'we must see everything', managed to understand that I couldn't cope with them around right now. I think they mumbled something about hoping to come back for the funeral as they left. As a mark of respect, they said, though obviously they didn't mean it. I wonder if they will still use our footage or not. They didn't say anything about that. I'm not sure I care either way at the moment.

The chateau itself now feels entirely overwhelming. What once looked like a fun and romantic project, building a fabulous life for us all, now feels totally insurmountable. I can't stay here alone. But we've sold up in the UK, and I don't know if I want to go back anyway. I don't know what to do.

'There's plenty of time to think about all that,' Tiggy says as I force this out between sobs. 'No rush at all. You need to look after yourself for the time being.' She takes my hand. 'Do you want me to see if I can help with paperwork? Did Nick have life insurance? Or a will?'

Fresh tears come. Tiggy is so kind. 'I'd love you to help,' I wail. 'But there's no will or life insurance.' We'd never thought about either of those things. It never occurred to us that anything would happen. We were young and healthy – we thought we were invincible. And as Nick didn't have a job when he died, I don't know if we'll be eligible for anything at all.

'OK,' Tiggy says. 'All this can be a bit tricky in France if you're not set up with . . . but now isn't the time. If there's anything you need me to do, sorting out the funeral, letting people know what happened, just shout and then leave it to me. Meantime I'm going to talk to a few people about helping you with the formalities.'

'Thank you,' I mutter hoarsely, tears dripping from my chin. 'I wouldn't know where to start. If you could arrange a funeral, that would be a huge help. And I'll give you a list of people who need contacting. Thank you.'

# 72

*November, Mozène*

**Aura**

The next few days pass in a blur of lying in bed, sitting in the kitchen and Helen placing food and drink in front of me at regular intervals. Sorrel has stopped asking about his dad, I'm not sure if he's finally realized what has happened or if he's already forgotten him. Helen occupies the boys most of the time. I don't know what I'd do without her. I can't focus on anything. There is too much to think about, so I don't bother thinking at all. I let it all wash over me. What will be, will be.

The investigation is ongoing, but the kindly police lady told me in broken English that it was likely to be ruled an accident. They're not sure whose gun he was shot by yet, apparently. The stupid boar had changed direction, everyone was all over the place and several guns were fired. Nick was standing somewhere he shouldn't have been. Bertie blames himself for taking Nick, and I wonder if he suspects he was the one who shot the fatal bullet. But even if it was, which it sounds like they will never know, I don't blame Bertie. I blame Nick, for going in the first place. If he had listened to me, and not gone off that day with the sole intention of watching a poor, innocent animal being slaughtered for fun, none of this would have happened. The leader of the *chasse* has sent me flowers along with *toutes mes condoléances*, but I'm not interested. They will no doubt be out hunting again next week, as if nothing had happened.

Considering what a short amount of time we've been in France, there is a good turnout for the funeral. In the end I agree that Seb and Chloe can film it; they say it would be good to 'pay tribute' to Nick in the programme and I just don't have the energy to argue. Everyone I've met so far in France is here, as well as several people I haven't met, or at least have no recollection of. I leave the boys at home with Helen again. They're too young for funerals – I don't want them absorbing that kind of negative energy. I can't believe this is the second funeral I've been to in as many months. I wonder what I've done to deserve this.

No one says it to me directly, but I hear people murmuring between themselves about the unlikeliness of having to attend two funerals for two relatively young men within such a short space of time. Especially when no one knows who killed either of them. I hear one particularly ridiculous woman speculating about whether it could be someone who doesn't like the English infiltrating the area. Utterly ludicrous, of course. Clearly someone killed Frank, but what happened to Nick was an accident, pure and simple.

Tiggy has been my rock. She organized the service entirely, she even found a traditional English hearse so that Nick's body didn't have to arrive in one of those horrible utilitarian black vans like Frank's did. I gave her my computer and phone so she could put together a photo montage for the screens in the crematorium, and she selected the music after asking me about key moments in our lives – Elvis Costello's 'She', which was the first dance at our wedding, John Lennon's 'Beautiful Boy', which I listened to as both Sorrel and Bay were born, and '50 Ways to Say Goodbye', which was 'our song' when we first met at university and is horrifyingly appropriate today.

Almost everyone here is local. I never knew my dad, and Mum died a few years ago – my inheritance from her allowed us to buy the house in London and, in turn, the chateau, which now feels like a millstone around my neck. Nick's awful parents are here, of course. They've never forgiven me for 'making' Nick get married so young, as they saw it, nor for the 'shame' of their first grandchild being born outside of wedlock, as they put it. They look terrible.

But his death hasn't brought me and his parents together, and neither will it. No hugs as we meet, not even a little pat on my shoulder from them. Just a taut half-smile from Roger and an enquiry about how the boys are getting on from Penelope. Not a single question about how *I* might be doing. The move to France was the last straw for them in their relationship with me, I think. They saw it as me taking the boys away from them. And, being avid church-goers as well as people who like to be seen to do things 'properly', they will be appalled that there are no hymns or prayers during the short service. Neither Nick nor I believed in a god and, even if we did, right now I don't feel I have much to thank Him for.

# 73

*November, Mozène*

**Aura**

After the service, there is a wake of sorts at home. I haven't contributed to its planning at all. Tiggy and Helen have made sandwiches and keep everyone's plates filled and glasses topped up while I stand bleakly, nodding and saying 'thank you' as various people I hardly know tell me how sorry they are for my loss and please do let them know if there's anything they can do to help. Penelope stands in the corner, primly holding her plate with her face like a slapped arse as she looks disapprovingly at the peeling paint and crumbling cornicing. Roger does magic tricks for the boys and it makes me shudder how they squeal in delight. Kids are so easily won over – they've no idea how rejected their grandparents made me feel since I met Nick.

After a couple of hours, everyone drifts off, including Nick's parents, who are staying in a local B&B, thankfully – they said it was to give me space, but I know it's because they think the chateau is too shabby for them. Tiggy and Helen tidy up and we have an awkward dinner together once the boys are in bed, the two of them faux-cheerful and talking about anything and everything apart from Nick and the funeral while I push food around my plate and stare into space.

After dinner Tiggy hugs and kisses me, promising to come back tomorrow. Helen says that if it's OK with me, she'd like to have an early night. I nod and say thank you again.

And then I am left alone in the kitchen.

Seb and Chloe leave early the next morning.

'Thanks for putting up with us,' Seb says. 'I'm only sorry it's turned out the way it has.'

He puts his hand on my shoulder and does that head tilt and sympathetic face everybody does that I've got so used to over the last few days.

'Until . . . well, until all this we really enjoyed our time here. And I hope you like the programme, once it comes out. We will make sure it's done respectfully, of course. Hopefully, in time, it will be something for you to remember Nick by. And nice for the boys to have so much footage of their dad?'

I nod, still numb. I could try to insist that the programme is canned but, right now, I don't have the energy. Plus, like Seb says, it might be something nice for the boys to remember Nick by. Because they're so young, I don't imagine they will have any proper memories of him when they are older.

'What will you do now?' Chloe asks. 'Will you stay here? Or go back to the UK?'

I shrug. 'I'm not sure. Probably stay, at least for the time being. I don't have anything to go back for. It's nice for the boys here, I don't want to disrupt them yet again. And I still like the idea of running a chambres d'hôtes. But whether or not I can do all this renovation on my own . . .'

My eyes fill with tears and Chloe looks awkwardly at the ground. Once again I feel totally overwhelmed. There's no way I can do this. I'll have to sell up and buy something small and manageable. Won't I? I just don't know anymore. 'Anyway,' I continue. 'Thanks for your . . . well, interest, I guess. I'll look forward to seeing the programme when it's ready. Safe journey.'

In the middle of the night, the lights come on again. The brightness wakes me immediately. I hurl myself out of bed, hit the switch with my fist and throw myself back under the covers, sobbing. I can't do this anymore, not on my own. There's no one to help me – no Frank, no Nick. I just can't do it. I'm going to have to sell what was to have been my dream chateau. Fresh tears come as I mourn the idyllic childhood I wanted my boys to have, my stupid husband who made so many mistakes but I loved anyway, and who died because he wanted to shoot innocent animals and fit in with the locals. None of this is my fault. It's just not fair.

My throat is sore and my eyes are like golf balls from crying. I've taken to staying in bed in the morning even once the boys are up and letting Helen sort them out. I simply can't face their cheerfulness first thing. I need time to ease into the day. I hear their joyful yelps downstairs and Helen's calm, gentle murmur. I close my eyes and try to go back to sleep.

# 74

*November, Mozène*

**Aura**

'I've decided,' I tell Tiggy, who arrives with yet another cake and a bunch of flowers when I finally surface at about 11 a.m. 'I've consulted the angels and I know what I'm going to do. I want to get rid of this place. It's too big to deal with on my own. It needs too much work. There's no way I can manage, and there are too many memories. Plus there's still weird stuff going on which creeps me out – the lights came on again last night by themselves. It's almost like the building itself is telling me I shouldn't be here. Nothing good has happened since we arrived. I think the best thing will be for me and the boys to make a fresh start somewhere else, in a more manageable property.'

Tiggy nods. 'That's understandable. Although, like I said

before, personally I think you should let the dust settle a little. You might feel differently in six months' time. And I know you haven't been in France long but you have lots of friends here – we can help you.'

I shake my head. 'No. I've decided. I feel better about it all now I've made a decision. Though even the prospect of getting estate agents round and dealing with all the formalities exhausts me.'

Tiggy squeezes my hand. 'If you're sure that that's what you want, I'd be happy to help. I don't know if you know this, but selling property in France isn't always as simple as it is in the UK. Did you set up a marital regime when you came over?'

'Marital regime? We were already married, ages ago.'

'Yep, I know, but when you buy a property in France, unless you've set up a specific marital regime, the children automatically inherit part of the house. Normally the notaire would tell you about all this when you buy,' she says, spotting my confused expression, 'but I guess some are better than others.'

'What?' I say. 'That can't be right. They're babies. They can't inherit anything, surely?'

She pulls a face. 'Their age doesn't make any difference. But let's not panic. It may be that you set this up and don't remember – it's only signing a piece of paper, it's not as if there's a ceremony or anything. If you give me all the details you have for your house purchase, I can pass it on to our notaire and find out for you. I imagine you'll need to sign a letter to say you give me permission to ask – they love an *attestation* for everything in France. I can draft it for you, if you like.'

I put my head in my hands. 'Oh God, why does it all have to be so complicated!' I lift my head again to smile weakly at Tiggy. 'Thank you. If you could ask your notaire, that would be a huge help. But just for argument's sake, what if we *don't* have this marriage contract? What happens then?'

'I'm no expert – I think it's better that we find out how you're set up, speak to the notaire and we'll go from there. If you give me whatever paperwork you have, I'll get on to it straight away.'

# 75

*November, Mozène*

**Aura**

Nick's parents are still staying locally and come over every day. They've said this is so they can support me and the boys, but they're no support at all – all they do is interfere and make snide comments.

'So have you given much thought to the future, Alison?' Penelope asks, sitting at the kitchen table, visibly sneering at the surroundings, as usual. She's always insisted on calling me by my given name, even though she's the only person who's ever used it since I decided to become Aura for short when I left for university. 'It'll be difficult to cope with a big place in this state of disrepair on your own.'

*Disrepair?* How fucking dare she? It just needs renovating, that's all.

In that moment I'm tempted to tell her I'm planning to stay just to annoy her, but I swallow down my anger and say: 'Yes, I have. I think I will try to sell and get somewhere more manageable.'

She takes a sip of her tea. 'That's good to hear. And where will you go? Perhaps you could get a little place near us? We'd love to see the boys more, and now that we're retired we could help out with childcare – I'm sure it's hard to think about it at the moment, but in time you'll need to go back to work.'

I can't imagine anything worse than living in their middle-class Home Counties dormitory town while they not-so-quietly disapprove of the way I'm bringing up my boys and generally interfere in my life. Absolutely no way. And aside from all that, I don't want my boys being infected by their mainstream, bourgeois ways and values.

'It's something to think about,' I lie, 'but I haven't decided yet. I may even stay in France, just not in this house.'

I didn't know people actually did this in real life, but she literally clutches her pearls. 'Oh no, dear. I don't see how that would work. How would you earn a living? We're happy to help out a little where we can, of course, but we don't have a lot of income anymore.'

No, just a fuck-off pile of tweeness worth at least a couple of million which you rattle around in selfishly, I think to myself, but I bite my tongue.

'You need to be able to support yourself and the boys,' she continues. 'It's disappointing to learn that Nick had no life insurance – I thought he was more sensible than that. And obviously all that . . . unfortunateness which happened and having to leave his job means you won't be entitled to anything from that.' She pauses. 'Such a shame,' she adds, in a way which seems to make her thoughts that somehow all this is my fault perfectly clear.

'I'm a counsellor,' I say tightly. 'I did the training. I just need to build up my client base. Or I could buy somewhere with some extra rooms so I could do Airbnb on a casual basis like lots of people around here do. I don't know. There are loads of options. Plenty of Brits live out here with their families and make a living one way or another. We own the house outright and don't need much. But with all due respect, Penelope,' I add, meaning with absolutely no respect whatsoever, 'it's much too early for me to be thinking about these things. At the moment I'm struggling just to get through one day at a time.'

She nods, gripping her mug so tightly that her knuckles have gone white. 'I understand. But I want you to know that the offer is on the table. We'd be happy to help with the boys as much as you like if you lived nearby. And as I said, I'm sure we could perhaps help financially to some degree if it meant seeing the boys more.'

Nice. We'll help you out, but only if we get to hijack our grandsons' upbringing.

'I don't think that will be necessary,' I say, but I feel a wave of despair crash over me. How on earth am I going to manage as a single mother? I was barely coping as it was.

'We'd love to play an active part in their upbringing,' Penelope adds wistfully. Unusually, given that she almost never touches me, she pats my hand. 'Think about it,' she implores. 'It would be good for the boys to have their extended family around them, in the circumstances.'

Over my dead body.

# 76

*November, Mozène*

**Aura**

'The default position in French law is that, on the death of a spouse, the children of the couple automatically inherit a proportion of the estate,' Tiggy's notaire, who fortunately speaks fluent English, tells me. 'In your case, as you have two children, sixty-six per cent. From your paperwork it is clear that you did not set up a marriage with the *regime de la communauté universelle*, or make any other provision to prevent this when you bought the property, so I'm afraid that is the position.'

'What?' I whisper. I don't understand. 'But they're babies. Can't we do anything about it? How can they inherit anything? They can't even write their own names.' Tiggy reaches over and squeezes my hand.

The notaire takes his glasses off and rubs his eyes with his thumb and forefinger. 'You have the right to stay in your current residence as long as you want. No one is going to throw you out, madame, you don't need to worry about that. However, if you want to sell, I or one of my *confrères* will have to make an application to a judge so that we can be sure you are acting in the best interests of the children.'

'But all that matters to them is that they're with me! I will always do the best I can for them! They're all I have now!' My voice is high and hysterical.

'Madame. I'm quite sure that is the case. And it is unlikely a judge would refuse any reasonable request when it comes to selling the house, especially because, as I understand, it is in need of a lot of renovation. However, these are the rules here in France, and this is what must be done. When the house comes to be sold at whatever point in the future, if the children are over the age of eighteen, their share becomes theirs to do with as they like. If you wish to sell before they are of age, you need to apply to the correct authorities who will ensure that the children's interests and rights are protected.'

'And there is nothing I can do about this?'

'It is a great pity when you bought the property that you did not consider looking at your marriage regime. It would have saved you a lot of heartache. I'm very surprised it wasn't suggested to you.'

Maybe it was. I don't remember. I've a feeling that because the house in London was bought largely with what I inherited from my mum, and because of how things were with Nick at the time, I felt safer keeping our assets apart. In case

337

I decided that I needed to leave the marriage after all. But that has now backfired quite drastically. I didn't consider what would happen if one of us died. We're young. Or, Nick *was* young. Death seemed so unlikely.

'And if I go back to the UK?' I press.

'That would be more complicated, but in effect, the same rules apply as the property is owned in France and your husband died while he was living here under French rules. I am sorry, madame. But try not to worry too much, if you want to sell the house, applying for permission is not difficult and can all be done easily by myself or someone like me. It is not like going to court as a criminal. I imagine you will need some time to think about all this, and I have another client arriving now, so unless you have any other questions . . .'

I push my chair back, fighting back tears. Tiggy stands up too. 'No. No questions for now. Thank you very much, you've been most helpful.'

'Wow, Aura, that's tough,' Helen says over dinner. She has made boeuf bourguignon and it is fabulous. She's a much better cook than me and I honestly don't think I could cope with the boys without her help at the moment. I keep worrying about when she is going to leave – she won't want to stay here forever – but I can't bring myself to ask her. I don't know what I'll do when she eventually goes and it's just me and the boys here all alone in this scary chateau which is falling down around our ears with weird stuff going on in the night. What on earth was I thinking, bringing us all here?

'Yep,' I agree. 'But there's nothing I can do about it now, apparently. It is what it is. So at some point or another I have to face the fact that the boys own most of my assets – I just have to hope they'll be kind to their mum in her old age! Or that I can marry a rich man next time round.' I laugh, but it sounds hollow.

'You're young, Aura, plenty of time,' Helen says. 'Who knows where you'll be ten years from now?'

'Probably here, still clearing out junk and covered in dust,' I say gloomily. 'It's so unfair. I feel like I've been trapped by the rules. I'm a prisoner. There's nothing I can do.'

She pats my arm. 'Don't be silly. I know it must seem impossible now, but you'll get through this. What about the immediate future – what do you plan to do?'

I sigh. 'I don't know. A couple of days ago I was dead set on moving away. But now I've found out how complicated it is, I don't know if I can face it. Plus, where would I go? I don't want to go back to London. A large part of me would still like to make a life here. Nick's parents are desperate for me to move to be close to them, but that's absolutely the last thing I want to do. They're horrible people and, while I get that they love the boys, I don't think they're a good influence on them and I don't want them having too much input into their upbringing. I wish I could just make it all go away.'

We both stare out of the window, listening to the rain beating down on the ancient glass.

'I think I know a way we can make it go away,' Helen says, 'but I'm not sure you'll like it.'

# 77

*February, London*

**Ella**

It's too warm here in the school hall now with all these people packed in and it turns out my snow-queen outfit isn't really made for dancing – I'm hot and sticky and I bet my hair is going frizzy too. Jack and Ethan come over. Jack is covered in a sheen of sweat and Ethan's looking a little wobbly on his feet. 'God, my sister is such a tart,' he says, but not without humour, watching her dancing somewhat suggestively with Mr Woods while he keeps his gaze fixed firmly on her forehead. Ethan scoops up a plastic cup of the punch and downs the contents in one. He pulls a face. 'That is REVOLTING!' he says. He puts his hand in his pocket and pulls something up, twisting his hand towards me so I can see what it is.

It's the top of a hip flask. 'Want a proper drink?' he asks me.

'Um . . .' I say, thinking back to the last time I got drunk. That didn't go so well – snogging Mr Dorian in the snow and then all the fallout from that. But it seems to have all gone away now and today is different. And it would be a shame not to celebrate the four of us all being friends again. Plus I could really do with some cooler air – I'm starting to feel a bit dizzy. 'OK. But not in here. I've been in enough trouble lately as it is.'

He pushes the hip flask back into his pocket. ''kay. I've got some tonic and stuff to go with it stashed in the art room if you don't want to drink it neat.'

'I should get Molly. She'll want to come too.'

'I'll tell her when she's finished dancing with Mr Woods,' Jack says. 'You can hardly march over now and ask if she wants to come out for a sneaky drink with him there, can you?'

Ethan waves his hand. 'OK. See you in a bit, Jack.'

Ethan weaves out of the hall and I follow. It's only then that I realize quite how drunk he is  - he can't even walk straight. 'Here we are,' he slurs, bashing the door of the art room open and barging in, 'Ethan's Bar.'

He rummages under a table where it seems he has stashed some plastic cups, tonic and more vodka, sets out two and clumsily pours our drinks.

He lifts a cup and I take one too. 'Cheers,' I say, as we tap them together and they make an indistinct, plasticky sound.

Ethan takes a large gulp and I do the same. I feel suddenly

self-conscious. I don't know Ethan all that well and I think this is one of the few times we've been alone together. Usually either Jack or Molly is with us. I feel weirdly shy, like I don't know what to say to him.

'So, Ella,' he continues, wiping his mouth with the back of his hand, 'what's all this stuff about you and Mr Dorian?'

'It's nothing,' I say airily. 'Someone made it up. Just a lucky camera angle in that stupid picture.' I can feel my heart thudding in my chest and my cheeks go redder. 'Why is everywhere in this school so hot?' I say, flinging open the window and sitting on the ledge. I take another glug of the vodka.

He nods. 'Lucky camera angle?' he says, with a weird leer. A wave of nausea washes over me and suddenly I feel a little frightened.

'Yes,' I say, as steadily as I can.

He gets up and moves to stand in front of me. He is so close that I can smell cigarette smoke on his breath.

'I really like you, Ella,' he slurs.

What? Where is this coming from?

'I like you too, Ethan,' I babble, 'But not . . . in that way and anyway, Jack and I have only just split up, I mean we might even get back . . .'

He shakes his head and fumbles in his pocket. 'Jack! My mate Jack. You were never bothered about him!' he hisses.

'Ethan, you're being strange. I'm going back to find the others.' I get down from the ledge and try to head for the door but Ethan stands in my way and says: 'Wait. I want to show you something first.'

I'm tempted just to ignore him and push past. But I'm a

bit scared to do that the way he's acting right now, like he's not himself, so I don't. Maybe he's taken something?

He draws his phone out his pocket and fiddles with it. He pushes the screen towards me. It is so close to my eyes I can't focus on it. 'See! You were never bothered about Jack! Look!'

I move back a little so I can see what he is showing me and as the picture comes into focus, My hand flies to my mouth.

It's a picture of me and Mr Dorian in the snow.

Kissing.

'Give me that!' I yell, trying to grab the phone from his hand, but he holds it out of my reach.

'I think Jack deserves to know, don't you? I think everyone deserves to know! That picture I put on Insta was only a taster – this is the main event!'

'Why would you do that?' I yell. 'How is this any of your business?'

He is suddenly quieter. 'Jack's my best mate. You were messing him around. And I thought if you weren't with him, then maybe . . . maybe . . .'

I feel a pang of pity. 'Oh, Ethan. I thought we were friends.'

He looks up at me with a glint in his eye and then back at his phone. He starts fiddling with it. 'What are you doing, Ethan?' I yell. 'Please don't! Don't send the picture! Tell Jack if you must but don't ruin Mr Dorian's life! It was nothing! Really! Just one kiss and we were both wasted!'

I launch myself at him and wrestle the phone out of his hand. I try to run away from him but there are tables in the way. He grabs me by the waist from behind with one hand and with the other prises my fingers off the phone.

It falls to the ground as the door flies open. 'What the fuck are you doing, Ethan?' Molly shouts. I freeze, as does Ethan for an instant, before letting me go. 'Leave Ella alone! What's wrong with you?'

Molly rushes over and helps me up, before bending down to pick up the phone.

'It's mine!' Ethan splutters. 'Give it to me!'

I see her glance at the screen,

Oh God.

Her face hardens. 'Is this what I think it is?' she asks, showing me the screen.

'I wanted to tell you, I really did,' I wail. 'But I couldn't! He made me promise, he said he'd lose his job . . .' Tears well and start coursing down my face.

'You promised,' she says, her voice low and tremulous. 'You promised nothing was going on, and you promised that you would tell me if it did. And here you are' – she thrusts the phone in my face – 'with your tongue stuck down his throat, and all the time you were telling me that nothing was happening! How could you?'

I lunge for it, throw it to the floor and smash my stiletto heel through it. That photo mustn't get out. It mustn't.

'What the fuck are you doing?' Ethan yelps.

'You can't show anyone that!' I scream. 'It . . . you'll ruin his life. He'll get sacked. It's not fair. On him. Or me. Please, Ethan. I'll buy you a new phone. Just don't . . .'

He looks at me in disgust. 'I wasn't going to share it. I just thought . . . God. It's gone now, anyway. No back-up, so you've got no worries for your precious Mr Dorian. You're mental, you are.'

'And a total bitch,' Molly snarls. 'The way you treated Jack. What did he do to deserve that? That's it for you and me. You were never really my friend anyway, clearly.' She gives me a look of pure disdain, grabs Ethan's arm as she leaves and drags him along with her, slamming the door behind them.

I pick up the pieces of phone and hurl them as far as I can out of the window. Tears start to flow and I feel sick. I open the window wide and sit cross-legged on the deep windowsill, breathing in the cool, fresh air. I put my head in my hands. I just want to go home. Back to Manchester, where everything was normal and easy. Go out with Tash and Lily. Get my brother to buy me dinner. Just not be here, dealing with all this.

# 78

*February, London*

Ella

A few minutes later the door opens. I hope it's Mr Dorian, but, of course, it isn't.

It's Jack. I rub my face with my hands. I hold my breath but I can't help it, another sob escapes.

He frowns and comes over to where I am still sitting on the windowsill. 'Sorry, just went for a wazz. What happened? Where are the others? Why are you crying?'

He touches my arm and more tears come. He moves closer and takes me in his arms. Oh God. It feels so nice. It's the first time he's touched me since the whole Mr Dorian thing. But now he's going to hate me.

'Hey . . . hey. Don't cry. What is it?'

I need to tell him. Ethan is so angry with me. And so is

Molly. One of them is bound to tell him about the picture of me and Mr Dorian. Or even show him. He said there was no back-up, but who knows? It's better he hears it from me.

'Jack . . . please don't hate me,' I hiccup.

He frowns. 'Ella – I know we've had our ups and downs and I wish you liked me as much as I like you, but I certainly don't hate you. We're friends.'

I shake my head. Oh God. I don't want to do this. But I have to.

'Come on, Ella. It can't be that bad. Tell me.' He is trying to sound reassuring, but I see something flicker across his face which makes me uneasy.

I steel myself. 'You know that photo on Insta?'

He pauses. 'The Mr Dorian one?' His voice sounds strangled.

I nod. 'I didn't tell you the whole truth about it. We kissed. But it was nothing. I'm so sorry. I didn't mean to . . .' I break off and start bawling like a child. I can't help it.

His face darkens. 'You and Mr Dorian?' he spits.

'I'm so sorry. It was only one time. No, twice, but one time was before . . .'

'You had sex with him?' he shouts.

'No! No! Nothing like that. We just . . . we just kissed. I know it doesn't make it OK, but we were really drunk.'

For a few seconds he stares at me with total contempt. 'You got with him? On the skiing trip? Like the Insta said? Like you categorically denied?' he asks coldly.

I nod miserably. 'I'm so sorry,' I sob, 'if I could go back and change things, I'd—'

347

He moves his face close to me. 'So you wouldn't let me touch you, didn't want to do those things with me because you were doing them with him,' he hisses.

'No! I didn't do anything with him, I—'

Jack roughly grabs one of my boobs and I yelp, trying to push him away but he doesn't move. My head spins. I've drunk too much. 'Did he do this?' he sneers.

'Jack, you're hurting me! Please, let me go!' I beg, 'I'm sorry! I didn't mean . . .' I uncross my legs to try to get down from the windowsill, to get away from him but I can't get past him – he is too close.

Still holding on to me, he presses his mouth on top of mine and forces his tongue deep in, biting at my lip. I wrench my face away.

'No, of course not. You'd rather do that with him than me, wouldn't you?' he leers, pushing his body against mine. I try to put my hand behind me to steady myself but the window is open and there is nothing there.

'I'm sorry!' I yell. 'Please, let me go.'

'Be quiet!' he screams back at me. 'Whatever you do for him, you'll do for me!' He takes a handful of my hair in each hand pulls it tight.

'No!' I scream, trying to wriggle away. 'Let me go!'

'Stop screaming!' he shouts, letting go of my hair with one hand and ramming it up under my skirt, so hard he pushes me backwards. I try to kick him away but as I lift my legs the movement unbalances me and suddenly I am falling. My calves are scraped by the edge of the ledge as my bodyweight pulls me over and there are a couple of moments of panic, and then nothing but pain.

# 79

*November, Mozène*

Aura

I am shocked. I wouldn't have thought Helen was the type even to think about doing something illegal like this, let alone go through with it. But she appears to be serious.

And the more wine we drink, the more sense her plan makes.

'Think about it,' she says. 'It's going to be a nightmare for you trying to get this place renovated by yourself. Don't get me wrong,' she says, leaning in closer and waving her finger in my face, 'I'm not going to leave any time soon. Not while you're so vulnerable. But we both know I can't stay here for ever.'

I nod. 'I know,' I say, brushing away a tear at the thought of her leaving. Oh God. How would I cope?

Helen pats my arm. 'Don't cry. It's going to be OK. We're going to sort it. But, going back to what I was saying before, even if you manage to get the renovation done, running a chambres d'hôtes single-handed as well as looking after your two boys? Total nightmare.'

Another tear falls. This time I feel so hopeless I don't wipe it away. I take another large slug of wine.

'Or if you sold it,' Helen continues. 'For a start, there's all that bureaucracy to go through. Instructing a notaire. Going to court. And once you've bought something else, the boys own most of it, so you can look forward to an old age in penury. Plus, how long is it going to take to sell something massive and ancient like this, unfinished as it is? Brits aren't buying in France the way they used to, and the locals aren't interested in these old piles – they want modern and functional with double glazing and central heating. It'll take ages to sell. Years. Unless you're willing to accept a pittance for it – and then you're back to square one. Only poorer.'

I stare at her helplessly, tears still streaming. It's all so awful. There's no way out. 'What am I going to do?' I wail.

She reaches over to take my hand and looks me straight in the eye. 'Think about this. If there was an accident – if the house just went – you could claim on the insurance and then do what you like. You'd get way more for it that way than trying to sell it in this state. And who knows? There might be some loophole you can exploit before you buy the next place, which means the boys won't automatically inherit while you're still alive. That way you could easily get something to suit you without having to go through the heartache of either selling or renovating this place. Wouldn't that be better?'

'Um, yes, it would but . . .' Is she really suggesting what I think she is? How would that even work? 'God, Helen, I don't know if I could.'

She leans forward across the table, her eyes gleaming. 'Why not? You and the boys get the life you want, the life you deserve, the life Nick would have wanted you to have. No one loses out apart from the insurance company, and no one cares about them, do they? Haven't you paid premiums all your life? Like all of us do, getting nothing in return? Now it's time for payback.'

I'm partly appalled, partly excited. I can't think straight. My head has been so foggy since Nick died. What she says makes perfect sense. But . . .

'I don't know,' I say. 'I'll have to think about it.'

Helen shrugs. 'Up to you. But I'm happy to help if you want me to. I don't want to see those little boys suffer.'

There is no noise that night. The Astrid is long gone, there are no dead animals appearing from nowhere and the bedroom lights stay off. Sorrel has stopped complaining about voices talking to him, and barely wakes during the night at all now he's back in my bed where he belongs. But even so, I don't sleep a wink. And by the morning, I have decided. I'm going to do it. It's the only way out.

Helen and I plot for several days. Apart from anything else, it's a welcome distraction. And if I ignore the horrifying nature of what we're planning and its illegality, it's almost fun. We spend hours googling 'how to make a fire look

351

accidental' and 'signs of arson' and the like, and Helen shows me how to delete my internet search history.

We make a plan. Given what has happened lately, we decide the best way to do it is to stage me being very drunk and knocking some candles over. 'A lot of this ancient furniture is incredibly flammable,' Helen says. 'And with all this half-rotten wood everywhere, the place will go up like a tinderbox.'

At Helen's suggestion I go to the doctor for antidepressants, partly because I think they might actually help, but also to make my story of not coping look more convincing.

But there is one important factor Helen and I don't agree on.

'I can't do it with the boys here,' I say. 'Let's send them to Tiggy's for a sleepover. We can tell her I need a full night's sleep without one of them waking me up. I'm sure she'd be happy to help.'

Helen pats my arm. 'I hear you. But it's going to look very suspicious if they happen to be out of the way on the night of the fire, isn't it? Especially when they're never usually away from you. Any investigator is going to find that fishy. And if the insurance claim is nullified, you'll end up in an even worse situation. Possibly facing criminal charges. We'll make absolutely sure they're safe, I promise. Don't forget, we're doing all this for them, aren't we? So they can have the life they deserve. There's no way I'm going to put them at any risk.'

I pull a face. 'Yeah. But I'd much rather they weren't here when it happens.'

Helen pulls her hand back and frowns. 'Do you really

think I'd let anything happen to them? Don't you trust me?' There is an edge to her voice that I haven't heard before and it makes me panicky. I need her to help me with this. She's the only person I have to support me, to help me with the boys. I can't lose her. It's too late to back out now.

'Of course I trust you. I just want to make absolutely sure they're safe.'

'They will be. We'll both make certain of it. They are the priority here, after all.'

# 80

*November, Mozène*

**Aura**

This is what we decide. The fire will be started around 10 p.m. in the little lounge I call the snug, which we have only partly cleared and is still crammed with flammable-looking chairs. Because it's in the centre of the house, close to the staircase, we figure this has the best chance of helping the fire to catch. Just in case, and to speed things up, we plan to soak some of the furniture with vodka and lighter fluid, distributing it carefully so as not to look suspicious. We'll buy cigarettes and an old-fashioned Zippo lighter, so it will look like I've been smoking.

I will light several candles and then use one to set fire to the chairs. By this time, Helen will be waiting outside with the boys, telling them we are going on an adventure. We will both leave our phones in the house, and eventually tell the police they were left behind in our rush to escape, and thus won't be able to alert anyone to the fire as quickly as we might have.

I will also leave my car keys in the burning room so we will have to walk, carrying the boys, to the next house, which is at least twenty minutes away. We hope that by this time the house should be beyond repair, best-case scenario. And if it isn't, I can get the work done courtesy of the insurance company and then put a newly renovated chateau on the market instead of a crumbling old wreck. It's win-win. For everyone.

I am nervous, and keep putting the big event off. Helen, on the other hand, seems excited by the prospect. We eventually fix a date – a Sunday, as we imagine there might be fewer *pompiers* on duty at the weekend which could perhaps delay their arrival, and choose a day with a decent weather forecast as we are going to have a long way to walk.

Tiggy has come over.

'You OK?' she asks. 'You seem a bit on edge.'

I wish I could tell her. But obviously I can't.

'I'm OK,' I say. 'It's just . . . all so hard, you know? I can't stop worrying about the boys, how all this is going to affect them. What their future will be like.'

Tiggy takes my hand. 'But what about you? How are you doing?'

I shrug. 'I'm as OK as can be expected, I guess. I saw the doctor and got some pills – Helen pretty much made me go. They're helping to take the edge off. I find I'm drinking too much in the evenings these days too, if I'm entirely honest. It's so lonely without Nick.' Helen asked me to drop this into conversation if I could, to reiterate how badly I am coping and make my planned drunken 'accident' seem more plausible. I'm quite pleased that I've managed to pull it off.

She nods. 'It's understandable – no one is going to judge you for that. And . . . have you decided what you're going to do? Did seeing the notaire help to clarify things at all?'

I sigh. 'I really appreciate you arranging that. And it's useful to know where I stand. But it all feels so confusing at the moment. I think I'm going to stay put for now, get on with the renovating as well as I can and simply remind myself now and again that it doesn't matter if it takes longer than I expected.'

I hate myself for lying to her, and her open, trusting face makes me want to cry. Do I really want to go through with this?

She squeezes my hand. 'I think that sounds very sensible. No need to rush into anything, is there? And I'm always happy to help out with the renovating. It will give me something to do. Now that the film crew has gone, you could look at getting in some more HappyHelp people. I know people who've had about six at a time. I'm not suggesting you have so many, necessarily, but a few extra pair of hands might be just what you need. It's not like you don't have the room for them here. And Helen's worked out really well for you, hasn't she?'

'She has. She's been amazing.'

'Have you heard any more from the police? Bertie said all the hunters had been questioned but they still can't be sure who shot Nick. He feels so guilty he's seeing a counsellor about it, and he's still worried he might be prosecuted. Or asked to resign. Even if they can't ascertain who fired the fatal bullet, in theory he was responsible for Nick as his guest that day.'

'I haven't heard any more. That's pretty much what they told me too, though, and that it was likely to be ruled an accident.' I pause. 'But please tell Bertie he shouldn't blame himself. I hope he's not prosecuted. If it's anyone's fault, it's mine. It was me that wanted to come here, to France. If it hadn't been for me dragging us out here, none of this would have happened. So much death – Frank, then Nick. I wish we'd stayed in London and just got on with things.'

A tear brims and rolls down the edge of my nose. Tiggy leans over and hugs me. I meant what I said about Bertie. But I don't mean what I said about blaming myself. Nick wouldn't have been shot if he hadn't gone out chasing innocent animals, and the only reason we had to come here was because of his stupid dalliance with a schoolgirl. But I want to play the grieving widow barely holding it together for Tiggy. I can't be blamed if I drink too much and get clumsy after all I've gone through lately, can I? It's Nick's fault I'm in the situation I'm in. Not mine.

# 81

*November, Mozène*

**Aura**

Sunday finally rolls around. The skies are clear and it's unseasonably warm, just as the forecast said it would be. I'm jittery and nervous all day and Bay won't stop crying. I guess he's picked up on my mood. Helen, on the other hand, seems calm as anything. I'm so lucky that she's so devoted to the boys and is helping me do this. On my own – I'm not sure what I'd have done. Probably sold the chateau for a pittance and gone back to the UK with the boys to live in some poky little flat, which would be all I could afford. Almost no one wants to buy these huge places, as I've learnt since I came out here. They're too much of a tie, too much of a financial drain. We've barely even got started and the way it's eaten through our savings is incredible.

It's better this way. A new start for us all. Maybe I'll stay local and buy one of those boxy, modern houses I was so sneery about when we were looking for our dream property. Something where nothing needs renovating and there's no DIY to do. Something with a small garden which will give the boys somewhere safe to play but that I can easily manage by myself. Maybe with a spare bedroom I can offer as an Airbnb for a bit of extra income. Certainly something much smaller and newer than this chateau, and less expensive so I can invest the rest of the money. Or maybe I could buy a small second property to rent out – they cost next to nothing out here, after all. Perhaps Tristram can advise me – he knows about that kind of thing. Or then again, I might go back to the UK, buy a house somewhere no one knows me for an entirely fresh start. There are a lot of options. But first, this has to be done.

Since Nick died I've loved having the boys back in my bed. I never wanted to kick them out in the first place, and now that he's not here there's no one to object to us co-sleeping again. Sorrel has stopped having nightmares and hearing voices, and we all sleep much better. I don't know why I let Nick talk me into making them have their own room in the first place.

The night of the planned fire, I read the boys stories until they fall asleep, as is our routine now. I then lie with them longer than I usually would, cuddling them and smelling their hair. Helen has promised me they will be safe and I trust her, but I still feel like I need to be extra close to them tonight. I've given them some homeopathic sleep remedies to help keep them calm.

359

Later, when I'm ready to set the fire, Helen is going to take them outside and wait with them until it's done. They will be sleepy and trusting enough not to ask too many questions. Helen will tell them it's a special game, a treat.

At first, she tried to persuade me to start the fire while the boys were still in the house and insisted we go up and get them right after the fire was lit.

'The closer we stay to the account we're going to give, the better chance we have of not being caught out,' she'd said. 'Especially as Sorrel might remember what happens and say something he shouldn't afterwards.'

But I refused, adamant that the boys must not be put at risk. It was too dangerous. The fire would blaze quickly if everything went as planned – the boys would be dozy and confused and unlikely to notice that Helen was taking them outside before the fire started. And even if they did, they're too young and incoherent for anyone to take much notice of what they say. They are very small – neither is particularly easy to understand at the best of times.

After I've finished reading to the boys, I go to find Helen in the kitchen. She's waiting with a bottle of vodka.

'Here you go,' she says, pouring large measures over ice cubes into two glasses, 'get stuck in.' She squeezes some lime juice into each glass and hands one to me.

We clink glasses and I take a sip. Ugh. I've never liked vodka. 'I thought you said you'd stay sober tonight?' I remind her.

'I will,' she says. 'Just one for Dutch courage. You, though, need to be visibly blotto so that when we go for help, your drunkenness is convincing. I imagine they'll give you a blood test too, or at the very least, a breathalyser. So, down the hatch!'

I drink it as quickly as I can, along with stuffing a handful of nachos in my mouth now and again.

'It'll have a faster effect if you don't eat,' Helen says, frowning.

'I won't be able to keep it down if I don't eat something,' I counter. With one more large gulp, I drain my glass and bang it down on the table. I'm already feeling the effects. 'Same again then, I guess,' I say, and Helen pours me another, even larger than before, plus a smaller one for herself.

'That's the spirit,' she says. 'Let's take these through to the snug and we can start setting the scene.'

The snug would have been a lovely room when it was finished, but now, it never will be. I'd envisaged it as a cosy little reading room once the chambres d'hôtes was up and running, a place for guests to read with a glass of red wine by a roaring fire on a winter's evening. I feel a pang of regret. It would have been gorgeous.

The cosy if somewhat dilapidated room is conceivably somewhere I might choose to sit and wallow in self-pity. We have left an ancient, moth-eaten chaise longue in here as well as two manky old armchairs with the stuffing coming out. Both look extremely flammable as they are, but we've added some lighter fluid as planned to speed things up. It's also one of the only rooms that still has curtains, which we figure will help with the flames.

A few days ago we went out and bought a batch of cheap scented candles with holders – tall, thin ones (both candles and holders) which could be easily knocked over. I chose purple candles in white holders, not that the colour matters, of course. We set them out all along the mantelpiece, as well as several on the small, spindly-legged table by the chair which I am going to pretend to have sat in for my drinking and crying.

I down my drink and Helen pours another, before chucking some of the vodka left in the bottle over the same chair. After all, it's more than conceivable that I would spill my drink in my drunken state, isn't it? She puts the bottle on the table and I stumble a little as I place the final candles and holders in position. My head is spinning and I feel sick.

'OK, I think we're nearly ready,' Helen says. 'Let's get the candles lit and then I'll go and get the boys.'

We light the candles with extra-long matches bought especially for the occasion. We don't speak, and it feels almost like some kind of religious ceremony. My vision is blurred and my hands are shaking. I only manage to light two or three candles while Helen efficiently lights the rest.

Forgetting that it is wet, I flop down into the vodka-soaked chair and feel the liquid seep into my clothes. Ugh. I think about standing up but it feels like too much effort. 'I'm not sure I want to do this anymore,' I whisper. It seems too huge – to burn down this chateau which has been here for hundreds of years. The chateau that we were going to renovate and make beautiful again. Restore it to its former glory. That was going to be our happy forever home. That the children were going to spend their idyllic childhoods in. That Nick and I were going to enjoy our newly fixed marriage in. What happened to all that?

'Nonsense,' Helen says briskly. 'It's for the best. You're

just drunk and can't think straight but that's fine – it helps our story stand up. Now, I'm going to get the boys, put their coats on and sit them on the front step. Once that's done, I'll come and help you knock some candles over and we'll get things moving. OK? You can't be carrying the boys down the stairs in the state you're in, it's dangerous.'

I put my head in my hands and try to protest – I don't want her leaving the boys on the front step on their own even for a short time – I'm sure that's not what we agreed – but I can't remember what we said and I can't get the words out. I hear Helen retreating and she's already gone. A couple of seconds later I hear her footsteps above as she goes into our room, and then whispering to either Bay or Sorrel as she carries him down the stairs and out of the front door. She then repeats the process with my second precious son. I picture them on the front step, confused and sleepy, bundled up in their coats. Sorrel will be sucking his finger with his squirrel held against his cheek and Bay will probably have dropped off again, his head in his brother's lap. I don't want to do this anymore. I try to stand up to go to them but my head spins, I'm wobbly on my feet and I crash back down into the chair.

After a couple more beats Helen reappears in the doorway. I lift my head to look at her. 'Are the boys OK?' I ask hoarsely. 'I want to see them.'

'They're fine,' Helen says, her words louder and more abrasive than I expected. 'I think we're ready to go.'

'No, Helen, I've changed my mind,' I croak, but my voice isn't working properly and she doesn't seem to hear me.

She picks up the candle closest to her and hurls it at the

ancient drapes, which instantly go up in flames. I didn't expect it to happen so quickly. I try to leap up but my head is heavy and it's a struggle to find my balance. 'Wait, Helen,' I plead as I force myself on to my feet and towards the door. With one sweep of her arm, Helen knocks all the candles from the fireplace on to the chaise longue below, which instantly sets ablaze. As I stumble towards the door she slams it shut in my face and I hear the key click in the lock.

# 82

*November, London*

**Seb**

The weeks spent at the chateau went brilliantly. The execu-
tive producer is really happy with our footage and literally
rubbing his hands together with glee at how things turned
out, with all the drama. He was expecting a simple story of
renovation with minor bickering and little setbacks – this
plot line will be a game-changer for *French Fancy* as a series,
and he knows it. He pretended to be shocked by Nick's
death for about five minutes but since it made most of the
UK papers (sample headlines; Death in Paradise and Byng
Bang Ding Dong – thanks, no doubt to the production
company press office) – he's been practically wetting himself
over the potential viewing figures. They've even found some
money in the budget for an outdoor advertising campaign,

which is practically unheard of for this kind of programme.

Chateau Ricane was originally going to be episode three in the new series, but they've now brought it forward as they want to open with it. I've been working eighteen-hour days to get it edited. It's my programme, I wanted to do all the editing myself, even if I've had to fast-track it a bit. It was agreed that I would edit as part of my contract. It was important to me.

The premise of the programme is 'we show it all exactly as it happens', according to the publicity. But in an edited show, things are never going to appear *exactly* as they happen, are they? It's just not possible. So being in control of the edit has allowed me to ensure certain people are shown in a certain light. That their true colours are absolutely evident. Editing is always my favourite part of the programme-making process, but especially so this time.

Every time Nick is dismissive towards Aura or Helen, the footage has stayed in. Most of the hard work he did around the chateau ripping out things, painting and renovating, gone. All the times he sat at the kitchen table complaining about something or bitching about the locals, in. Most of the cute footage of him playing with his two boys, gone. It's such fun. Almost like playing God.

Bertie suggesting Nick join the hunt was a gift to me. It was the second chance I needed. Especially after my attempt to kill Nick at the Hallowe'en party had failed. And after all the care I'd taken, purchasing a large knife in a bog-standard supermarket, along with a few other items, and paying in cash so it would be virtually untraceable, then stashing it in my camera bag and waiting for a moment when he was alone. When I caught sight of the big black cloak and scythe heading in the direction of the portacabin loos while everyone else was watching the fireworks, I knew this was the chance I'd been waiting for all night. I put my latex gloves on, slipped in behind him and stabbed him in the back. Some might call that cowardly, but it was no better than he deserved. Except it turned out I'd picked the wrong Death, and it wasn't Nick at all, it was that poor sap Frank. I feel bad about that, obviously, but needs must. From what I understand, no one will miss the guy too much anyway, not now he's been exposed as a perv. Chloe and I were questioned, along with all the other party-goers, and I gave the police access to all our footage of that night. I explained to them that we don't film constantly, so the gap in filming at the time that Frank was murdered was just one of many that evening, as they could see. I shot the grand finale of the fireworks display, which somewhat appropriately formed a heart dripping blood against the night sky, after I had stabbed Frank. But we wouldn't need more than a few seconds of the display for the programme so I hadn't filmed the whole thing, as I told them. And obviously it would have been weird to have been shooting outside the loos, away from the party, so there was nothing of use to them in what I'd captured. They weren't suspicious when I told them I couldn't remember exactly where I'd been when Frank was stabbed – it had been a very busy evening and I had been all over the place.

But back to the day of the hunt. Chloe was in charge of filming because I was taking part in the shoot. It couldn't have gone better. The crack of dawn start had already put her on the back foot – she's never at her best first thing in the morning. The drizzle and cold meant she was already bored, pissed off and not concentrating properly by the time we got to the woods. The mist made it difficult to see clearly. And then Nick choosing to go for a leak when he did – what a godsend that was. I'd have done it anyway though. I would have shot him. I'd have found my moment at some point – it would have been easy enough. Hunting accidents happen more regularly than you'd think. But with everyone firing their guns like that, and all the guns being pretty much of the same type, they never did work out who fired the fatal shot. Especially as I'd brought my own along because, well, you never know. When I left the UK, knowing that I needed to kill Nick, I hid it in the van, just in case. I used my own gun that day – I switched it earlier in the morning with the one that Bertie lent me. The ballistics people found it all very confusing, but ballistics is never an exact science at the best of times.

Bertie seemed privately convinced it was him who fired the fatal shot, as well as fretting over the fact that Nick was officially his responsibility. A few of the red tops went full throttle over his presence that day, taking the opportunity to reveal his affair which was, apparently, common knowledge around Westminster. But I don't feel bad about that – he deserves it. He's a lecherous old perv whose sweet wife Tiggy deserves much better. Now that the affair is public, maybe she'll find the strength to leave him. Maybe she could even shack up with Celia, like she clearly wants to. I hope so.

I've been through all the footage of that day carefully, as

did the French police, and there's nothing to implicate me. I've since got rid of the gun, of course – I dropped it in a river during a stop on our drive back to the UK while Chloe bought sandwiches. Any other day I'd have given Chloe a bollocking for her shoddy filming, missing a key event like someone being killed. She had the camera trained on Thea at the time, for some reason, so she didn't see anything.

So, I will get away with it, just as that bastard got away with killing my sister and causing my mum to have a total breakdown. The inquest recorded an open verdict, which is often what they do when they think a death is a suicide but can't be 100 per cent sure. But as far as I'm concerned, it was murder.

With the so-called 'incident' happening at Ella's school the way it did, the DNA of literally hundreds of people was all over the room. Nick's DNA was found on her clothes, but he had danced with her earlier that night, so that wasn't enough proof that anything untoward had gone on.

Jack, her kind-of boyfriend, told the police she'd said she wanted a few minutes to herself in the art room because she was upset at that pathetic excuse for a man ignoring her all evening, only dancing with her when Molly forced him to. According to the investigation and the inquest, Ella fell while she was alone in the room. She had been drinking, and they decided she probably fell out of the window while getting some air.

But does that sound likely? I don't think so. I don't think she fell. I think she jumped, because of all the stress that pathetic excuse for a man caused her. Or perhaps Nick pushed her – worried she was going to tell someone what had really happened between them. I'll probably never know but either way, as far as I'm concerned, he killed her.

Mum had told me about the stuff that had happened at school, the Instagram post and all that. When I asked Ella about it, she insisted there was nothing going on, but I didn't believe her. Ugh. Even the thought of him perving over her still makes me want to hurl.

He always denied everything – said she had a crush on him, happens all the time in schools. The CPS decided not to prosecute – they said that while there were rumours of an incident on the ski trip, there wasn't any evidence. It was all hearsay, a photo that could be explained away, with both parties claiming nothing untoward had occurred. Reading between the lines, I think the authorities decided, given that Ella was already dead, and in light of perv-face's exemplary record, it wasn't in the public interest. Basically, they couldn't be arsed. He was a small story in the paper for a few days and he apparently 'agreed to resign from his job', but that was it.

I spoke to her Manchester friends at her funeral – I've known them since they were all tiny. Before her death, Ella had been miserable. He made her miserable, causing all that trouble with the stuff on Instagram, leading her on and then casting her aside. All so upsetting for her. Absolutely the last thing she needed when she was at a new school, away from her friends, knowing no one. She's dead, it's his fault, whether she was pushed or she jumped is kind of irrelevant now. He's finally got what he deserves.

I wish she'd confided in me. I hadn't been in touch as much as I should have before she died. We were close when she was still in Manchester. She was my little sister, and I protected her. She wanted to live with me when Mum moved to London, but Mum wouldn't have it and, realistically, I didn't have the space or time to make sure she was behaving herself. We still spoke fairly often after the move, but we were both always busy, especially me, and I regret not making more time for her.

After Ella died, I read in the paper that Nick and his drippy wife Aura had decided to start a new life in France. I followed her on social media using a fake account. Since she shared pretty much every spit and cough of their move, it was easy enough to find out where they would be going.

My original plan had been to head out to France on holiday, find him and, one way or another, ensure justice was done. I hadn't been there for Ella enough when she was alive, but I could take revenge now she was dead. Maybe that would make up for my failing her, at least to a degree. As well as for what he'd done to Mum, who still isn't well enough to continue in the job she'd strived for her whole career. She's signed off sick for now, but I imagine eventually they'll find a way to get rid of her. So he's not only killed my sister, but ruined my mum's life too.

I hadn't decided on details, but I've watched enough *CSI* and worked on enough true crime programmes to have a few ideas about how to kill someone and get away with it. Plus I already had my gun, if need be. It's easier than you'd imagine to get a shotgun licence, especially if you're a member of a shooting club like I am.

And then a TV mate mentioned he was execcing on this programme and that the wife of 'that perv teacher' had applied to be on it. He was all set to turn her down, until I told him ratings would go through the roof if they handled it right. Even talked him into giving me a job on the programme – Ella had a different surname to me, being from a different relationship of Mum's, so he never made the connection.

It was tricky being around Nick in France, trying to pretend to be nice when all the while I wanted nothing more than to smash his face in, but it helped to see how miserable he was. Aura barely let him touch her and as far as I could see, they kept out of each other's way as much as possible. She almost seemed to shudder when he came near.

I think he regretted the move. The chateau was a horrible, creepy place. I don't believe in the supernatural, but some of the stuff that was happening there freaked me out. The dead animals, the music going off in the night, the lights switching on and off at random. Aura accused me of setting it up to make the filming more interesting, but it was nothing to do with me. I still feel a bit spooked by some of it.

I turn back to the screen. Chloe has finally caught up with the action and I hear a muffled gasp from her as she zooms in on Nick's prone body, his pathetic cock hanging out of his flies. I won't be able to get away with leaving this shot in the final cut, but seeing him dead on the ground and knowing it was me that put him there feels good. I've finally done right by Ella and Mum.

# 83

*November, Mozène*

**Aura**

'Helen!' I try to shout, but my voice comes out as a weird slur. 'What are you doing? Let me out!'

The window is now a wall of flames where the drapes have caught alight, and the chaise longue has gone up like a bonfire. The air is thick with smoke and it's difficult to breathe. I pull my T-shirt up over my mouth but it doesn't make any difference. I bang on the door but my arms feel like lead and I can barely lift them. 'Where are the boys?' I plead.

'They're fine,' Helen snaps from behind the door. 'I put them in the car to keep them safe and warm. I gave them a little sedative with their evening milk earlier so they won't wake up.'

'What?' I ask. 'What did you give them?'

'None of those stupid sugar pills of yours. An antihistamine – something to make them properly sleepy. Nothing dangerous. I'm not going to harm innocent children. Not like you. I put something stronger in your vodka too. And in case you wonder why you may have been feeling particularly out of sorts lately, I've been slipping a few extra pills the doctor gave you into your food for days now, to make it harder for you to think. Belt and braces, and all that.'

A buzz of adrenaline makes me feel slightly more lucid, though it is still hard to focus. I don't understand what she means about me harming children. 'What? Why? What are you talking about?' I demand. 'I've never hurt a child. Never would. Please, Helen,' I bang on the door again but my arms feel weird and floppy. 'Let me out. We can talk about this. Whatever you think I've done, there's been a mistake.'

I cough and pull my T-shirt further up over my mouth, but it's useless. It's not making any difference. I sink down to the floor, remembering from some safety course I did at work that in a smoke-filled room, the air is clearer lower down. I bang on the door again. 'Please, Helen . . .'

'There was no mistake,' Helen says. 'My daughter died.'

What? What daughter? Why has she never mentioned this before?

'That's awful, Helen,' I slur, trying to keep my mind and voice clear in spite of my panic and brain fog. 'But I never met your daughter. I didn't even know you had one. I don't understand why you're blaming me. Please, let me out and we can talk about this.'

374

The window. Maybe the window. The curtains have as good as burned away now. If I get over there, I might be able to escape. I start to drag myself over on my stomach, as low to the ground as I can. The smoke is so thick now I can barely see and my lungs feel like they are burning.

'Shut up,' Helen snaps, 'from here on you can just listen. Little Angels? The nursery where you sent your boys? I don't imagine you ever met my daughter – things like pick-ups and drop-offs were too menial for someone like you. Nick would have met her though – my daughter Indy and Sorrel were good friends. Nick never met *me*. I rarely saw any of the other parents – poor Indy was first in and last out most days. Not because it was beneath me to pick up my child, but because as a single mum, I had to work long hours to support us both. I didn't have the nice short days of a teacher like Nick or a *counsellor* like you.'

I don't say anything and continue trying to drag myself towards the window.

'Are you still listening? I hope you haven't died just yet. I want you to know what you did. Or rather, what you didn't do.'

I've no idea what she's talking about. The woman is clearly mad. How did I not notice? Why did I trust her with the boys? Why did I never question why a woman of her age was living like a backpacker? Oh God. I need to get out of here. What has she done with them? Where are they? I try to take a deep breath but the thick air burns and makes me cough again.

'Oh good. You're still there, for now at least. Yes, Indy and Sorrel were firm friends. She adored him. Never shut

375

up about him at home. He was always in the pictures she painted – she'd always point him out to me. Perhaps Indy was in his too. I imagine if you'd stayed in London longer, and oh, of course if she hadn't died, we'd have eventually got them together for a play date. If you'd ever taken enough interest in your boys for five minutes to know what they wanted, that is.'

Indy. It rings a vague bell. I try to take another breath, but breathing is becoming almost impossible and I can't see a thing. My fingers touch the wall – the window is right above me.

'Sorrel and Indy spent a lot of time together, according to the nursery staff. Playing Duplo was their favourite thing, did you know that? Sweet really – barely two years old and already with their own likes and dislikes and forming little friendships. Kids are amazing, aren't they?'

I pull on the windowsill to haul myself up. Every part of me hurts. My head is swimming and I feel the air get hotter and the smoke more dense as I lift my head, still sitting on the floor.

'Indy never ceased to amaze me. She was so ill when she was tiny. She had cancer. Heart breaking, seeing her suffer like that. I'm sure you can imagine, though I doubt you'd care.'

What is she on about? Of course I care. A child with cancer. How tragic. Maybe it was the stress of that which sent Helen mad? Which she clearly is. I pull myself up further and manage to touch the window handle, but the heat sears my hand and I have to pull it away. I take off my T-shirt and wrap it around my hand.

'The way she got through the cancer – so stoic. Never complained. Rarely cried. And guess what? After several rounds of chemotherapy, she was in remission. She was going to be OK. It felt like a miracle. Kids are so hardy. At least, they can be.'

Even with the T-shirt around my hand, I can feel the flesh burning as I finally manage to wrench the window open towards me.

'When I told Indy she could go back to nursery, she was so excited! Such a sociable little girl – she loved it there. And even more so when she met little Sorrel. She always looked forward to seeing him.'

I haul myself up further and try to push the ancient shutters open. I try and try, but they don't budge. I want to scream in frustration but nothing comes out. I can't breathe. I drop to the floor again, but it's the same down there. It's all smoke – no air.

'You still there? I nailed the shutters closed earlier, in case you were thinking of getting out that way. If the investigators notice – though I doubt they'll be able to tell, given how well this is going up so far – I'll say you nailed them together for security, what with being freaked out by the weird stuff going on in the night. I did a few others too for authenticity. Clever, huh?'

'Please . . .' I whisper. 'Please help me . . .'

'But then Indy caught measles. Pretty much all the babies at nursery did, as you know. It didn't take much investigation to work out it came from your kids – the nursery is ridiculously slack with their IT security and it was easy to hack the records.'

I can't see. I can barely hear. I don't even have the strength to take another breath.

'So most of the smaller babies at the nursery, too young for MMR, caught measles from Sorrel and Bay because you thought you knew better than science. Because you didn't want to "pollute" your children's bodies with things you don't understand. No, something like vaccination isn't good enough for you and your children. The nursery should have pulled you up on it when you didn't get round to handing in their medical records, but sadly, they didn't.'

Everything feels like it's closing in.

'Indy had only just finished chemo and hadn't yet had her MMR redone. So she was unprotected, like the babies not old enough for their jabs. They, thankfully, managed to fight it off, though I believe one has been left with some hearing damage. Indy, though, her immune system was too weak. Can you imagine what it's like to watch your child die of encephalitis in hospital, Aura, when you know it was entirely preventable? When she's already endured chemotherapy and fought off cancer? When her tiny little body has already been through that too? Can you? Can you imagine that? Aura, are you still listening?'

# 84

**Helen**

I know everyone says this about their children, but I mean it when I say that Indy was my whole life. I'd given up on meeting the right man and decided to have her by myself, through IVF, before it was too late. It wasn't a decision I took lightly. But my job was stable, I'd been there a long time and they offered a generous maternity package. I knew that once Indy was born I would need to return to work and she would need to go to nursery. As she was to be my only child, it would be good for her to socialize with other children anyway. But outside of working hours, I would devote my every waking minute to her. I figured that, in many ways, the absence of a partner could be a positive thing for a child. No one competing for my attention. She would be number one in my life and all my love could be lavished on her. She would never have to share.

My second round of IVF was successful, which was better than the odds for my age. I had budgeted for five rounds. When you've managed to buy your house at the right time, live alone, have frugal tastes and don't have much of a social life, it is easy to save.

My pregnancy had its ups and downs and I imagine it would have been less tiring had I done it when I was younger. But I bore the nausea, back ache and puffy ankles without complaint because I knew this was exactly what I wanted. I couldn't wait to meet my baby.

She arrived two days after my due date and I fell in love with her immediately. The early months were tiring but I got her into a good routine quickly so that we could both enjoy our time together as much as possible before I went back to work. I breastfed her in bed in the mornings, watching her little rosebud mouth working away, stroking her hair and marvelling at her tiny nails, thinking how lucky I was.

I went to antenatal classes because I wanted to be as informed as possible about how best to look after my baby but I was never one of these people that met up with the other mothers in Starbucks after the birth to moan about sleepless nights and block all the space between the tables with an enormous buggy. I relished my time alone with Indy, taking her to the park and feeding the ducks with her. Pushing her on the swings. We did some classes such as baby yoga and baby massage, but I only did these for her benefit – I wasn't interested in socializing.

I took endless photos of her. She was so beautiful. And then . . . one day I noticed a white glint in one of her eyes in a photo. I felt sick. I'd read about this. I knew what it might be. I took her straight to the doctor's surgery – I begged and pleaded until they gave me an emergency appointment.

There were tests, scans and more tests and a couple of weeks later, I got the diagnosis I'd been dreading. Cancer. Retinoblastoma. 'But please try not to worry too much, Ms Summers,' the doctor reassured. 'It's rare, but in the vast majority of cases, very treatable.'

Six months of chemotherapy followed. Indy was in and out of hospital. It was awful seeing her so weak, so vulnerable. Heartbreaking to make her endure this treatment which so often seemed to be making her sicker.

Work was amazing and gave me compassionate leave on full pay so I could be by her side. And after six months of chemo I got the news I was waiting for – she was clear. She'd need regular tests, but the doctors and the statistics indicated that she should be OK.

But by that time I had no choice but to go back to work. I couldn't take compassionate leave for a child who was no longer sick. Indy had started at nursery before she was diagnosed – I'd visited every single one in the area, and she was signed up to the best one I'd found. Montessori, with a friendly atmosphere and an excellent OFSTED report. I would rather have stayed at home with Indy indefinitely but financially that wasn't possible. I wanted the best for her and hoped to send her to private school, but it was only me and her so I needed to earn money. I spoke to the doctors at the hospital, and they agreed that Indy was ready to go back to nursery and be with other children – it was important for her development.

I cried the first day she went back. And the next, and the next. But she made a new friend, little Sorrel, and was always smiling when I picked her up, babbling away about the fun she'd had. As the days went by, it got easier. When we got home I would make her dinner, then we'd play for a little while before her bath and bedtime. It was so cosy. Such a lovely way to finish the day. The other mums at nursery were always moaning about having to do tea, bath and bedtime and how monotonous and stressful it was, but I loved it. I looked forward to it all day, every day.

And then one day there was a notice on the door of the nursery when I picked Indy up. 'There has been a case of measles in the nursery. Please monitor your children carefully and keep them at home if they show any symptoms.'

My heart leapt into my mouth. Indy hadn't yet been revaccinated – it was too soon after her chemo. I rang NHS Direct as soon as I got home and they told me not to panic but to keep a close eye on her. I could barely think of anything else.

I rang into work sick the next day and kept Indy with me. I googled frantically so I knew what to look for. And for a few days she seemed fine. But then she was grumpy and tired. There was a rash. An earache. A high temperature which I couldn't get down.

I took her to A&E and she was put on a drip. She fell unconscious as her brain swelled. She was intubated. I held her hand. A few days later, she died. My little Indy was gone. I felt like my life was over.

# 85

**Helen**

Nothing mattered anymore. I seriously considered suicide. After all, what was there to live for now? But then, I got angry. Indy had been taken away from me. She had beaten cancer, but this entirely preventable disease had taken her. Someone would pay.

It was easy enough to find out which child at the nursery wasn't up to date with their vaccinations – everyone already knew anyway. It was Sorrel.

Aura by this time was a kind of local celebrity for all the wrong reasons, thanks to her pervy husband and the never-quite-proved stuff that went on with that schoolgirl. Lots of kids at the nursery had older brothers, sisters and cousins at the school where her husband taught, so I'd heard all the gossip. Even if Aura's Facebook hadn't already been open, I'd probably have known about her move to France from the local grapevine. But as it was, thanks to quietly stalking her on Facebook, I knew her moving date, and then following a bit of research on Google Maps, the exact house she was buying. I could find out pretty much everything but her bra size. Some people are so stupid.

I sold my house and paid off the mortgage – without Indy I didn't need a proper home. The not-inconsiderable equity left me with plenty of cash with which to travel. I joined all the various expat Facebook groups Aura was in using a fake profile with an image I'd downloaded off the internet and a new gmail account. When she started wittering on about the pros and cons of the HappyHelp site, I knew that was my way in. I booked a one-way flight to Toulouse and got a HappyHelp placement fairly local to Aura's new house, so I'd have a reference to get me in with her. After that I kept an eye on the noticeboards. It didn't take long before she was begging me to come and help. By the end of the summer, all the students have gone and volunteers happy to work for literally no pay are much fewer and further between. And she was clearly desperate.

To start with, I wasn't sure what I was going to do to her and her family. First, I thought I'd spook them a bit. I set alarms on the Astrid to make it play music in the night and later installed a device in the light switch to switch the lights off and on via an app. Hilariously Aura thought Seb was doing it all. Seeing how rattled she was made me feel better, but it wasn't enough. I knew I needed to do more, but wasn't sure what.

At one point I thought I'd have my revenge by taking away one of her children as she had taken mine. Perhaps an unfortunate 'accident' – it would have been easy enough to arrange, with Aura begging me to take them off her hands at every possible opportunity. When I asked to borrow the car to drive them to soft play, I was planning to crash it or drive into a river. At that point after Indy's death, I still didn't care if I lived or died, and I would have been happy to give up my life in the interests of making Aura miserable.

But once I was in the car with the two boys, it felt wrong to hurt them. They were sweet and innocent with their whole lives ahead of them, just like Indy. If I hurt them, that would make me as culpable as Aura. I couldn't take their lives away from them. They didn't deserve it. She, however, did.

It was that sad old letch Frank – who was quite clearly listening in on Aura via the Astrid – who first gave me the idea of talking to Sorrel at night via a speaker hidden in the floorboards. I didn't do it for long; my intention was to unsettle her, not him, and I like to think I made it up to Sorrel. We had a lot of fun together. Way more than he ever had with Aura, who was too wrapped up in herself to pay either of her sons any attention.

And then Nick died, and Aura fell to pieces. All it took was a few crushed-up pills in her food and some gentle drip-drip suggestions from me about how hard her life would be in the crumbling chateau all on her own with the boys and how much easier life would be for all if it was gone. And the rest is history.

# 86

*Six months later*

**Helen**

'Lelen?' Sorrel says. 'I did dees for you.'

He hands me a bunch of dandelions and I hold them to my nose, pretending to smell them.

'They're lovely, Sorrel, thank you,' I say.

He grins at me, picks up his squirrel and toddles off towards the beautiful house in the Home Counties where we now both live. He's such an adorable little boy, and I feel so blessed to spend time with him and Bay every single day.

After we'd 'escaped' from the chateau on the night of the fire, I walked to the nearest house with the two boys as slowly as I could (although there's no option other than going slowly when you're carrying two sleepy children) and called the police and fire brigade. Almost nothing could be saved from the chateau and Aura was formally identified from her dental records. I told the police how worried I'd been about her, how I thought she could be suicidal. That she'd talked about wanting to kill herself since Nick's death, that I'd made her see a doctor and she'd been prescribed antidepressants. That I suspected she was taking too many. That I had been awoken by the smell of smoke, grabbed the boys and taken them outside. That I'd put them in the car, which had been left unlocked as usual, given the rural location, but the keys were in the flaming house. That I'd tried to go back in to get to Aura, but by then the flames were too intense. Obviously I didn't tell them I'd posted the key to the snug back under the door once it was clear she was over by the window and unconscious. Such a sad turn of events, I'd reflected. Those poor little boys.

In the absence of any other family or any will, it was inevitable that the boys would be taken on by Nick's parents. We'd already met a few times at the chateau after Nick died and then at Aura's funeral. I sought them out, offering to come and work for them as the boys' nanny 'for continuity in this difficult time for them,' I had said. As I had already given up my job anyway, it would suit all of us well.

So here I am, nanny and, to all intents and purposes, full-time mother to these sweet little boys. Of course they're no substitute for Indy, no one could be. But I'm making myself indispensable to Penny and Roger, who, while fit and healthy, are approaching their seventies and will increasingly need my help with the two boisterous little boys now in their care. One of the first things I did was make sure they caught up on all the vaccinations they missed. They will grow up loved, safe and happy, and with the best chance of staying healthy. They will be brought up according to my values, not Aura's stupid, selfish ones. It's what they deserve.

As I go back into the kitchen to find a glass of water for Sorrel's dandelions, he hurls himself towards me and wraps his arms around my legs.

'I love you, Lelen,' he says.

I cradle his head. 'I love you too, Sol. Tell you what, why don't you call me Mummy from now on?'

# Acknowledgements

The first draft of this book was written largely during the first lockdown of 2020 in between walks (within 1km of home, of course) when it was lovely to have something concrete to get on with. So first thanks go to Phoebe Morgan at HarperCollins for your faith and enthusiasm for *The Chalet*, as well as for including a second book in my contract on the strength of a paragraph. And of course thank you for the new contract! Sorry for the fangirling but you are the type of editor every author dreams of. Huge retrospective thanks also to Fliss Denham, Rachel Quin, Sophie Churcher and the rest of the HarperFiction team for helping to make *The Chalet* such a success – I loved every step of the way and it achieved way more than I could ever have expected thanks to you all.

Thank you to Gaia Banks at Sheil Land for your usual patience in reading my very rough first drafts, securing the foreign deals (yay!), negotiating the new contract and putting up with all my questions. Thanks also to your Shiel Land colleagues Lucy Fawcett for dealing with the film and TV side, and also Alba Arnau and Chloe Woods.

Thank you to *The Chateau* beta readers Eve Ainsworth, Sarah Wells, Jackie Wesley and Hannah Parry who I think read when I'd got about two-thirds of the way through? All of you helped shape the book in some way and I hope you approve of how I finished it.

Thank you again to copy editor Anne O'Brien for tidying up my words and flagging my continued over-use of 'just', 'really' and 'a bit', and to Claire Ward for another brilliant cover.

It takes an (online) village to write a book, so thanks to my IRL and virtual friends (and friends of friends) who have helped with many, many questions along the way ranging from words teens use and nursery care to gun law and medical questions, as well as music choices, names, pedantic grammar queries and much more. Any mistakes or inaccuracies are, of course, my own. Plus thank you of course for keeping me company and making me laugh when I should have been actually been writing *The Chateau*, and for throwing your support so fully behind *The Chalet* when it was published – it meant a lot.

Thank you to the bloggers and reviewers who were (largely!) so enthusiastic about *The Chalet*, and to Anne Cater of Random Things Tours for organising such a great blog tour. I read every single review and really appreciate you taking the time to share your thoughts, both with me and with other readers. I always love to hear from you, so please do keep in touch via @catherinecooperjournalist on Insta,

@catherinecooper on Twitter and @catherinecooperauthor on Facebook.

Thanks to Toby for lending me his toddler self and Dodo to appear as Sorrel and his squirrel (not that I asked!) and to Livi for being so excited about the books.

Finally, thanks to Alex for everything - especially for taking me seriously when I first said I wanted to move to France all those years ago. Though I'm still relieved we didn't buy an actual chateau xx.